How to Tame a Wild Rogue

"Good morning, Mr. St. Leger. I trust you slept . . ."

Her eyes flickered. Dropped to his torso.

And then it struck him: his rolled-up shirtsleeves exposed a brazen amount of skin from fingertip to elbow. His throat was partially on view, too.

For God's *sake*.

He suddenly felt like an ape in all his bronzed and hairy bareness. He thoroughly resented it.

"They're *arms*, Lady Worth," he said on a hush. "I suggest you move closer to the settee if you feel a swoon coming on. I cannot guarantee I will get to you before you topple out of your chair."

She courageously turned her head toward him again.

"As valuable as that advice undoubtedly is, Mr. St. Leger, I'm not a swooner by nature. Please forgive me. I was just a bit startled, as I'd forgotten I was sharing quarters with a man who isn't a gent—"

She bit her lip. Torment and regret and apology flashed in her widened eyes.

His rank and ramping incredulity fair pulsed during the ensuing silence.

"If you think implying I'm not a gentleman will hurt my feelings, I've good news for you," he said, his voice low and silky. "My heart is as hard as my thighs."

Also by Julie Anne Long

JULIE ANNE LONG

How to Tame a Wild Rogue

THE PALACE OF ROGUES

AVONBOOKS

An Imprint of HarperCollinsPublishers

HOW TO TAME A WILD ROGUE. Copyright © 2023 by Julie Anne Long. All rights reserved. Printed in the United States of America. No part of this book may be used or reproduced in any manner whatsoever without written permission except in the case of brief quotations embodied in critical articles and reviews. For information, address HarperCollins Publishers, 195 Broadway, New York, NY 10007.

First Avon Books mass market printing: July 2023

Print Edition ISBN: 978-0-06-328091-5
Digital Edition ISBN: 978-0-06-328093-9

Cover design by Guido Caroti
Cover illustration by Kirk DouPonce, FictionArtist.com
Cover images © iStock/Getty Images; © Shutterstock

Avon, Avon & logo, and Avon Books & logo are registered trademarks of HarperCollins Publishers in the United States of America and other countries.

HarperCollins is a registered trademark of HarperCollins Publishers in the United States of America and other countries.

FIRST EDITION

23 24 25 26 27 BVGM 10 9 8 7 6 5 4 3 2 1

Acknowledgments

MY GRATITUDE to splendid editor May Chen; to Avon's talented and hardworking staff; to my stalwart agent, Steven Axelrod, and his wonderful staff; and to my beautiful communities at Instagram and The Pig & Thistle After Dark, whose joyful enthusiasm and support make me feel as though I *might* be doing something right.

How to Tame a Wild Rogue

Chapter One

෨෨෨ර

*H*E'D BEEN born on a night like this: the sky
choked with black clouds, the wind banshee-
screeching through cracks and rattling windows
in their frames like a costermonger who'd caught
hold of a thieving urchin.

Or at least that's the sort of thing Lorcan St.
Leger liked to tell whatever audience he held in
thrall at a given moment.

"It's how I got so strong and so ugly, you see,"
he'd say. "I was born screaming into a headwind.
And I've fought against headwinds me whole
life."

He didn't actually know precisely when or
where he was born. But he'd come to understand
that a personal myth could be as useful as armor.

Experience told him the impending storm
would be long and violent and his skin prickled with not unpleasant portent. His ship had
reached harbor just ahead of it; and while his
crew had dispersed at once to inns or brothels,
captain's business had kept Lorcan out later than
he'd anticipated, and by the time he'd reached
the nearest inn the last room had been taken. He
needed to find shelter soon, but the only other
possibility for lodging nearby was a storied

brothel he knew of mainly through misty, prurient reminiscences shared by sailors over the years. He'd seen the building once, years ago; gargoyles lined the roof edge.

So that's where he was headed. In a pinch, he supposed, he could take shelter in the livery stable he'd passed. God knew a man could keep worse company than horses.

Now and again the fitful wind whipped clouds away from a full moon, and fragments of his surroundings were illuminated: the eyes of a slinking cat, the sheen of greasy water atop an open barrel, a lantern hook outside a shop door. Nearly every shop and dwelling had taken their lamps in. He hadn't seen another human on the street for nearly a quarter of an hour.

Only cats, rats, and Lorcan St. Leger would walk the streets near the London docks unafraid at this time of night.

In St. Giles, as a child, he'd learned that a moment's distraction could mean death. Terror had been the whetstone against which he'd honed his reflexes and wits. How to find hiding places and escape routes, how to fight, when to ingratiate, when to intimidate, how to barter and steal—he leveraged his lessons into strength, and then into power. By the time he was scarcely more than twenty years old he'd built a shadowy empire from one end of England to the other of men and women who would have killed for him.

He'd made sure they'd never needed to. Brutality was the fastest way to the gallows, after all. The quickest way to get caught. And it was no substitute for strategy and cunning or for razor-sharp judgment of character. Lorcan wasn't above it, of course, if it was the quickest solution to a sticky problem of disrespect or immediate threat. And he'd tolerated no nonsense from the various earls, viscounts, and other nobs who'd been his customers and whom he'd easily charmed. They paid cash on the nail or they got nothing.

And no one ever crossed him twice.

In exchange for their fealty, he'd given his meticulously chosen crew trust and respect. He listened to their needs and paid them promptly and well. They'd repaid him with adulation and iron-clad loyalty.

Those days were behind him. He was more than a decade older than when he'd begun; he led a different life; he had a different crew. And yet still he instinctively moved swiftly and nearly soundlessly through the dark, his every sense on alert.

He froze when he heard a muffled thump from a few feet away.

It was the sound of something—or someone—falling to the ground in the narrow street up ahead.

He flattened himself against the building wall. Pistol in hand, he inched soundlessly toward the alley. Then peered around the corner.

Very little surprised him anymore.

But about fifteen or so feet ahead of him, into the alley separating two buildings, a woman was lowering herself out of a second-story window on what appeared to be a braided bedsheet.

On the cobblestones below her he could just

make out a small, dark, oblong shape. Likely a valise or knapsack she'd thrown to the ground before her descent. The source of the thump.

He decided to pause to take in the spectacle as though it were a puppet show.

Her feet flailed a bit before she gingerly came to rest on the top of a stack of crates pushed up against the building wall.

She was still a good seven or eight feet off the ground.

And she'd run out of bedsheet.

Lorcan wasn't quite certain *what* manner of escape he was watching, but he found himself rooting for her just the same. The wildness in his soul could not help but admire the wily people of the world, the ones who tried and got away with audacious things. He was disinclined to judge. No one knew better than he did what desperation could inspire even a saintly person to do. He possessed a moral code, after a fashion, but his first instinct was always to help. At least the first time.

The moon and a rude gust of wind conspired to hurl her cloak and skirts upward and dropped them again, but not before revealing a pair of elegantly curved calves wearing surprisingly good embroidered stockings.

"I once gave a pair of stockings much like those to a mistress," he said idly.

The woman flattened herself against the wall and froze.

But her breath formed swift white puffs in the frigid air.

One hand remained fisted around the sheet. The wind whipped the hood from her head. She yanked it back over her head with the other.

He moved carefully closer. He could now hear her terrified breathing.

"Madam," he mused, "it looks as though you're in a bit of a bind."

Perhaps because this was self-evident, she didn't reply.

"If what you've just tossed down is a satchel full of silver plate, you'd best hurry. I should hate for their rightful owners to awake and shoot you." Now he was having a little fun at her expense.

"Why would I take silver plate?"

Her voice was a shock. Low-pitched, exquisitely refined, every word as precise as a cut gem. It was like stumbling across a diamond necklace in the dirt.

"Oh . . . lass . . ." he said pityingly. "First day at thieving?"

"I'm not thieving." She actually sounded indignant. "Some . . . blighter . . . moved the barrel that I . . . that I planned to . . ."

"Blighter!" He was amused. "You'll never get to heaven using that sort of language."

And then he became brisk. "I believe you're going to have to jump. And I'm going to have to catch you, because the sound of human bones crunching against cobblestones puts me right off me feed."

She said nothing. The only movement was the

lashing of her cape about her ankles. It snapped like a sail in the wind.

"My offer is not indefinite, madam. Jump or be caught stealing, it's all the same to me."

DAPHNE FINALLY RISKED a look over her shoulder.

For a chilling moment she saw no human at all. Only layer upon layer of shadows, all in various shades and textures of black.

It was as though the night itself had been speaking to her.

Fear seeped into her bones like an icy fog.

And then, at last, her eyes were finally able to distinguish the outline of what appeared to be a very large man.

Her slamming heart squeezed into an icy fist.

His face was a pale blur, shadowed by a beaver hat. The rest of him was all in black.

And then, as if he could read the run of her thoughts, she detected a fleeting glint. Perhaps a flash of teeth.

Daphne bit her lip. Her heart slammed like a boot kicking her over and over again in her chest. She had planned it all. And wasn't planning one of her gifts? Over the span of two days, she had noted the crates. Calculated their heights using her own height as a comparison. Measured the sheets. Tested their strength by looping them around the bed frame. Surreptitiously measured the distance between the crates and the barrel. Noted the easy hop from the barrel to the ground.

And between the time she'd gone in this evening and the moment she'd gone out the window, somehow, for some reason, someone had moved the barrel.

And if that wasn't a metaphor for her entire life, what was?

"I'm going to count to three."

His voice seemed to come from everywhere and nowhere. So deep, so resonant, so quiet. So nearly disinterested. As if this was a matter of everyday business for him.

He could be anyone. A murderer. A rapist. A Samaritan. A hallucination.

"One . . ."

She'd already dropped her valise to the ground. She could not afford to lose a single thing in it, particularly one critical letter. He could have stolen it, she told herself. He hadn't yet.

She was positive she couldn't pull herself back up to the window again.

Moreover, she thought she might prefer to break every bone than to suffer the indignities that stalked her inside.

She considered sending the man in search of a barrel.

"Two . . ."

Her palms were wet inside her gloves. Nerves robbed her limbs of sensation. Her teeth clacked from terror. She considered whether it mattered at all whether he murdered her. For a mad instant death sounded like blessed respite from the relentless, capricious buffeting of her life.

"Three . . ."

"God help me," she whispered and leaped into the dark.

HE CAUGHT HER first by the shoulders, then she collided with a chest like a wall of bricks. Huge arms snapped around her and he staggered backward two steps. He regained his balance swiftly.

And then neatly, gently, he placed her feet on the ground.

He hadn't even grunted. One would have thought he spent his days catching flying women.

He didn't release her at once. Which was all to the good, because her knees were like water.

She remained motionless within the confines of his arms. Winded, weak with mingled terror and outrageous elation, mindless with relief. Whoever this was represented shelter and safety.

He smelled of woodsmoke and cheroot smoke and damp wool.

When she felt his chest move with a breath she was mortified to realize her hands had reflexively curled into the wet wool of his coat like a cat's claws. Her forehead was pressed against his waistcoat button.

Mortification scorched away elation, then sanity swept in. She was instantly wildly terrified to be in the grip of a strange man.

He sensed it. He released her at once and stepped back.

"There now. Are you sound?" His voice was more efficient than kind. But it was a little of both.

"Y-yes. Thank you." Her voice was frayed.

"Nothing I wouldn't also do for a drowning cat," he said amiably. "After that, it's up to the cat to survive another day, if it can manage it. God-speed, madam."

Lorcan touched his hat, pivoted, and strode three steps away from her.

Impulsively, he glanced back.

She remained rooted to where she was, statue still, it seemed, staring blankly at the wall in front of her.

He took two more, slower, steps.

Then stopped.

He pivoted.

He debated with himself over whether to ask the question. He did not have to care. He frankly didn't *want* to care.

But she looked so stunned. And very alone.

"What are your plans?" he said evenly.

She gave a start and staggered backward, away from him.

"My plans are not your concern, sir." She said it politely but firmly.

But her voice trembled.

Well, he thought. Truer words were seldom spoken.

"There won't be a sane or sober hack driver on the street in this weather," he warned.

"Which is just as well, as I planned to walk."

"I see. To . . . where, precisely?" He languidly swept an arm to indicate the black night laced by labyrinths of alleys. Here and there, blurry pin-pricks of light interrupted the dark. Lamps that would soon be snuffed either by their owners or by the relentlessly building wind. When the storm broke in earnest, not even the watch would be out on the streets.

The woman took a breath and drew herself up to her full height. The top of her head had reached about to his collarbone, and she smelled of good soap. He'd noted this when he'd held her. "Sir, I've nothing worth taking in any sense of the word. If you do not plan to rob or—or—otherwise—me, I'll just be on my way. But I am grateful for the assistance and I hope no lasting damage was done to your person by its collision with mine. Goodbye. I'll . . . think of you fondly from time to time."

It was just the sort of bracingly acerbic speech Lorcan appreciated.

She sounded more exasperated than fearful. Given where she was and what she was doing, she ought to be both. A sane woman would be, anyhow.

When he said nothing, she snatched up her bag and began walking.

She rounded the corner out of the alley and continued walking at a brisk clip, the heels of good walking shoes echoing in the dark, her bulging valise thumping against her thigh. Increasingly fat raindrops bashed down on the top of her hat and bounced off, glinting. She was soon barely visible in the misty wash of darkness and weather.

He had the strangest sense that he was watching someone wade suicidally into the ocean.

"Christ," he muttered. Irritated.

He couldn't allow it.

He followed, quietly. Stealthily. At a distance.

She made what appeared to be a decisive turn around a corner toward Lovell Street.

Seconds later, he heard the scream.

DAPHNE FLUNG HER body back against the building wall.

A knife was pointed at her throat and a mouth was open in a dark snarl inches from her eyes. "I'll just take yer baggage, now, won't I—"

Something darted out in her peripheral vision.

Her attacker howled in pain as the knife flew from his hand.

She heard it slice the air in cartwheels and land with a metallic *clink*.

Her rescuer seized a fistful of the attacker's coat in one fist and hoisted him until his boot toes scraped the cobblestones.

"ARE. YOU. MAD." Three vicious slaps whipped the would-be thief's head to and fro. Three words were delivered like barked orders.

The shocking sound of flesh striking flesh cramped Daphne's stomach.

"God have mercy . . ." Her attacker moaned. "Lordship? I didna know you were back in London—I didna know she was yer doxie, Lordship—dinna kill me—God save me—"

Lordship?

"Cease your whining. Preying on a wee woman alone," he hissed. "I should slit you like a fish. Go on. Get out of here."

He opened his hand as though dumping a chamber pot. The man dropped to his knees with a gut-churning crack. He crawled a few inches, then righted himself, and half scrambled, half stumbled away. His footfalls echoed, then faded, then were gone.

Her large rescuer didn't precisely brush his hands briskly together. But he seemed no more nonplussed than if he'd just taken a broom to a dusty cottage floor.

They regarded each other in silence for a moment.

"I'm sorry you were obliged to experience that," he said finally.

But she couldn't speak. The efficient, competent brutality of it had bludgeoned her witless.

Her fear was transcendent and arrived delayed and so total it was almost anesthetizing.

No thought or feeling could get through. She couldn't seem to form words.

He waited.

Finally, she opened her mouth, and as if waiting for her to do that, a tiny sound emerged.

It regrettably bore more resemblance to a whimper than a word.

Her back was literally against the wall. She realized it didn't feel dissimilar to the man's front.

A wall would not save her if he wanted to break *her* in half. She was certain he could.

She was shivering nearly violently now.

An overhang protected her somewhat from the ever-swifter downpour.

He remained where he stood, a dark dripping statue.

"Madam," he said quietly. Patiently. His low

voice penetrated the hiss and splat of rain like a cello. "The streets here at night are as full of sharks as the ocean. My bones tell me a storm will be long and brutal. The ones I've broken never lie. Do you have a destination? Are you meeting someone?"

He could break her in half if he wanted to, she thought again. Slit her like a fish, she supposed.

He hadn't yet.

"One hundred feet." Her wobbly voice shocked her. She sounded like someone else entirely.

"I beg your pardon?"

She cleared her throat. "It's about one hundred feet from here. I counted it off, you see, when I . . . The building. I can find it. It's white . . . there are little . . . little . . . gargoyles on the roofline, and a sign on chains . . . I saw the rules in the tobacconist's, and I liked them . . ."

She stopped, because her ability to speak had run out.

He was quiet. She wondered if he was considering the possibility that she was quite mad.

"Are you certain you want to go there?" He sounded careful.

It wasn't the question she was expecting.

"Yes."

Another odd pause. "Are you . . . looking for employment?"

And now his words seemed strangely, carefully uninflected.

It was a curious question.

Oh God. She wondered whether he was about to make her an uncomfortable offer.

"I hope to find shelter there."

This was the truth. Employment would have to wait. But it could not wait for long.

"As do I. In exchange for escorting you safely there, I should like the answer to a question."

"You may ask it," she said.

She wouldn't promise to answer it. And she didn't intend to give him her name. It was bad enough that he'd witnessed perhaps the most ignominious event of her life yet.

"Why were you climbing out of that window in the middle of the night?"

She considered this. "Because I couldn't remain where I was a moment longer."

After a moment, his smile appeared again, that white flash in the dark. He gave a short laugh. But it sounded almost like approbation.

The rain was falling faster now, the drops larger and messily splatting, as if the sheer weight of it was tearing a rent in the sky wider and wider.

"I've a question for you, sir." Though her voice was stronger now, it still wobbled.

"Very well."

"Are you, in fact, a lord?"

He paused.

"What do *you* think, luv?" he said ironically.

She didn't dare say what she thought.

And after a moment he said: "Shall we?"

For the second time that evening, she moved away from the wall and toward him, and it felt nearly the same as leaping from a crate.

Chapter Two

⟨෴⟩

THE LITTLE white building glowed like a candle flame among all the low dark ones crouching around it.

"Oh, thank God," she breathed.

Those were the first words either of them had uttered for one hundred feet. She had a feeling they were both invested in a certain anonymity, for reasons of their own.

The lamp hadn't yet been taken in from its hook. It was miraculously still burning, even as the flame juddered. Her escort leaned his head back in an attempt to read the sign, which was impossible, as it was dancing and twisting on its chains in the winds.

Daphne rapped on the door.

She jumped backward when something hit the door with a soft thud from the opposite side.

There was a sound of a scuffle and a male expostulating.

The peep hatch flew open.

A large, pale eye appeared, blinked, then inspected them.

"Good evening." The owner of the eye sounded a little winded, if cheerful. "Welcome to The Grand Palace on the Thames. What can we do for you?"

Daphne found the young woman's voice—the cadences of a good servant in a fine household—very reassuring.

"Good evening," Daphne said in her best Lady of the Manor voice. "We're hoping you've rooms to let. I saw your advertisement and it seemed very clear that this is a fine establishment, indeed."

"Oh, how *lovely*!" The young woman sounded genuinely delighted. "You'll want to have a chat with our proprietresses, Mrs. Hardy and Mrs. Durand. As we're very exclusive, you see."

There ensued the scrape of a bolt being shot, and the door swung open upon paradise: a black-and-white marble foyer shining beneath a chandelier dripping with crystals. Blessed warmth rushed out and embraced them as though they were prodigal family.

They were ushered in by a young woman wearing a white cap which had tipped sideways on her blond head, as if she'd just collided with something.

Behind her stood a tall young man wearing understated blue livery and a harried expression. Both of them sported flushed cheeks.

"My name is Dot."

"I'm Mr. Pike."

They spoke at precisely the same time, which seemed to fluster them into silence. Their mouths then set in twin, stubborn lines.

Mr. Pike inhaled audibly and at length, seemingly mustering patience. He offered a smile. "Would you like me to take your wet wraps so you can warm yourselves next to the fire while you wait for Mrs. Durand and Mrs. Hardy?"

The foyer was flanked by what appeared to be two rooms; he gestured to the one on his left.

Daphne and her rescuer surrendered their hats and dripping wraps to the footman—her cloak, his dark, many-caped greatcoat, his beaver hat, her bonnet—and the maid named Dot watched him bear them away. Her expression confusingly suggested Mr. Pike had just robbed her.

"Have you indeed rooms to let, miss?" her escort prompted.

She turned with a start to them. And then she went still and studied them with what appeared to be unabashed fascination.

"We've a suite available. It's very nice and a bit . . ." She lowered her voice as if she were confiding a delicious secret. ". . . *dear*."

Daphne's stomach clutched. A suite. Singular, she'd said. Perhaps only one room.

"A suite includes more than one room?" her companion cleverly asked.

"*Three*, sir." She glowed as she imparted this marvel. "A sitting room, and two rooms for sleeping."

This was marginally better.

"And the doors properly close and lock?"

"All of our doors and windows properly close and lock," Dot informed him proudly. "And all of our hinges are well oiled, and our flues are clean." Dot seemed to have interpreted this question as a matter of housekeeping. "I'll go and tell Mrs. Hardy and Mrs. Durand that you're here."

She whirled and thundered up the stairs.

By the time Lorcan and Daphne arrived at their door, a bitter, relentless January wind had been soughing and moaning through previously un-suspected cracks and crevasses of The Grand Palace on the Thames for nigh on a fortnight. It seemed no room was exempt.

"It sounds like a Peruvian whistle," Mrs. Pariseau had said one night in the sitting room, with startling specificity. She was one of their very first guests, a spirited widow who seemed possessed of a great store of arcane knowledge, so everyone assumed this was correct.

"Sounds a bit like my digestion," Mr. Delacorte reflected in the smoking room. Anyone who had spent time with Mr. Delacorte there could attest that this was also correct.

"It sounds a bit like you when I make love to you," Captain Hardy murmured into Delilah's neck while they were in bed one morning, listening to a low moaning created by the wind, and she'd given him a playful little swat.

"It's like the incessant chatter of a guilty con-science," Lucien, Lord Bolt, marveled on a hush to his wife, Angelique, as they lay awake one night, listening to it.

"Well, when you think about some of the things this building has seen . . ." Angelique murmured.

In the scullery, the wind had once groaned so sorrowfully and so harrowingly Dot had taken such a fright that she now refused to enter it alone, or at night. The very notion of ghosts both terrified and thrilled her, but she also found it thrilling to be terrified. She liked to imagine she was a heroine in a Horrid novel.

All in all, the creaks, cracks, sighs, and whistles made Delilah and Angelique feel as if The Grand Palace on the Thames suddenly milled with unseen guests. Which was unsettling, as the ones they could see were challenge enough.

Delilah and Angelique had lately been forced to admit to themselves that they had made a series of rare miscalculations. Flush from their success of letting a room to a scandalous opera singer in exchange for a spectacularly profitable night of entertainment, they had taken a chance on a charming, blushing, coltish trio of young German musicians who agreed to play in the sitting room at night now and again in exchange for a reduced rate on their rooms. They were polite, they spoke little English, and they played like angels.

But they ate like oxen. With terrifying, unanticipated speed and gusto. Mr. Delacorte's waistcoat button had popped twice as a result of efforts to keep up. Even Helga, who hailed from Germany and was inclined to be indulgent with anyone who appreciated her cooking, had been alarmed. She'd been compelled to frantically replan menus and shopping lists and budgets.

When they weren't practicing Mozart exquisitely in the annex ballroom, Hans, Otto, and Friedreich laughed uproariously amongst themselves in the sitting room and flirted with the maids. All Delilah and Angelique had to do if they wanted to discover why Rose or Meggie

hadn't yet finished the dusting was to follow the
sound of giggling.

And then there was Mr. Angus McDonald,
a somber, flame-headed Scottish scholar they'd
admitted because they found his brogue a thing
of great beauty, a sound like rough water tumbling over rocks on the misty moors. Which
meant, unfortunately, they often could scarcely
understand him. During his interview, they had
mistaken what proved to be a certain unyield-
ing dourness for appealing gravity. And he said
things like "He's an awfy scunnersome laddie"
and "Whit dae ye pit in clapshot?" which they
suspected might be faintly insulting, but they
could mostly only nod and smile, as not even
Captain Hardy nor Mrs. Pariseau was fluent in
Scots Gaelic. They felt rather terrible about it,
but he was meant to stay only a fortnight, and
he had been given the room over Delacorte. The
encroaching storm likely meant Mr. McDonald
was going nowhere soon, unless it was mad,
driven there by Mr. Delacorte's snoring.

And if Mr. McDonald and the German boys
occupied opposite poles, in between were their
husbands, who were at the moment moodily
smoking in the gentlemen's smoking room and
talking in low voices of worrisome things they
clearly didn't want Delilah and Angelique to
hear. Captain Hardy, a legendary former blockade commander, and Lucien, the bastard son of
a duke who had made a fortune at sea, were now
partners (along with Mr. Delacorte) in an import
endeavor, the Triton Group. Their ship carrying

silks and spices from the Orient was nearly a fortnight overdue in port. This was the source of their
muttering. Any number of things could have happened to *The Zephyr*. Taken by pirates or sunk by
a storm. A lightning strike might have turned the
mizzenmast into a torch. Mutiny. Illness. Tsuna-
mis. Sea monsters.

For more than a week Captain Hardy and
Lucien had been away from home for long hours
in meetings with investors and merchants and
insurers, as well as helping to sandbag storage
warehouses in preparation for the anticipated
storm.

"It's going to be a bad one," they'd grimly
predicted.

The ladies had prepared as best they could.
Menus were planned that wouldn't involve fre-
quent trips to market; a little library of books and
games, like Spillikins and decks of cards, were
collected and installed in rooms, and embroidery
silks and yarn and oil pastels were stockpiled in
case a guest wished to pass the time knitting or
drawing.

Such had been the steadily gathering tension at
The Grand Palace on the Thames, Captain Hardy
had taken to mostly speaking in tense monosyllables even to his wife, as if to offset the relentless vigor of the German boys. And he was never
loquacious at best. Delilah could scarcely bear it.

So Angelique and Delilah went after the drafts
the way Gordon, their fat, striped cat, went after
mice, because moisture was the cancer of an old
building like The Grand Palace on the Thames,

and it was one of the few things they currently could control. Mr. Pike, their prized new footman, had been so helpful in that regard. But he, too, needed to be fed, and male servants were taxed.

When the first raindrops finally began to fall it was almost a relief, and Angelique and Delilah looked up alertly at the familiar and portentous sound of Dot scrambling up the stairs and set aside their mending as she burst breathlessly into the room.

"We've visitors who would like to let a suite."

"A suite!" said Delilah. "Well then. What are they like, Dot?"

"She is a lady. And he is a pirate."

She gazed at them with a look of happy expectation.

Delilah and Angelique exchanged glances.

"Dot," Angelique began carefully. "Are you certain you aren't confusing the two of them with the story Mrs. Pariseau read in the sitting room the other night?"

"She is a lady." Dot, the former worst lady's maid in the world and current cherished-if-occasionally-bewildering member of the staff, was a trifle indignant. She did know her ladies from her not-ladies. "She talks just like you and Mrs. Durand, elegant, like." She liltingly imitated them. "Her cloak is good wool, but not in the first stare of fashion. Her shoes are well made but the toes are worn and she has all of her teeth and a nice smile. But she's very pale and her eyes are like this." She bracketed her own with her fingers and stretched her lids to illustrate someone who looked as though they'd had a tremendous surprise. "And he is a pirate," she concluded firmly.

Delilah heard Angelique draw in a long, audible breath. As if she hoped if she sucked in enough air she'd find some nourishing patience somewhere in it, the way a whale took in krill.

Dot fanned out a hand and with the other counted out qualities on her fingers. "He is wearing a gold earring. And I think there's a ruby in it! An earring! I ask you! His hair is *this* long"—she pointed to a place below her ear—"and it's black as a raven's wing! His teeth are bright. He is enormous." Enormous was a word she'd lately taken to using as often as possible. "Black as a raven's wing" she'd absorbed from one of the Horrid novels they'd read aloud in the sitting room at night. "And . . ." She paused, to heighten the sense of drama. "He has a scar from here"—she slowly drew it with her fingertip along her own face—"to here."

They had to admit, their potential new guest sounded somewhat piratical. It wasn't out of the realm of the possible, given that their pristine little boardinghouse was located near the docks. Even pirates had to disembark their ships sometimes.

She paused. "He seems pleasant, however," she added, dubiously. "Pirates aren't usually, are they?"

Angelique furrowed her brow. "Hmm. Did you inspect him for parrots, Dot, or wooden limbs?"

"No," Dot admitted, dejectedly.

"And they're a married couple?" Delilah was

already untying her apron and smoothing her skirts in preparation for going downstairs.

"Well . . . she's a lady alone with a man late at night and she said 'we are looking for rooms.' And I told them we had a suite of rooms available and it was dear, and they said 'that will do.'"

Dot was hardly entirely naive. But neither Angelique nor Delilah wanted to enlighten her as to the variety of interesting reasons a Lady with a capital "L" might be compelled to take a room with a pirate for just the night. Most of those reasons did not *quite* align with their vision for The Grand Palace on the Thames. Every now and then a man brandishing a crumpled, yellowing menu of prurient services would appear at the door and request the Vicar's Wheelbarrow. He would be sent packing with an admonishment to *read the sign*. Granted, the building's past did still haunt the sign in the form of a single word: "rogues," still faintly visible behind the elegantly lettered "The Grand Palace on the Thames."

"Well, we'll just go and have a chat with them, shall we? Will you bring in tea?" Angelique hung her apron on the hook near the door.

Usually this request prompted Dot to hop delightedly and bolt back down the stairs.

She remained rooted in place.

Angelique's and Delilah's eyebrows launched in tandem.

"Before we go down . . ." Dot took a deep breath. "I've something unfortunate to tell you."

Delilah and Angelique said not a word to each other. Nor did they meet each other's eyes.

The silent words "Oh, God" throbbed in the air.

"Very well," Angelique finally ventured.

"It gives me no pleasure to report it," Dot warned somberly.

"You can tell us anything, Dot," Delilah said gently as Angelique's eyes flared a caution at Delilah. In truth, neither of them was certain they could withstand hearing all of Dot's thoughts. It would be like taking all the medicines in Mr. Delacorte's case. Hallucinatory. Headache-inducing. One might never be the same after.

Dot took another deep sustaining breath and exhaled.

"Mr. Pike cursed near the front door."

Angelique and Delilah carefully refrained from meeting each other's eyes.

"I see," Angelique said gravely.

"It was the word that begins with a 'b' and ends with an 'ucks,'" Dot expounded.

So . . . bollocks.

"Right beneath our *chandelier*," she pressed on, when they said nothing. She made it sound as though he'd urinated upon the holy sepulcher. The chandelier was, in fact, practically sacred as far as Dot was concerned. Below it, the words "The Grand Palace on the Thames" had first been uttered. Dot had been included in that magical moment and she never forgot it.

With great patience, Delilah suggested, "Did you perhaps step on Pike's foot again, Dot?"

Dot hesitated. "His foot was the only part of him that arrived at the door before I did. I didn't see it there when I arrived."

She gazed innocently at them, which was no challenge for her as she'd come into the world equipped with eyes like dinner plates. She was blossoming in interesting ways since they'd all moved into The Grand Palace on the Thames. While they rather liked her emerging initiative and competitive streak, it was becoming clear they might need to guide and prune it the way one might coax roses over a trellis, before it ran amuck and sprouted into full-blown guile.

"He almost stepped on mine just the other day," she defended, correctly interpreting their expressions again. "And he's a good deal . . . taller." The word "taller" drifted a little wistfully when she said it.

Pike was indeed tall. And fit. And probably anybody's definition of handsome.

If only he wasn't her nemesis, was the implication.

After the long and fruitless and frustrating search for a footman, Mr. Pike had been their reward at the end of a thrilling, harrowing episode at The Grand Palace on the Thames involving an earl's runaway fiancée and a spymaster. And all the maids had been beside themselves with glee. Until Dot realized he would be competition.

"Dot, even fine, upstanding men might curse if trod upon in just the wrong place," Delilah informed her.

"Oh, I didn't know that." Dot absorbed this information for a moment. "What is just the wrong place?"

"No. We're not going to give you advice on

how to torment Mr. Pike," Angelique said firmly. "You are the senior employee, he is new, and as such we should like you to arrive at a compromise with Mr. Pike whereby the door is answered promptly and politely and no one comes away from it limping."

"Am I in *charge* of Mr. Pike?" she breathed. Her face had gone radiant with possibility.

"No. But you are by way of a mentor. Someone who is kind enough to share their experience with a new person on staff." Angelique, the former governess, was always a little stricter than Delilah, who never objected, as the two of their methods combined had proven to be effective.

"I see," Dot replied, only a little deflated.

"Perhaps he's still sore from the last time you trod upon him," Delilah added. "*You* might even curse under such circumstances."

"I would *never*," Dot vowed, after the fashion of a martyr.

"Good to know, Dot," Delilah humored. "Thank you for telling us about Mr. Pike. Will you go and make tea for our potential new guests now, please?"

Dot bolted down the stairs again.

AND WHEN DOT vanished up the stairs, Daphne and his Lordship at last turned to look at each other in the light of the chandelier.

Whenever a surge of emotion tempted Daphne to avert her eyes from something, some stubborn, pilgrim quality of character compelled her to confront it with a steady gaze instead. She wanted to be brave. Permanently brave. She thought perhaps the more she worked at it, the braver she would become. It seemed the best way to ensure she was never frightened or hurt again.

"When you look at me like that, I feel like you can see into every crevice of my mind," Henry had once told her with a little laugh.

She'd been warmed clear through. She'd thought he'd found it charming.

So even as she felt her every muscle contract against this man's sheer sensory impact, she didn't look away from him.

And he was fearsome.

His face had the stark drama of a landscape shaped by elemental forces, battering seas and brutal winds and the like. Shadows lurked in the little valleys beneath cheekbones hard and high as fortress walls. Black whiskers glinted on his box-cornered jaw. Thick, dark brows hung over deep-set eyes. A majestic nose presided over all of this.

And a bright, white scar snaked like lightning from the corner of his eye to nearly his chin.

Perhaps that's how he'd gotten so adept at knocking knives from hands. Someone in his history hadn't missed. He'd probably decided that was never going to happen again.

His mouth—long and surprisingly beautifully shaped, the lower lip unequivocally sensual—curved in a patient, sardonic smile.

He likely knew what she was thinking and gave not one damn. There probably wasn't a thing or a person a man like this would need to worry about.

What an enviable condition.

His expression gave no clue as to what he thought of her.

She suddenly felt small and ridiculous and plain next to him. As if the two of them were costumed for a pantomime. But who was she anymore, after all? She'd slipped and lodged in that awkward gap between social strata. Tumbling down further was unthinkable; her efforts to extricate herself merely seemed to wedge her in more tightly.

He turned away from her and inspected the room into which they'd been ushered.

It was soft and pink as a maiden's blush in the firelight and so achingly cozy a lump formed in her throat.

The crystal chandelier had fallen in love with him: it picked out a blue gleam in his hair, the glint from the gold hoop in his ear, and sprinkled a few rainbows on his black coat. His hair fell to his collar and was tucked behind his ears.

"It looks like a granny's house," he murmured, bemused. "This place was once called The Palace of Rogues. It used to be a bordello."

She recoiled. "You thought you were escorting me to a *bordell*—"

They pivoted at the soft swish of wool skirts and the brisk click of heels on marble. A blond woman and a brunette, side by side, wearing welcoming smiles.

No.

It couldn't be.

Shock fleetingly warped the room before her

eyes. Then it merged with disbelief and shame and embarrassment before they all settled in an icy-hot pool over her heart.

Of all the things Daphne dared to waste a moment wishing for over the years—that Henry would have been an only child, for instance, so that his brother would never had needed a governess, that her father had never learned how to play five-card loo—this wish was perhaps the most fervent of them all: that a trap door would open beneath her. Because her pride was an open wound. She sincerely felt she hadn't the strength.

And yet, like all the moments that had preceded this one, she would need to face it anyway.

"Good evening. Welcome to The Grand Palace on the—"

The dark-haired woman stopped abruptly and her hand flew to her mouth in shock.

She slowly lowered it.

"Oh, my goodness," she breathed. "Lady Worth? *Daphne?*"

Chapter Three

‹❦❧›

DAPHNE'S BODY knew what to do before she knew which words to form; her knees dipped in a curtsy.

"Delilah! Oh, my goodness . . . what a pleasure . . . I cannot believe . . . that is . . . it's been so long. Forgive me . . . ought I to call you . . . Lady Derring?"

Mortified heat rushed into her face. What an appalling hash of a sentence.

There really was no gracious way to say, "The last time I saw you, you were about to marry an earl, and now look at you! Here at a boarding-house by the docks not one hundred feet away from where I was nearly robbed."

It had been perhaps eight years. Funny how time races when juggling one disaster after another.

And to think her life had once been orderly and elegant and scripted. Belatedly she realized it was because she'd seldom been presented with social situations that defied convention.

Daphne was—had been—perhaps still was?—Delilah's social superior in every way: in wealth and stature and family name.

But Delilah had possessed a different sort of social supremacy: she was beautiful. It had proved to be Delilah's impoverished family's salvation.

Daphne had not ever resented her. After all, they were united by the tension that beset all women: the rest of their lives depended upon making perfect matches. Daphne had money and stature; Delilah had eyes like a doe. These were what they brought to the marriage mart and her doe eyes had helped Delilah captivate the Earl of Derring.

And furthermore, the last time Daphne had seen Delilah, she'd been so certain of her own future, so satisfied with how she envisioned life unfolding with Henry, it was simply impossible to begrudge a poor knight's daughter the attentions of an earl.

Delilah's cheeks sported bright pink spots, too. She'd apparently wisely opted for silence instead of attempting a sentence. But she couldn't stop her famously lovely dark eyes from moving wonderingly between Daphne and the man standing next to her as if she'd been presented with an equation impossible to solve.

"Life has been eventful indeed in the intervening years," Delilah began with a little laugh. "It's an honor to be able to welcome you to *my* home."

Delilah had been to Daphne's home for teas and picnics and assemblies. They had liked each other. And yet both had been aware that Daphne had been extending graciousness and charity to the poor daughter of a knight.

"I'm not certain whether such news would have reached you, but the Earl of Derring passed away not long ago. I've remarried. I'm known as Mrs. Hardy now."

"I had not heard. I'm so terribly sorry for your loss." She grasped hold of this platitude gratefully.

Intriguingly, Delilah hadn't qualified the earl's passing with a "sadly."

"I'm very well and happy," Delilah added hurriedly, and, Daphne thought, with a frisson of defensiveness. "My husband is—" She pressed her lips together, then gave another little laugh. "Oh, for heaven's sake! Forgive me. Do let me start over, Daphne! In my delight and astonishment in seeing you again I have quite forgotten my manners. Allow me to introduce my dear friend and fellow proprietress of The Grand Palace on the Thames, Mrs. Angelique Durand."

So, Delilah, a former countess, now ran a boardinghouse near the *docks*.

The golden-haired Mrs. Durand curtsied. "How do you do, Lady Worth?"

Hers was another soothing accent: it spoke of education and refinement.

"A pleasure to meet you, Mrs. Durand." Daphne's knees recognized those words as a cue for another curtsy.

Throughout these exchanges, the large, fearsome stranger who had apparently thought he was leading her to a bordello remained so quiet and watchful he might have been one of the gargoyles lining the roof.

There fell the inevitable awkward pause, during which torment ramped in Daphne.

Because the three of them were such well-bred

ladies, and as such were bound by and observed the social rituals and niceties, Daphne knew what they expected her to do next.

But she couldn't do it.

More specifically, because she hadn't the faintest idea what to say.

Delilah prompted gently, tentatively, "Dot tells us you'd like a suite. How lovely! This must be your . . . husband?"

In truth, there wasn't *quite* an ellipsis' worth of hesitation before she said the word husband.

But the minute pause fair echoed like a chasm.

Because they all knew there was only one acceptable answer.

And it was the glimmer of hope in the words that cut Daphne so savagely: Delilah hoped Daphne had not plummeted so far in life that she was now the unmarried lover of a large pirate. Delilah clearly hoped that her life was as happy as her own apparently was, when it was patently not.

If Dot hadn't already made it clear to Mrs. Durand and Mrs. Hardy she was amenable to sharing a suite with this man, and if anyone else at all besides Delilah had asked the question, she might have been able to spontaneously invent an alias and a story. An alias had been her plan, after all, when she'd gone out the window.

But she didn't know Delilah well enough to tell her the truth of her life as it was now. Moreover, her pride wouldn't let her.

And the truth was scaldingly painful, humiliating, frightening, and messy. To tell it properly she would need to start with what had happened with Henry. She in fact knew no one intimately enough to entrust with her truth, unless it was Henry. He'd once been the beating heart at the center of her everything. Everything else had been a tributary that ran to and through the fact of him.

There was the shorter truth: *Oh, this man? I found him in an alley while I was leaping from a window, right into his arms!*

And as another second ticked by Daphne realized that chasm of silence had a crumbling edge. The man standing next to her was a terrifyingly unknown quantity. In less than an hour, she had come to believe he was capable of anything.

He proved her correct by doing the most shocking thing of all.

"Aye, just call me Mr. Lady Worth. For indeed, I am Daphne's proud husband."

He bent his big frame in a bow so low, slow, and graceful it flirted with parody. It was a sensual caress of a bow.

Daphne noted that Delilah and Mrs. Durand were at once transfixed.

When upright he said, "I more typically answer to Mr. Lorcan St. Leger. It is indeed a pleasure to meet any friend of my wife's. Thank you both for welcoming us to your establishment. I understand The Grand Palace on the Thames is very exclusive and it's easy to see why."

It was such a pretty speech it was almost impossible to believe he'd recently hissed a death threat to a knife-wielding thug. If she'd closed her eyes, she could almost believe he was a gentleman. Almost.

Relief and humiliation and relief again visited her in violent succession, like those slaps he'd applied to the thief. He'd solved a problem and created another.

But wasn't that the run of her life lately?

Daphne realized she had never before outright, baldly lied to anyone. A lie made up out of whole cloth. And in a moment of startling epiphany, she realized it was because she'd never really needed to. She wondered how many things she would be willing to do if she were cornered. If self-righteousness was really just the bastion of the comfortable.

"Thank you, Mr. St. Leger," Delilah said. "That is very kind of you to say."

Both Mrs. Hardy and Mrs. Durand were regarding him with the sort of fascination and amazement to which he was no doubt accustomed.

Which made her wonder what sort of men *they'd* married.

Another silent interval ensued.

Aplomb was in short supply in the pink room.

"Well. Daphne!" Delilah turned to her. "My goodness. I suppose we can both attest that life certainly takes turns we do not anticipate. As do our hearts, I expect," Delilah added, delicately.

It was a tremendously kind thing to say.

"Aye," Daphne croaked. Absurdly. After a long moment.

She could not look at Mr. St. Leger.

"We thank you for your kind words, Mrs. Hardy," St. Leger said soberly.

"Thank you, Mr. St. Leger. Please, do have a seat. Dot should return shortly with the tea, and I expect you'll both need it. Perhaps you would like a little brandy to take off the chill?"

"We are so grateful for your hospitality," he said again. "Brandy would be most welcome."

We. The word clanged against her ear. "We" had meant something else altogether to her once, something nearly sacred. It had belonged to her and someone else.

She was painfully reminded of the shelter and promise in the word. Because even though hearing it abraded her soul a little, she was oddly, pathetically grateful for the moment to be part of a "we."

"How DID THE two of you meet?"

It was a perfectly reasonable question, one not typically met with the mute stares with which she and Mr. St. Leger presented them.

"Would you like to begin, my dear?" St. Leger prompted, gently.

My dear. Oh God. She should probably prepare herself for more of this. She would probably need to issue endearments of her own.

She hesitated.

Then she cleared her throat. "Well, we met on a night much like this one . . ."

She turned toward him, tentatively.

". . . stormy and thrilling and a little bit dangerous. Just like me, my darling wife is fond of saying," he added.

"Ha ha!" Daphne laughed cautiously. "We do have our little jokes."

Delilah and Angelique smiled patiently.

"Alas, the missus has *quite* domesticated me," he said with every evidence of satisfaction.

Which was funny, because by virtue of settling onto a pretty pink settee, he looked twice as feral as he had before.

Mrs. Hardy and Mrs. Durand watched, appearing somewhat spellbound, when he slowly leaned back and crossed his legs.

He surreptitiously nudged her with an elbow.

"It's a rather long and very bit of a, well, *personal* story, in truth," she began. "You see, I had come to London for a visit. And I . . . I found myself in a bit of a predicament, and in need of some urgent assistance. In part because I had dropped something very important to me . . . and there he was. He simply refused to take no for an answer when it came to helping."

"I could not possibly leave such a lady dangling in distress," he said humbly.

Miraculously, Delilah and Angelique appeared content with this halting little story.

"And I am grateful for this quality in him," Daphne added.

This was true. However complicated that gratitude. However much she wished no one on earth had witnessed her ignominious window escape.

She turned toward him and looked up. "And then, after one look at his . . ." *Earring. Scar. Glower. Eyes. Lips. Black, black hair.* She faltered. "One look and I . . ."

His eyes mesmerized her. By rights they ought to be black and fierce, but they were surprisingly light and clear. Shades of mossy green shifted into golden brown. They reminded her of the eyes of a wild animal, perhaps a fox or a wolf, in that they seemed ageless and remote. The eyes of a creature whose acquired wisdom and instincts and experience were entirely alien from her own.

But gradually, before her eyes, they took on a gleam of wicked amusement.

It occurred to her that Delilah and Angelique probably thought they were blissfully lost in each other's eyes rather than paralyzed in indecision about which lie that wasn't a lie to tell next.

He freed her from his gaze by turning to their now riveted audience. "One might say it was destined."

She nodded. "Destined," she echoed weakly.

This story, remarkably, seemed to touch both Mrs. Hardy and Mrs. Durand. They were both now wearing indulgent expressions.

"We've had more than a little experience with destiny here at The Grand Palace on the Thames," Delilah reassured her. "And we have both met our husbands under unusual circumstances, haven't we?"

"Indeed," Angelique said. "And we're both very happy."

"My favorite memories usually begin with unusual circumstances," Mr. St. Leger said, probably truthfully.

"It's so good to know you are well and happy, Daphne," Delilah said.

"Very kind of you to say," Daphne replied. "And you as well. It certainly seems like serendipity to see you again on a night that portends to be as brutal as this one. L-l-orcan's bones tell him," she explained hurriedly, absurdly thrilled to have an actual fact to impart. "About the weather."

She mentally kicked herself for the stutter. She keenly felt the tiny embarrassment of using his first name.

Lorcan nodded sagely. "How well she knows me."

"What brings the two of you to The Grand Palace on the Thames this evening?" Mrs. Durand asked.

"Well, my ship reached harbor yesterday, ahead of the storm. I've been in London all day conducting business. Daphne had earlier seen an advertisement for The Grand Palace on the Thames in a shop. It sounded like just the sort of fine, cozy place she'd like to stay."

Good heavens. He not only remembered her disjointed babbling, he'd managed to interpret it correctly.

The mention of a ship was interesting, indeed.

Unless he was a pirate.

Angelique and Delilah exchanged a satisfied glance.

Daphne glanced toward the doorway at the

sound of clinking. Dot was approaching at a stately pace, bearing a rattling tea tray laden with a pot and porcelain cups.

Delilah cleared her throat. "Your ship, Mr. St. Leger. Are you a . . ."

Dot froze like a statue on the threshold. Her breath appeared to be held.

"A privateer, Mrs. Hardy. For nigh on three years."

(It was a crestfallen Dot who delivered the tea tray, which rattled more profoundly on descent, but did not crash.)

It seemed ridiculous to feel relieved that her fake husband was not, in fact, a pirate, but she needed a blessing to count.

She knew what privateers did. It was piracy of a sort, sanctioned by the crown, supplementing the work of the navy. Capturing enemy ships for cargo and ransoming crews. Dangerous. And often very, very lucrative.

"And do you travel with your husband, Mrs. St. Leger?" Mrs. Durand set about pouring and handing cups around.

Daphne went still.

Mr. St. Leger had just said his ship had docked. Her heart picked up a beat.

"I have indeed traveled with him," she said carefully.

One hundred entire feet, unless one also counted the air distance from the crates to his chest.

Surely it was unseemly to feel triumphant each time she managed to tell a lie that wasn't a lie.

She wondered if this indelicate instinct for survival at any cost had simply lain dormant until it was needed.

"Life on a ship with your husband!" Angelique exclaimed. "How thrilling that must be."

Daphne smiled at her. "It is unlike anything I've ever before experienced."

"She's surprisingly resourceful in risky situations." St. Leger sipped his tea. The little white teacup looked as crushable as an egg in his big hand.

"That doesn't surprise me," Delilah said stoutly, thereby surprising Daphne. "Perhaps you already know this, Mr. St. Leger, that Daphne was the lady of her house from the time she was . . ."

"Eleven years old," Daphne completed.

"Isn't it remarkable?" was what St. Leger smoothly chose to say. "I suspect it's how she became so resourceful."

Daphne turned to Angelique. "My mother passed away then, leaving just my father and me and my brothers."

"I'm so sorry. I lost my mother at a young age, too," Angelique told her.

The warmth of commiseration bound them all for a moment.

And then Delilah surprised her again. "My mother always pointed you out as an example of fine young ladyhood I should strive for."

"How delightful for you," Daphne said dryly. "I'm so sorry."

Angelique and Delilah laughed.

"Everyone admired Daphne for being so

clever when we were younger," Delilah, who had been admired for being beautiful, added wistfully.

The compliment made Daphne flush. "I didn't realize. It isn't always particularly valued in a woman, cleverness."

"No truly strong man is frightened of a clever woman," St. Leger said.

Thus ensuring he was at once bathed in fond looks of approbation.

"Angelique is very clever, too," Delilah said proudly. "She speaks five languages. She was a governess."

That word. Even after all these years it was like a quick shiv prick to Daphne's rib.

The tiny shock of it blanked her mind for an instant.

When Lorcan's earring glinted in her peripheral vision she realized he had turned to look at her because a little conversational lull had set in.

Daphne was practically an Olympian at composure regaining. She'd had a lot of practice.

It began with a deep breath, which she took.

Suddenly everyone pivoted toward the sound of boot heels swiftly crossing the marble foyer.

And into the room without preamble swept two of the most strikingly handsome men Daphne had ever seen.

Delilah and Angelique rose to their feet.

But not before they exchanged a quick "what on earth?" glance.

Lorcan slowly rose to his, too. Daphne followed suit.

Daphne noticed Lorcan's hand flex at his side. As if he were regretting the absence of a sword.

Her arms went cold with nerves.

"It seems our husbands have blessed us with an unexpected visit," Delilah explained. And while the word "husbands" was rich with wry warmth, the word "unexpected" was given an interesting emphasis. "Allow me to introduce mine, Captain Tristan Hardy."

The man with cool, silvery eyes and close-cropped hair bowed.

"And my husband, Lord Bolt," Angelique announced.

Bolt's dark hair was longer; he had a long, fine-boned face and unusual green eyes. And he bowed, too.

Both were tall, slim, broad of shoulder, and fierce of expression. Both were profoundly different in appearance in nearly every other way, from their clothing to their posture.

Delilah and Angelique scooted together to the middle of the settee so their husbands could flank them, as it seemed clear that neither intended to leave.

"Last time we met, Lord Bolt," St. Leger said slowly, "we were dispatching pirates in the Atlantic."

Bolt's fixed regard evolved swiftly into delighted recognition. "St. Leger! Almost didn't recognize you without a sword at your hip."

"Funny, I always picture St. Leger wearing a noose."

Captain Hardy said this so lightly that it was a moment before the words registered among those gathered.

And when they did the silence and stillness was so abrupt it sucked the air from the room like a gasp.

Chapter Four

✦

DELILAH SLOWLY turned her head toward her husband.

Who had eyes only for Lorcan St. Leger.

Mr. St. Leger was also engaged in not blinking.

Daphne gave a nervous little laugh. "Oh, yes. Mr. and Mrs. Blackguard! That's us." Some wayward impulse prompted her to pat her fake husband on the knee.

The collision of her hand and his thigh reverberated through her bones clear to her teeth.

She might as well have struck a rock.

Her hand lay still, momentarily stunned like a bird that had slammed into a window.

Long enough for the wily opportunist to cover it with his own.

Her lungs seized. She could hardly snatch the hand away in front of the tribunal deciding their fate.

They both looked down.

Her hand had all but disappeared beneath his.

The entirety of her being seemed to congregate to where their skin met.

Never mind that for the first time in her life her hand was a mere shocking few inches away from the clothed penis of a man she'd met in an alley.

It was pantomime affection and a liberty taken. By rights she ought to be infuriated, but in her exhaustion, she could not sort out the proper indignation from the clamor of things she felt. She felt two things: a gruesome remnant of bitter regret that it was not Henry's hand; and, despite that—despite everything—strangely, obscurely comforted.

To her horror, her eyes began to burn with tears.

She looked up to see that the eyes of both women had gone meltingly soft.

A little puzzled shadow had appeared between Lord Bolt's brows.

The cool steel of Captain Hardy's regard was now not reserved only for her fake husband. He was watching her, too.

Captain Hardy struck her as the sort who missed nothing and never softened.

She was increasingly certain he had a very good reason not to, when it came to Lorcan St. Leger.

Who finally, gently, lifted his hand.

She withdrew her own gingerly from his thigh and tucked it away at her side.

"Daphne—the former Lady Worth—and I knew each other as girls," Delilah explained to Bolt and Hardy.

"A pleasure, Mrs. St. Leger," Captain Hardy said.

Daphne nodded. "The pleasure is mine, Captain Hardy."

"I suspect you are all amazed that such a fine

lady as Daphne agreed to wed a great ugly brute like me. But I am no coward so I made free to ask her. I every day endeavor to be worthy of her favor."

Such a humble, courtly speech. So nearly archaic in its cadences. As she watched that particular fairy dust known as charm settle over nearly every person in the room, she was reminded of why she distrusted it. It was so often employed to obscure a real truth, or to . . . *maneuver* someone.

Or maybe she just envied it. She'd more than once worried she possessed no charm. Ceaseless responsibility had made her habitually briskly efficient. A shyness that no one suspected in her sometimes made her seem too stiffly formal or too earnest. And feelings of all kinds visited her with such force she sometimes went mute from them, which had always seemed to her a weakness to be disguised and managed. For if she had ever been valued for anything, it was for her steadiness.

And while her intelligence was fierce, like her father's, her wit often had bite.

None of these qualities seemed to add up to winsomeness.

Her cheeks had gone warm.

Everyone had turned to her for her reaction and she had yet to say a word.

Somehow, she found the right ones. "You can see how he won me."

Most of the people in the room smiled warmly.

Too late she thought she ought to have protested, with perhaps a playful little arm swat, something to the effect of "Nonsense. You are neither ugly nor a brute."

She was no longer certain of the definition of either of those words. Her imagination had somehow not extended to the existence of a man like Lorcan St. Leger.

"And we're so grateful to know you've a list of sensible rules. The missus loves rules," he assured Delilah and Angelique.

Well. It wasn't untrue.

"Opposites do tend to attract," Captain Hardy said pleasantly.

Daphne went warily still.

"Indeed. I imagine that's what attracted a countess to a blockade captain from St. Giles," St. Leger countered just as pleasantly.

Both of them were smiling.

Neither of them were blinking.

Daphne's stomach contracted as another infinitesimal silence formed and settled in.

It was like watching two people fence with silk rapiers. It seemed only a matter of time before someone was hurt.

Delilah turned to her husband again. She seemed as unsettled as Daphne was, which was proof that something was awry.

But Captain Hardy's gaze remained fixed on Mr. St. Leger like a hound pointing at a hare.

Did Captain Hardy know how dangerous Mr. St. Leger could be?

He must know. Perhaps that was why he was watching him.

Daphne's heart clogged her throat.

"My husband was indeed a blockade captain," Mrs. Hardy told Daphne, proudly. Carefully. "And now he and Lord Bolt and our guest Mr. Delacorte are partners in an import endeavor called the Triton Group. They own their own ship."

"Isn't that a coincidence," Lorcan said. "Twelve frightening and competent men call me captain now."

There was a silence.

"You're a privateer," Captain Hardy said flatly.

He didn't bother to disguise the emphasis on "you're."

"For the past three years. Quite a successful one."

"For whom do you sail now that the war is over?"

"For England during the war. Now I've a commission from Argentina. I'm back in England to pay off the rest of my ship. She'll be all mine." He paused, and smiled. "She's called *The Rogue*. A converted merchant ship outfitted with guns."

"That's how I met St. Leger. His crew helped us fight off pirates off the coast of Spain some years back," Lord Bolt told everyone gathered.

Angelique gave a subtle little shudder at the notion of her husband fighting off pirates, while Delilah ventured to her husband, "Tristan . . . can we assume that you and Mr. St. Leger have also already met?"

Captain Hardy didn't reply.

So Lorcan did. "Hardy and I first knew each

other when we were mere boys. Last time we met we shared a drink or two. Discussed the problems of the world. Seems a thousand years ago now, doesn't it, Hardy?" Lorcan said pleasantly. Ironically.

"And somehow like only yesterday, too," Captain Hardy replied.

Another odd little silent interval ensued.

Daphne cleared her throat. "Your rules are so elegantly printed." She gestured with the little card she'd been given to read. "One just wants to sit and admire them." This was a patently inane thing to say, but it did the trick of changing the subject.

One quick glance at their rules had, in fact, brought home to her how deep in she and her fake husband Lorcan were.

"We've thought about framing them and hanging them in all the rooms," Angelique told her.

"What a clever idea. Perhaps one or two done in needlepoint?"

"Or in elegant calligraphy!" Delilah suggested.

Suddenly every man present tensed with wariness as all the women seemed poised for a lively discussion about the domestic arts.

Delilah noticed and, with some apparent regret, decided against such a digression. "Daphne . . . if I may I ask . . . how fares your family?"

She hesitated. "My father is well." She was pleased with her choice of word. It wasn't untrue, and revealed nothing, really. "My brothers are touring the continent." She had no idea where her brothers were currently, though her best guess was Paris. Their last letter had been sent from there, nearly a month ago. They'd been gone nigh on half a year.

"It's lovely to know your father is well. I confess I often thought of how you managed your father's home so brilliantly for so many years, when you were so young. My mother aways held you out as an example."

"Oh, what a joy that must have been for you," Daphne said dryly.

Delilah laughed. "Truthfully, I always considered you the very model of graciousness. Everything in your house seemed to me so beautiful and so harmonious. When I inherited this building from my first husband, it was quite the proverbial sow's ear. But I confess I thought about you a time or two, Daphne. I told myself if Lady Worth could manage that grand house as a little girl, Angelique and I could certainly create a silk purse from a tumbledown building. It has all turned out better than we dreamed."

Daphne was motionless as the words sent grief and gratitude washing through her.

She could at least still see the house that Delilah had so admired from the caretaker's cottage, where she now lived with her father.

"Thank you," she said finally. "I am touched. And I am so pleased for you, Delilah. It's a beautiful place. It very much seems like a home."

Both Angelique and Delilah glowed.

"You're the first person I've seen from our village in a very long time," Delilah admitted. "I confess we've been very happy here in London at The Grand Palace on the Thames, with our friends and loved ones."

She cast a fleeting, searching look up at her stern, handsome husband, who returned it with a swift inscrutable one.

"Well," Angelique said, cheerfully. "Dot no doubt informed the two of you that The Grand Palace on the Thames is an exclusive establishment. And it is, in that we care so much for the happiness and comfort of all of our tenants that we like to have a little discussion first regarding whether we think a new guest would be a happy fit for all concerned. But I think under the circumstances we can forego our usual—"

"Delilah, I should like a private word with you and Angelique."

Captain Hardy didn't apologize for the interruption.

Daphne's heart clenched again. Both Angelique and Delilah slowly turned to Captain Hardy, their faces carefully expressionless.

Lord Bolt was staring at him, too, one brow upraised.

Next to her, she could feel Lorcan St. Leger's great, hard thigh tensing.

Oh God. Daphne silently prayed.

"We should be grateful to stay with you for the duration of the storm," Lorcan said pleasantly. "I think this will pay for a suite and any other conveniences."

And Lorcan slowly, with great ceremony freed

the gold earring from his ear and placed it on the table.

It twinkled next to the teacups.

IN SILENCE, THE four of them crossed the foyer to the sitting room, home of the Epithet Jar and a pianoforte, and scene of merriment, spirited discussion, cutthroat chess matches, innuendo, mock pirate battles, and lovemaking.

They stopped in the center of the room.

"Absolutely not. He is not staying here."

They spun to stare at Captain Hardy. The only other time Delilah had heard her husband use that voice was when he was addressing soldiers.

Neither she nor Angelique wished to encourage him to *ever* use it on them.

Only one of them was married to him.

And so Delilah pulled in a breath. "It's clear you've some history with Mr. St. Leger, Tristan. And while he admittedly cuts the sort of figure that can give a person pause—"

"You don't think he's handsome?" Angelique said.

She froze and her eyes flared in amazement, as though a ventriloquist had suddenly commandeered her mouth.

Everyone at once transferred their astonishment from Captain Hardy to her.

"Do . . . *you* think he's handsome?" Lord Bolt ventured. He seemed to be holding his features carefully still.

Angelique laughed lightly, gave herself a little shake, and waved her hand dismissively. "I honestly have no idea why I said that. I suppose I'm a little flustered, as Delilah and I are usually the only two participants in discussions about whether to admit guests. We're unaccustomed to being escorted across the foyer by two stern men like prisoners being marched to the gallows."

It was a jest.

And yet it was not.

Neither Captain Hardy nor Lucien took this subtle but unmissable hint. They remained rooted to their places.

Lucien's eyes remained fixed wonderingly on his wife.

Captain Hardy returned to staring almost accusingly at his.

Delilah interjected soothingly. "More to the point, present *exceptionally* attractive male company notwithstanding, we do not make a practice of admitting guests based on their physical appeal, nor do we stand about and rank it before we make a decision about who we allow to stay with us. And by we, I mean me and Angelique."

Thusly Delilah and Angelique reestablished that they were the voting bloc. This had been accepted without controversy or comment by both Captain Hardy and Lord Bolt from the moment they took up permanent residence at The Grand Palace on the Thames.

The silence this caused was a delicate and somewhat wary sort.

"Please listen to me," Captain Hardy said in a voice so insufferably reasonable Delilah clamped her teeth together. "I can tell you definitively that St. Leger looks like what he is, and that's a damned scoundrel."

It was a startling accusation from a man who never made them lightly.

"Tristan. The Epithet Jar is right *there*," Delilah said weakly.

But Captain Hardy's current mood was clearly impenetrable to jests.

"I felt the word would help press my point home. And did you note the theater with the earring? I think he was trying to goad me. That thing is worth several hundred pounds."

"Is it the earring? It's his earring, isn't it?" murmured Lucien to his wife.

Angelique sighed and gave his arm a squeeze.

"If you'll recall, Angelique and I pawned our jewelry to create The Grand Palace on the Thames. Buying things with jewelry is rather a tradition here. Though of course we can't accept it. The earring."

"Can't we?" Angelique murmured regretfully.

It was worth about a dozen times what Mr. St. Leger would owe them for even a fortnight's stay.

"Hopefully Mr. St. Leger has some English currency at the ready," Delilah said.

"Do you know what kinds of men wear earrings?" Captain Hardy persisted. "Pirates and blackguards. Do you know why? So if their dead bodies wash up on a foreign shore, whoever finds them can pay for a funeral with the gold in their ears. And do you know why they're liable to wind up dead on foreign shores? They are far more likely to murder and be murdered."

"It's a practical way of storing one's wealth, when you think about it," Lucien contributed. In a devil's advocate way.

"While I remain grateful for the many exciting ways in which you've expanded my horizons, Tristan," Delilah said so dryly Captain Hardy's lips finally twitched toward a smile, "here is the conundrum. Though I haven't seen Delilah in nigh on a decade, I am personally acquainted with her. I've been to her *home*. Furthermore, I know her family, and they are quality."

"What sort of quality? The Lucien's father sort, the Duke of Brexford, who is a right bastard, or the 'you' sort, quality to the bone?" Captain Hardy said to Delilah.

"Aww," Angelique teased him softly.

Captain Hardy cast his eyes sharply at her. He was never going to be comfortable exposing the tenderest contents of his heart to anyone but his wife.

And even then, he still struggled.

No one objected to his assessment of the Duke of Brexford, because it was simply true that he was a right bastard.

"I'm talking about character, Tristan," Delilah said. "That's what we mean when we discuss 'quality' here at The Grand Palace on the Thames. For instance, we think Mr. Delacorte's character is of the highest quality."

Mr. Delacorte was one of their very first guests. He was a salesman of remedies from the Orient, which he sold to surgeons and apothecaries up and down England, a lover of donkey races and festivals involving the pursuit of greased pigs, and he mostly confined his flatulence to the smoking room, for which they remained grateful. And while he was also a partner in the Triton Group, he coped with his worries rather differently than Captain Hardy and Bolt did. For instance, tonight he'd gone to a pub to sing bawdy songs and he hadn't yet returned. Which was unlike him. He was very close to missing curfew, and he'd never before missed it.

"And here is the thing, and why I'm concerned about Daphne," Delilah continued. "The last time I saw her—just before I married the Earl of Derring—she was engaged to the son of the Earl of Havelstock. Henry, his name was. And in truth, I cannot say we were close—she was always my social better, and her family was so much grander than mine. But I do think we liked each other. She seemed very happy last I saw her. Absolutely radiant. I wonder what happened?"

"Havelstock?" Lucien mused. "I've spoken to him at White's. He's besotted with his beautiful wife. Word has it that she was his younger brother's governess."

There was a moment of total silence honoring the potential crushing of a heart.

"Oof," Hardy said quietly.

Delilah glanced with concern at Angelique. She'd been a governess once. While her circumstances had been similar, things had gone rather more badly for her.

Angelique's expression had gone unreadable.

"Well," Delilah said carefully. "We don't actually know what took place. Perhaps she broke the engagement herself. I feel it isn't my place to pry. We should not assume. But Angelique and I know full well—too well—what it's like for life to crash down around our ears, and how it feels when you finally find the person who feels like home. She seems to have chosen the husband of her heart. Which takes courage. Sometimes even fortitude," she added dryly. Pointedly.

"While that may, in fact, be true," Captain Hardy said with irony, not wholly unamused, "I believe 'the husband of her heart' coordinated a smuggling operation between France and London so sophisticated and efficient that we were never quite able to prove it. Primarily silks and liquor. It seems to have ceased operations about three years ago. Coincidentally when he allegedly became a privateer. His nickname on the streets is 'your Lordship.'"

This time silence fell like an anvil.

"You *believe* he headed a smuggling operation." Delilah said it gingerly. After all, her husband, and the men in his command, had been legendarily ruthless about breaking the chokehold the many and often violent smuggling gangs had on English towns. He'd been so very good at his job he'd bartered his heroism to the king in exchange for a visit to The Grand Palace on the Thames. His Majesty had briefly parked his majestic behind on the settee in the sitting room of The Grand Palace on the Thames.

One of the thousands of ways, large and small, that Captain Hardy had proved his love for Delilah since he'd met her.

"Am I certain of this?" Hardy said. "Yes. Could I ultimately prove it?"

But it seemed Captain Hardy couldn't bring himself to say the word "no."

Lucien said thoughtfully, "I only knew St. Leger to be incredibly skilled with a sword, for which I had cause to be grateful at the time. But if Hardy says it's true . . ."

The unspoken part of that sentence was, "it must be true."

And it probably was.

Both Delilah and Angelique desperately wanted it to be untrue.

"But what is he like?" Delilah asked on a near hush. "Was he violent or unpredictable when you knew him?"

"All men are capable of violence," Captain Hardy said shortly. "You ought to know this by now."

Yes. She knew this. And Delilah had witnessed firsthand what Captain Hardy would do to a man who threatened her.

"But he isn't likely to go door-to-door in the building robbing our guests at pistol point."

This time his pause was lengthy. "No."

"What is he *like*, Tristan?"

"He's intelligent and shrewd. Charming and well-connected. Efficient, organized . . ." Captain Hardy sighed. ". . . probably even brilliant. And we considered him dangerous, because the men who reported to him would do anything for him." Captain Hardy recited this flatly, as though he'd said it before. "And we couldn't get a single one to betray him, through any means."

"Interesting," Delilah said. "It sounds like the two of you are more alike than you are different."

Lucien gave a short, astounded laugh and closed his eyes and shook his head to and fro slowly. He knew exactly how Captain Hardy would hear that.

But Delilah had learned the language of her husband's body, the shift of light across his eyes, the twitch of a brow. She'd memorized them over every precious moment they'd so far spent together. And though they had all been under-standably under considerable strain for a fort-night, something unfamiliar lurked beneath the tension of his mood. It might even be pain, which puzzled her.

Delilah knew she was her husband's weak-ness. So while it wasn't easy, she returned his now icy, incredulous stare with a melting one.

"Tristan . . . He's currently a free man, con-victed of nothing, apparently, who seems to have a *reasonably* respectable trade, charming manners, and is protective of his wife, who ap-pears very fond of him. I should think these are qualities with which you can identify. And surely you aren't suggesting the daughter of an earl married beneath her?"

This was a startling and skilled feint. Of the four people standing in the sitting room, two of them had, by societal standards anyhow, married beneath them: Delilah had been a countess when she'd married a blockade commander. Lucien was a viscount and the bastard son of a duke, who'd ac-quired his own wealth and had married a former governess who was also the former mistress of an earl. Viewed through the eyes of society, they were unlikely matches, indeed.

But all of them believed they'd made the right and only choices of spouse for themselves.

A flicker of rueful appreciation for Delilah's tactics briefly interrupted Captain Hardy's determined stoniness.

"Perhaps he's like Lucien, and all it took was the right woman to inspire him to change his wicked ways," Angelique suggested into the breach.

Lucien snorted good-humoredly.

"And if he is a privateer," Delilah added, "it means St. Leger now works for the crown, as you did."

Captain Hardy stared at his wife in stunned silence for a full three seconds.

"I . . . what on . . . not at *all* like I did." His voice was practically arid with disbelief.

Delilah laid her a hand on her husband's arm. "Tristan," she said softly.

After a moment, he took a breath.

His tension eased; he simply couldn't help it when she touched him.

But only a little. Not entirely.

"Tristan . . . people *do* change. Look at Lucien, for instance. All of the *ton* hated him at one time."

"Hated?" Lucien was startled.

"Passionately disapproved of, more precisely," Angelique amended diplomatically.

This was true. When Lucien had been captured and thrown in the Thames to drown one midnight a decade ago, no bastard son of a duke had ever been more notorious or more beloved of the broadsheets. Tempered by battle and struggle, he'd returned, with a fortune of his own, and was now generally considered quite reformed and civilized by all the members of White's.

"We appreciate and respect your concern. Truly. But as we've all discussed before, the decision about whom to admit into The Grand Palace on the Thames has always belonged to me and Angelique. And I simply can't countenance sending either of them back out into the storm. Especially Daphne. *He* strikes me as a man who can take care of himself, regardless. Whether the two of you would like a say in who is admitted to The Grand Palace on the Thames is a conversation we can have another day."

The unspoken words were, "and we can tell you right now how that conversation will go."

"I agree with Delilah," Angelique said gently.

And just like that, all four were in uncharted waters. It was truly the last place any of them wanted to be after a fortnight of relentlessly increasing tension, filled with sleeplessness, uncertainty, eerie drafts, worry, rambunctiously cheerful Germans, and on the threshold of what might well be the storm of the decade, which would seal all of them up together for at least a week.

"Delilah . . . *Pike* came to get us when he got one look at the man. He did the right thing."

Captain Hardy had clearly been saving this for last.

Perhaps he hadn't meant to say it at all. But he

was accustomed to winning and he knew how to do it.

Delilah and Angelique froze.

They were both careful not to look at each other. But the news was frustrating and infuriating.

It certainly answered the question regarding why Captain Hardy and Lord Bolt had suddenly appeared in the little reception room uninvited.

But Mr. Pike, their footman, was meant to report to *them*. He ought to have brought his concern straight up the stairs to the little sitting room.

Granted, he might have been worried about being stampeded by Dot.

It was one more controversy in a week characterized by them.

"Are you questioning our judgment?" Delilah asked evenly.

"Yes," Captain Hardy said, with infuriating patience. As if this should have been self-evident.

A fraught, taut little silence ensued.

"So you and Bolt are saying our new footman has better judgment than either I or Angelique do."

Delilah said this deceptively pleasantly. As if giving him one final opportunity to scramble to take it back.

Angelique drew in a surreptitious breath. Very few people ever guessed that Delilah, who was almost unfailingly kind, gentle, sensible, and good-humored, possessed a temper. Angelique knew it.

So did Captain Hardy. He'd once—it seemed

so long ago now—been coolly evicted from The Grand Palace on the Thames at Delilah's behest. And at the time, he'd deserved it.

Lord Bolt's eyes widened in a warning to Captain Hardy.

He was no fool, Captain Hardy. Damned if he replied, damned if he didn't, and he knew it.

He chose wisely.

He took a half step toward his wife. "Delilah . . ." He'd lowered his voice.

Everything he knew and felt about her was in the way he said her name. Unshakeable love, humor, a peace and passion and understanding neither had dreamed they would know in this lifetime.

But it was shot through with an ache, and something like an exasperated plea.

They seldom argued. They were both so *reasonable*. They both had muscular senses of fairness and a healthy respect for rules.

He was a private man. There was more he wanted to say, and he was telling her he would not say it in front of Angelique or Bolt, as much as he liked them.

And just like that, she wanted to protect him from making himself vulnerable. She couldn't help it.

But Delilah was suddenly unnervingly certain she would never again win an argument if he was really determined to win. He was a man for whom ruthless vanquishing of foes had been a way of life.

"Tristan . . ." she said hurriedly. "I know what

you're about to say. I *know* in the past I've erred on the side of giving someone—well, two someones— the benefit of the doubt and it turned out rather badly. It was how we met, in fact. But I am not as naive about people as I once was, in large part thanks to you. And I so want it to be true that Daphne is happy and safe. And . . . and . . . loved."

Her voice dropped on the potent little word.

No one spoke. Tension and unspoken things held all of them fast.

A long, four-way stare concluded when Captain Hardy's head fell back on a sigh.

Then he swiped his hands down his face in frustration.

It was capitulation. For now.

But they all knew this conversation, and all the silent things that simmered throughout it, was far from over.

"Even if the temptation to go on a murderous rampage overtakes him, with you and Lucien and Ben Pike here, we have naught to fear from him. Even Dot knows how to shoot," Delilah reminded him.

"She still hasn't quite mastered the aiming part of shooting," he said grimly.

"She can be surprisingly valiant. She was once prepared to defend my possessions with a hatpin. Before all of this. Before I met you."

Captain Hardy and Lord Bolt exchanged an unreadable look.

As friends and business partners, they had their own silent language now, too. As did Delilah and Angelique.

"Did any of you notice how Lady Worth looked at her husband?" Angelique said softly to Delilah, who nodded. "Don't they seem oddly suited?"

The four of them gazed across at the pair sitting on the settee. They appeared to be murmuring to each other.

"I have a feeling Delacorte will love him," Captain Hardy said finally, grimly.

This seemed probable. Delacorte loved nearly everybody.

DURING THE FEW minutes the four residents of The Grand Palace on the Thames debated their fate, Lorcan and Daphne had, in fact, remained silent, siloed in entirely separate thoughts. Mere inches separated them on the settee; she hadn't shifted away from him, nor had he shifted away from her. She was afraid the four people across the foyer would take note of it and become suspicious if she did. And she was still so weary and chilled, despite the proximity to the fire. His big body gave off heat, and at the moment, she was nearly as impartial to the source of it as a turtle basking on a rock. He smelled like woodsmoke, cheroot smoke, and night air, mingled with what she recognized as wet man. Distinctive, not unpleasant.

Three possibilities bound her in a sort of Gordian knot: they would both be asked to leave, thanks to whatever it was that bothered Captain Hardy about Lorcan St. Leger; St. Leger would be asked to leave, and she would be obliged to tell Delilah that she couldn't afford a suite; or they would be invited to

stay, and she would find herself in a suite alone with
Mr. St. Leger.

She'd once scrupulously planned household
budgets down to the ha'penny, made sure the mi-
nutest details of the family home, from curtain
pulls to hinges on the doors to locks, were in perfect working order. She had hired and fired servants; she had arranged seating charts and menus
for dinner parties and more. All of this and more
had mostly been her responsibility since she was
eleven years old.

But she hadn't the faintest idea how she would
endure or respond to any of the possibilities at
this moment facing her. Her mind felt blank as a
tundra.

He finally murmured, "Mr. and Mrs. Blackguard?"

She didn't reply. Her nerves were so raw she
could feel the entire path of her own breath as it
traveled into and out of her body.

"What did you do to upset Captain Hardy?"
she finally said.

For a moment she thought he was so lost in
thought he hadn't heard her.

"'Upset,'" he repeated thoughtfully, finally,
with great amused irony. As if he'd never heard
a quainter word.

Chapter Five

❧

A FEW MINUTES later Daphne found herself following Lorcan St. Leger up the stairs to the suite of rooms that Mrs. Hardy and Mrs. Bolt proudly referred to as the annex. The earring was back in his ear; as it turned out, he was in possession of pound notes to pay for their room, after all.

Captain Hardy and Lord Bolt had not reappeared.

The tall young footman had graciously insisted upon carrying her valise the entire distance. Daphne supposed this temporary relief of a little burden was part of what made The Grand Palace on the Thames exclusive. He would have carried Mr. St. Leger's as well, if Mr. St. Leger had let him.

Mr. St. Leger carried his own portmanteau in one hand. She suspected he was capable of carrying the footman under the other arm, if the mood took him.

Daphne's heart lodged in her throat at the foot of the stairs and remained there for the duration of the climb to their door. She felt a little as though she was floating above her own body, watching the little procession. She thought, "My goodness! Going up to a room with a strange man is the last thing on earth Lady Daphne

Worth would do," as though she were another person altogether.

She watched his back for any clues to the man she hadn't yet ascertained from his front. His well-tailored coat stretched clean and smooth as a pelt across his shoulders. Each time they passed by the lit sconces (wax candles, from the looks of things, not tallow—another little luxury), she caught the glint of a strand of silver in his black hair. His boots were beautifully made and very well worn.

And by the time Mr. Pike turned the key into the lock, her heart was thumping so hard it nearly choked her.

Mr. St. Leger hadn't said a word for the duration. He was obviously preoccupied, as well. Or perhaps he viewed her as luggage, something he'd inadvertently acquired and was now obliged to ferry from place to place.

When Pike proudly flung open their door (which, she noted, didn't creak; the well-oiled hinges were polished to a gleam, the sort of detail she was accustomed to noticing), she saw a long, handsome settee upholstered in blue brocade arranged in front of a merrily leaping fire. Heavy wool curtains fell to the floor; paper striped in pale blue climbed to the picture rail. Several little tables paired with chairs were scattered about, suitable for writing letters or playing Spillikins or alighting at to devour the scones they were told would be arriving in the morning.

Remarkable what a few pounds could buy.

She desperately hoped he didn't think it would also buy him a woman.

The two closed doors would be the bedrooms.

"The fires have been laid in the rooms and they should be nice and cozy," Mr. Pike told them. "Do ring if you would like tea before eleven o'clock this evening. Otherwise, we shall see you at breakfast. So delighted to have you staying with us."

"Thank you, Mr. Pike," she said as graciously as if this was her very own home.

He seemed an enviable servant, the sort that were always a challenge to find and keep.

The sort that Daphne's family had lost one by one.

The door clicked shut behind him.

They turned to face each other.

"Mr. . . ." She paused for a breath.

"Blackguard?" he completed helpfully.

". . . St. Leger . . . I should like to make something clear."

"I am all anticipation." Though he looked, in truth, somewhat impatient.

She drew in a breath to steady her nerves.

Then another.

He watched her with great patience.

"While I am grateful indeed for the shelter tonight and for your assistance, I hope you shall not construe my presence alone in this suite with you as . . . that is . . . I hope you do not think that your generosity has purchased certain . . . ah, benefits, beyond the amenities. That is, I should like to tell you that you should not assume my presence in this suite with you is an agreement to . . . and while I did in fact t-touch your knee, for which I sincerely apologize, it was in the spirit of . . ."

The array of subtle emotions—astonishment, irritation, hilarity, anger, bafflement—that flickered in swift succession across his remarkable face made her falter to a stop.

A sort of detached amusement was what settled in at last.

Throughout he regarded her the way a lion might regard a mouse darting to and fro between its paws. Mildly amusing, a bit presumptuous and a trifle irritating, possibly not worth the effort to lift a paw to smash.

Her face was hot.

He said nothing for a moment.

"Virtue is *quite* the millstone, isn't it, Lady Worth?" he finally said on a sympathetic hush. "You would have spared us both that little speech if you could only allow yourself to say, 'I hope you don't think you purchased rights to . . . ravish me.'"

He rolled the "r" extravagantly and ironically. She had the distinct sense that the delicate pause was less to spare her sensibilities than to give her an opportunity to imagine the word he really wanted to use.

He was mocking her, but not scathingly. She sensed she did not signify enough for him to scathe.

She remained mute. Mortified.

"Allow me to give you the benefit of my experience," he continued, still politely. "Life is, on the whole, short, brutal, and unjust. And I expect if you ever do relinquish your virtue, you'll wonder what all the fuss was about."

She gave a short dark laugh. "Oh, *thank* you. Spoken like a man. Both the lecture about your 'experience' and your astonishing blithe ignorance of the societal value of so-called virtue to a woman. And what makes you think I haven't relinquished it?"

God above, Daphne, she thought.

Why? Why *would you say a thing like that?*

Because his assumption was insufferable. It flattened her to a mere type. It made the real dramas and terrors and hopes of her life seem cheap and ordinary.

And frankly, she'd hoped to shock him.

He merely performed a skeptical, pitying, "Come now, Lady Worth" head-tip.

"To your concern. How should I put this?" He cast his eyes ceiling-ward briefly. "We might as well be two different species, aye? What sense would that make? Furthermore, my appetites do not run to unwilling women. At the moment your hair is standing up as fuzzy as a pussycat in the midst of a fright, and that's no way to seduce a man."

She met his gaze steadily.

The little creases at the corners of his eyes had deepened. That was the only way in which his steady, challenging expression had changed.

She nearly sprained all of her muscles in an effort not to clap her hands to her head and frantically smooth.

She desperately wanted to wake up from a dream in which she'd been standing in a strange room with a large pagan who had "appetites" and somehow knew the difference between "willing" and "unwilling" women. She was hardly completely naive. But her knowledge of debauchery was primarily gleaned from Greek myths in which fleeing maidens turned into trees to avoid the terrible fate of ravishment and luridly accomplished Renaissance canvasses filled with fleshy nude people writhing in gossamer draping.

Mr. St. Leger would not look out of place in one of those paintings. Or as a satyr, for that matter.

"In other words, you're quite safe from me, Lady Worth," he clarified when she said nothing. He still sounded insufferably amused, and a little distracted now. As though he was nearing the end of his willingness to humor her with conversation at all.

Despite everything, the emphasis on the word "quite" landed on the raw.

"Understood," she finally said. Somewhat faintly. "Thank you for the . . . clarification."

He nodded politely. "But I should warn you that patting a man's knee might just give him wicked notions."

"Do forgive me, Mr. St. Leger. I suppose you can always put your head out the window and let the rain extinguish your inflamed passions."

His eyes went bright as lit windows when he smiled, delighted.

She cleared her throat.

"I should like to thank you for . . . for understanding the awkward social circumstances into which I had inadvertently walked when Mrs. Hardy recognized me. And for leaping selflessly into the fray, as it were. I expect the last thing you wanted to do this evening was acquire a wife, given that you hoped to take lodging in a bordello."

It was as stiff and awkward an expression of gratitude as anyone had ever uttered. It also marked the first, and God willing, the last, time in her life she'd used the word "bordello" in a sentence.

But every person deserved the dignity of appreciation, regardless of their motives. She understood the terrible subtraction of being taken for granted, as though one was a mere utility, like a fork or a barouche. She was uncomfortable simply taking.

His expression grew more and more inscrutable as she spoke. He studied her a moment longer.

"While virtue may be a millstone, pride has its uses. And pride is about all you've got left, ain't it, lass?"

He said it ironically.

Her throat seized up.

It was possible his startling astuteness was just instinct. Perhaps he knew this about her the way a fox might learn a thousand different things by sniffing the wind.

But she *hated* that he was right, and that he knew it.

Suddenly, exhaustion was like mud sucking at her ankles.

"Why don't we talk in the morning about how we intend to maintain our marital charade for the duration of our stay here? Assuming this is how you mean to go on," he said.

"Very well."

He turned away, put his hand on the doorknob to the room. He froze like that a moment.

Then he pivoted a crisp half turn.

He seemed to be considering what to say as he studied her.

"If you'll indulge my curiosity, Lady Worth. You thought that I assisted you from a second-story window in the dead of night in a storm, then dispatched a thief who set upon you, all in order to keep you alive long enough to ravish you in this peculiar little fairy land of a boardinghouse with *rules* and apparently stocked with everyone we once knew?"

He did sound curious, and not accusatory. They were different species, after all. He was trying to puzzle out her customs.

When he put it that way, she could see how it would seem churlish. She flushed.

"I . . . have stopped assuming anything at all about men and their motives. But in my experience, they often do just what they want with little thought to the consequences, particularly with regards to women. And forgive me if you don't strike me as the sort given to . . . charitable works."

Surprisingly, he half smiled at this. As if she'd just delivered a surprise he did not object to.

After a moment he said, "You were fleeing a man."

Startled, she replied, "Yes."

"Not a husband." It wasn't inflected as a question. How did he know? Was he the type of man who could tell a spinster at forty paces? Perhaps all men could.

If she hadn't felt desolate before, she did now.

How much information did she owe him?

And then she realized she ought to define to him who she was. To more clearly draw the boundaries of her character, and class, and station.

"The husband of an older, nearly deaf gentlewoman to whom I was briefly serving as a companion as she traveled to London to meet up with him, a position for which I was to be paid. He thought my duties ought to extend beyond the ones described to me. He was hovering in the room outside of my bedroom door, otherwise I would have made a more orthodox exit."

Thusly she dryly summarized what had, in fact, been harrowing, frightening, and exasperating.

"Why would a gentlewoman, as you say, choose to stay in a room near the docks?"

Daphne took a breath. "The gentleman in question runs to extreme thriftiness. They were rooms over a shop owned by his solicitor, and he was offered the lodging for no cost."

He dipped his head in a slow nod.

She sensed a dozen other questions were gathering in his mind.

But his expression changed not at all. It was clear this man was difficult to shock. Read one way, it was a strangely reassuring quality. Her own steadiness was all about effort, an effort she struggled to conceal.

His was different, she understood. And unnerving therefore. Because it seemed an earned quality. One would have needed to experience quite a few unthinkable things to achieve an unshockable condition.

What manner of man was Lorcan St. Leger?

"Why *did* you help me?"

"Damned if I know." He sounded sincere, and puzzled. "God saw fit to make me do penance for past misdeeds, I suppose. And perhaps because I suspected you'd say things like 'blithely ignorant,' which is just about the funniest thing I've ever heard."

He reached again for the doorknob.

"My apologies for the 'damned,' my lady, but there's naught on the little card of rules about cursing in the rooms."

He winked at her and vanished into his room.

She heard the door lock immediately. As if he was afraid she might rush into the room and touch his knee again.

ONCE DAPHNE WAS behind a locked door she stood, motionless, to see which of the thousands of emotions she'd struggled to hold in check all night would sift to the surface first.

She was surprised to discover it was exultation. It was weak and short-lived, like the last bubble to drift to the top of a glass of champagne. But there it was.

She'd successfully gone out a window on a *sheet*. There was a trick to alternating one's feet that transformed it into a sort of ladder. A sort of puzzle to it. And she'd done it! If she ever needed to climb out a window using a sheet again, she'd be prepared.

She wished it seemed unlikely.

She'd not only gone out the window on a sheet, she'd apparently found the limits of her own self-sacrifice, which had heretofore seemed limitless. Not even to help her beloved father would she allow Mr. Daggett to squeeze the bottom of the daughter of an earl.

She didn't know what she would tell her father when she returned home. Especially since she hadn't yet been paid.

Lorcan St. Leger was precisely right. Pride was about the only thing that stood between her and ruin. Pride was the thing that had sent her leaping into the dark into the arms of a stranger, and pride was why she now had an enigmatic fake husband who was possibly a criminal. Pride was the boat she frantically paddled even as the steep Waterfall of Doom loomed to pull her over.

She couldn't imagine why fate should take such an interest in her. She had been dutiful and uncontroversial. She hadn't fatal beauty or reckless habits. Apart from her mother dying when she was young, there had been no warnings, no inklings, that her life would be happy to a certain point, and a disaster thereafter. That the scalding shame of Henry's perfidy would be just the first of a seeming endless cascade of shame. More shame when she'd learned that her father was in desperate financial straits, more and more during the gradual peeling away of all of the trappings of their station, the servants, the horses, the house— scarcely noticeable at first, and then, terrifyingly swift, like the sands of an hourglass. More when she'd been compelled to discreetly find a renter for their home while she and her father moved into the caretaker's cottage. Still more when she'd taken what had seemed to be an easy enough little job as a companion to Mrs. Leggett, only to discover what men like Mr. Leggett thought he could do to women who needed to take easy enough little jobs. She'd never before taken a job. It wasn't what the daughters of earls did.

"You do not always have to know the *why* of things," Henry had once told her, affectionately. Or so she'd thought. He'd said this when she'd tried to tell him why she loved oranges.

Because that was just it: she usually did thoroughly know. Why things moved her or did not. Why she liked or did not like them. Why things happened. She was filled with thoughts and feelings and no one had any use for them.

Now she wondered if she'd merely made Henry tired.

To her, the "why" of things enriched the good things in life, and made the bad things bearable, or at least more interesting.

If she'd known why any of this was happening, could she have somehow traced it to the beginning? Could she have stopped it?

At what point does a person going over a waterfall realize that paddling is futile? At what point does the attempt to forestall the inevitable seem ridiculous to anyone watching from a distance—that frantic scrabbling in midair before the plummet to doom?

Was she already laughable?

She wondered at Delilah's journey from countess to boardinghouse proprietress. Had there been an interval of awkwardness and terror between her old life and the improbable one she'd embraced? Had Captain Hardy already been waiting in the wings to snap her up? Were the rules she'd written a clue to the contentment with which she glowed?

Because reading them only reminded Daphne that "pride goeth before a fall."

She lifted the little card left on the charming and plain writing desk and read:

All guests will eat dinner together at least four times per week.

All guests must gather in the drawing room after dinner for at least an hour at least four times per week. We feel it fosters a sense of friendship and the warm, familial, congenial atmosphere we strive to create here at The Grand Palace on the Thames.

All guests should be quietly respectful and courteous of other guests at all times, though spirited discourse is welcome.

Guests may entertain other guests in the drawing room.

Curfew is at 11:00 p.m. The front door will be securely locked then. You will need to wait until morning to be admitted if you miss curfew.

If the proprietresses collectively decide that a transgression or series of transgressions warrants your eviction from The Grand Palace on the Thames, you will find your belongings neatly packed and placed near the front door. You will not be refunded the balance of your rent.

Gentlemen may smoke in the Smoking Room only.

They were reasonable rules, of course. Comforting. Even genteel. The kind of rules a lady raised according to the etiquette and mores of fine society would compose.

But nearly every one of them meant she would need to convincingly pretend to be married to Lorcan St. Leger in front of an audience, and God help her and him.

She blew out a long breath.

Tucked in a walking shoe in her portmanteau was a plump letter she'd received from the Earl of Athelboro, whom she'd met once a half year ago, and with whom she'd spent a pleasant enough few hours when he'd visited her father. It had been sent to her care of Mrs. Leggett, and she'd needed to pay the postage with her dwindling funds when she fetched it only yesterday. She was down to just enough money to pay for a cheap room and a mail coach home.

The Earl of Athelboro had a weary smile and a countable number of strands of hair left on his head. He was fit enough, if gone to comfortable plumpness; outwardly, at least, he exhibited none of the usual habits that would lead to self-ruin. And he'd just been widowed for the second time. He'd fathered five children on two countesses, and they were all motherless now. She thought she knew what the letter would say.

She didn't dare open it yet. She was too weary to think; she hadn't any strength left with which to entertain either crushing disappointment or elegiac relief.

Best to read it by the light of day.

She swiftly transferred her clothes to the little wardrobe in the former Delilah Swanpoole's improbable boardinghouse. She smoothed the skirts of dresses that were two seasons too old but still fit beautifully, gently folded away her stocking, her shawls, her night rails, tucked away her slippers. She always took scrupulous care of everything and everyone she cared about.

It had never seemed to matter much to anyone except her.

She did it, anyway. She loved, anyway. She couldn't help it. When she loved, it felt to her fathoms deep. It took the whole of her up. Surely this ought to count for something? But she had never loved ostentatiously or dramatically. Perhaps that had mattered to Henry? Surely one could not help but notice the ocean if they stood next to it, even if it was still?

Loving anyone had not yet done much but crush her.

She performed her ablutions and got out of her dress and into her night rail and crawled beneath the covers of a clean and comfortable bed to await the rest of the emotions she'd kept at bay. They would be her company tonight.

LORCAN HAD SLEPT in holds of ships strung with hammocks filled with sighing, snoring, farting men. He'd slept stuffed in beds in rooms packed with several families, and on fetid streets tucked behind barrels, pulling his toes in so the rats wouldn't conduct their battles across his feet.

But he'd never *lived* with a woman for more than a week or so—and that was only if "living with" meant the same thing as "enjoying athletic carnal marathons"—but he expected it would be a bit like navigating a room that also contained a small, temperamental animal, perhaps a feisty squirrel.

He had long ago given up attempting to guess the ages of people; he only knew that happy people tended to look younger, and misery and hardship tended to etch itself into features. People living in squalor were capable of happiness, and people living in palaces were often perfectly wretched. Lady Worth was perhaps thirty years old, if he had to guess. Her face was pale and pinched, as if she were withstanding a good deal, or holding *in* a good deal. The only color in her complexion was the lavender crescents beneath her eyes.

But when she'd turned her face up to him on the settee her eyes had given him quite a jolt. They were the color of good whiskey shot through with firelight, and a surprisingly fierce spirit looked out of them. She was frightened, but she was a fighter, he would warrant. She was angry—more accurately, probably, indignant—at whatever hand the world had dealt to her and was struggling to regain her footing in it while keeping the shreds of her dignity intact.

What an abasement to have to pretend to be married to a man like him.

How she must be suffering.

He half smiled. Mordantly, but not entirely without sympathy.

He would not want to be married to him, either.

Lorcan knew exactly who he was. Her opinion of him could never possibly have a bearing on his opinion of himself.

When all was said and done, he'd really rather not have to live in a suite with her, but he'd brought it on himself, and it was of almost no consequence to him. And the acquisition of a fake wife was probably the reason he had shelter at all tonight.

Of more consequence was being confined to a building that also contained Captain Tristan Bloody Hardy.

He realized he was pacing and forced himself to stand still.

What a shock that must have been for Hardy to see him cozily ensconced on a pink settee, chatting with his pretty wife, a cup of their very good tea in his sword hand.

And yet that bastard hadn't so much as twitched a brow when he'd seen him.

Bloody granite, as always.

God, he'd liked that man.

Just a little more than he'd hated him. But even hating him had felt more like sport. The way one hates the opposing team.

Perhaps being recognized by the vermin who would have cut Lady Worth's throat for her had been a portent. Perhaps there would never be such a thing as "the past."

Lorcan investigated his accommodations and discovered the bed was spectacular; the pillows were like angel bosoms, the mattress generously buoyant. He learned this by testing both with light thumps of his fist. No dust or insects rose.

Everything was so clean he was half-reluctant to sully it with his sweaty body.

He paused to rub a corner of the knit coverlet between his fingers, thoughtfully. It was soft and tightly knit of good wool dyed blue. Even now, when he could well afford it, some part of him remained cynical about and somewhat mistrustful of comfort. As if it was something he still needed to earn.

He located the chamber pot (painted all over with tiny flowers, apparently to make the maid's job less odious). A pretty little pitcher (painted with pink roses, very nice) was filled with water, and a knit cloth (blue) was beside it.

He yanked his boots off and lined them up before the hearth. He stripped swiftly and installed his clothes with care in the wardrobe. The room was warm and the air felt soft on his naked body. He stood a moment, allowing it to settle over him, and closed his eyes. He hadn't been lying about his aching bones: they reminded him of the brutal life he'd led and they warned him of storms. They were merely part of the general ambiance of his life, the usual sights and sounds and sensations. He noted them; they hurt, but they slowed him not. He paid no more attention to the aches than he did to the creaks of the house. He soldiered on, as always.

He performed some swift splashing and scrubbing of his sweatier body parts, and then he climbed into bed to let the soft mattress absorb some of the great weight of simply being alive.

As he did, he listened to the building groan and sigh in the wind the way all old buildings and ships do.

After a moment it was clear it was perhaps the quietest place he'd ever slept in his life. How ironic would it be if the quiet kept him awake.

The sough of the wind. The steady tick and splat of rain against glass. The intermittent creak and pop of wood swelling or settling.

Entwined with all of it a steadier sound he could not quite identify. Perhaps a cat meowing? Or distant laughter?

No. He realized it was weeping.

In the room next to him, Lady Worth was weeping.

Quietly. In a constrained way.

"In a constrained way" was likely how she did everything. Likely she simply couldn't help it. It was how she'd been raised, like a Japanese bonsai tree. Confined to a precise, decorative shape.

Something had obviously blown the lady far, far off course, the way they sometimes discovered dazed, frazzled birds far from their native lands perched on the rigging when they were out at sea. Refugees from storms.

Life was suffering, he could have told Lady Worth. She'd fast lose that sense of suffering if she gave up the notion of how things ought to be and instead dealt with them as they were. They never did, though, the gentry. He in fact had counted on this, and prospered from it. They wanted what they wanted, war or no war. They wanted life to go on as it always had, with no sacrifice, no obstacles, and often, no expense. They might have their precious manners and rituals, but morals never got in the way of this wanting.

He'd made certain they got what they wanted. Silks and liquor, mostly.

In St. Giles, morality was a luxury. Or rather, it was subject to interpretation. When you came from nothing, when you had nothing, when everything around you conspired against your very survival, you soon learned what you could transform into currency. And for Lorcan, that was his wits.

The trouble with Captain Hardy was that the army had shaped his sense of moral rightness and it was now as rigid as his spine.

And people tended to break along the places they could not bend.

He didn't suppose he could fault him. It was a matter of luck and luck was fickle. They had been boys together, for a short time. Tristan had found work when he was ten years old as the assistant of a naval commander, and this was what had shaped him.

If Lady Worth was a bonsai, Hardy was the mast of a ship. He had found a way out of St. Giles and into the daylight of respectable society.

While Lorcan had been left to find his way in the shadows.

And he'd learned dozens of invaluable things: How to sail. How to lead. How to charm, when necessary, bully when necessary, how to skillfully negotiate. How to manage money, and to invest it. How to speak French and German and Spanish. He'd learned byways and alleys all up and down the coast of England, and he had friends everywhere. Enemies, too.

He'd been proud of the way he'd conducted his work.

Seeing Captain Hardy was a bloody unwelcome reminder that he'd never been proud of the work.

There came the day when Lorcan was approached by a man off the coast of Cornwall he quickly suspected of being less interested in commerce than in spying for the French. He'd bartered the man's name to a bloke who worked in intelligence at the Alien Office, a certain Mr. Christian Hawkes, a man whose morals were as situational and as pragmatic as Lorcan's, for a privateer charter. And Hawkes had made sure he got one.

Because he'd wanted a chance to work in the daylight, too.

And now Lorcan was well on his way to being wealthy.

He didn't know if he believed in portents. But perhaps seeing Hardy again was a way to measure how far he had come. A way to remind himself that he'd done it almost entirely on his own. That not even a proud man like Hardy had been able to outsmart him. That there was likely nothing he couldn't have or do now.

His consciousness began to drift, the sound of Lady Worth weeping dissolved into and became all of a piece with all the ambient sounds of his life so far, rain and the crash of waves, weeping and laughter and screams, gunshots, laughter, moans, flesh striking flesh, the snap of sails, and he slept.

Chapter Six

✎✎✎

"*I*'M SORRY I'm so late to bed," Delilah whispered to her husband as she climbed in next to him. "Delacorte finally came home, but he brought Lord St. John Vaughn back with him, because St. John couldn't get a hack back to St. James Square in this weather. Apparently, St. John went with him to sing songs in pubs. If you can believe that! We had to put him in a suite."

Angelique and Delilah had been none too pleased about this. But they could hardly throw out the young heir to an earl. Delacorte had done the right thing. And they knew St. John's parents, the Earl and Countess of Vaughn, would pay for their son's lodging. They were good people.

"Do you remember the time Gordon brought in a live mouse and put it in his food dish, and the poor thing ran around the room and tried to climb the walls and the furniture?" Angelique said. "I think that's what St. John will be like after a few days trapped inside due to the weather."

St. John was young and very handsome, and reveling in this was his favorite pastime. He enjoyed making young women blush and basking in their attention, gambling modestly in gaming hells and buying fine horses. He quickly grew bored when deprived of any of these activities. He was rather indolent, but not fundamentally a bad sort in any other way. His family was lovely and rich and it wasn't his fault his father was an earl, not really.

Learning chess had been an act of desperation born of boredom during his first visit, and this was how St. John and Delacorte had forged an unlikely bond—Delacorte had taught him. Their former guest Mr. Hugh Cassidy had fallen in love with St. John's sister Lillias and whisked her off to America. He missed his sister, and would not outright admit it. Delacorte missed his bosom friend Mr. Cassidy, and said so all the time. He missed everyone when they left. This, too, rather bonded them, though Mr. Delacorte had found Lillias unnerving.

"Tristan?" Delilah whispered, tentatively. "Do you want to talk about our earlier conversation?"

He remained silent.

He was either sleeping . . . or pretending to sleep. His head was turned away from her. Usually, by morning, she'd find his face close to hers, on her pillow. Usually, instinctively, they turned to each other the moment they climbed into bed, even if they were half-asleep.

She felt a chill unrelated to the lowering fire, and turned down her lamp.

By HABIT LORCAN usually rose as the sun was just a narrow gleam at the horizon. The mouse-quiet maids had clearly already been in, judging by the scent of freshly brewed coffee wafting into his room from the sitting room.

He got his trousers and boots and shirt on and emerged from his room cravatless and coatless and yawning to a surprise.

Lady Worth was sitting at a little table near the window.

She'd opened the curtains to reveal sheets of falling rain.

Her dress was a shade of deep yellow, beautifully fitted, bands of dark brown braid trimming the long sleeves and wrapped below a lovely swell of bosom. Last night's fuzzy hair had been tamed and prettily coiled up and pinned on top of her head in that clever way women seem to be born knowing how to do. It was a rather decent color. Warm gold, like a weathered doubloon. A few strands had made a break for freedom and spiraled lazily at her temples.

She looked pristine in the gray morning light.

The toes of brown slippers peeped out from beneath the hem, and one of them was tapping idly, as if she was listening to a waltz in her head.

One would never have guessed he'd found her last night in an alley.

She seemed to be reading a letter.

He rested his eyes on her the way he might any quietly lovely thing.

From somewhere beneath the armored plate of his soul, an ancient memory twinged: the shock of the first time he'd seen a fine lady stepping out of a beautiful carriage. He'd been a small boy. He hadn't fully comprehended how very, very lowly his place was in the world until then.

In that instant, he'd decided to become anything but lowly.

He watched her toes and thought: he'd never learned how to waltz.

"Good morning, Lady Worth."

Her head shot up. She offered a tentative smile. "Good morning, Mr. St. Leger. I trust you slept . . ."

Her eyes flickered. Dropped to his torso.

Then she jerked her head toward the window, and before his eyes, hot color flooded her cheeks.

Bewildered, he dropped his eyes swiftly to ascertain his cock wasn't peeking out of his trouser fall, because surely nothing short of that warranted such a reaction.

She cleared her throat. ". . . well."

She was still showing him her profile.

And then it struck him: his rolled-up shirt-sleeves exposed a brazen amount of skin from fingertip to elbow. His throat was partially on view, too.

For God's *sake*.

He suddenly felt like an ape in all his bronzed and hairy bareness. He thoroughly resented it.

"They're *arms*, Lady Worth," he said on a hush. "I suggest you move closer to the settee if you feel a swoon coming on. I cannot guarantee I will get to you before you topple out of your chair."

She courageously turned her head toward him again.

"As valuable as that advice undoubtedly is, Mr. St. Leger, I'm not a swooner by nature. Please forgive me. I was just a bit startled, as I'd forgotten I was sharing quarters with a man who isn't a gent—"

She bit her lip. Torment and regret and apology flashed in her widened eyes.

His rank and ramping incredulity fair pulsed during the ensuing silence.

"If you think implying I'm not a gentleman will hurt my feelings, I've good news for you," he said, his voice low and silky. "My heart is as hard as my thighs." He paused, then added, "How *is* your hand this morning, by the way?"

A fresh swath of hot color joined the first over her cheekbones.

For a moment he thought he'd vanquished her aplomb.

"I confess I was less concerned about devastating you than I was about committing a lapse of good manners," she said finally, coolly.

He hated to admit it, but he liked everything about this sentence, perverse man that he was. Its elegance, its humor, its bite.

"So, you're suggesting one can't be a gentleman while also strolling about with their sleeves rolled up to reveal their strong, sinewy forearms." He feigned confusion.

"Not in front of women to whom they aren't actually married." She explained this gently and apologetically, a missionary to a Heathen.

Which might have been enraging, if it was not so hilarious.

He was peculiarly touched by her gentleness.

"Probably because their scrawny aristocratic forearms embarrass them," he suggested.

They locked gazes for a tick or two.

"No doubt," she humored.

He smiled at that.

And for a moment, she also seemed in danger of smiling, too. But she was clinging to tension the way she'd clung to that sheet out the window of the building she'd escaped.

He gestured to the chair opposite her, mutely asking for permission to sit. Lady Worth was just going to need to endure the primitive assault of his bare arms.

She nodded cautiously.

On the table sat two scones on two little white plates. Two cups flanked a carafe of coffee. A little bowl of sugar and the little pitcher of cream appeared untouched.

He peered and discovered that she took her coffee black. This was a little like discovering she drank whiskey neat.

He would usually take good coffee however he could get it, but he liked a pinch of sugar in his, so he spooned a bit into the bottom of his cup.

And to his surprise, she lifted the pot and poured for him.

Her wrists were delicate, her fingers slender. The deft prettiness of the gesture disarmed him, and he was not generally in favor of feeling disarmed.

"Thank you," he said pointedly, to prove he was not an ape.

She nodded and returned to her letter. A little dent of concentration had appeared between her straight, slim, emphatic dark brows.

"By the way, if you'd rather not look at my arms, you can look me in the eyes, instead, Lady Worth."

With a great ironic show of humoring him, she lowered her letter and tipped her head back.

Her eyes were almost golden in the morning light, and they canted a bit at the outer corners, like almonds, or perhaps teardrops. The elegant arch of her cheekbones reminded him of cathedral windows. Her mouth was wide and pale pink and soft looking, her jaw a clean, sharp angle, her nose straight and perhaps a bit long.

She wasn't the sort of pretty everyone would agree upon, he decided. The uncontroversial, indisputable sort. The sort that their proprietresses, Mrs. Hardy and Mrs. Durand, were.

He was reminded, for some reason, of a bust he'd once seen of Eleanor of Aquitaine, who'd been a powerful queen. Though he thought this was more about the way she held herself, and her general air of purposefulness and confidence, as though she was accustomed to never being free of either authority or burden.

Her gaze suddenly flickered uncertainly in response to something in his expression.

She dropped her eyes to her letter again. He noticed she possessed a veritable little forest of dark lashes.

"Did Mrs. Hardy and Mrs. Durand issue a fresh batch of rules?"

"It's a marriage proposal." She didn't lift her head.

"I see. Get a lot of those, do you?" he said mildly.

She didn't reply but her flush deepened. The curve of her cheek reminded him of a china cup, smooth and gleaming.

"All those pages to say, 'Lady Worth, will you be my bride?' It must be because he uses a thousand words to say what he could say in about ten."

"Then it will be a match made in heaven, clearly." She said it dryly. But somewhat abstractedly.

She looked up again, finally.

"It's a good offer," she said stiffly. A trifle defensively.

Which suggested that while torrid romance wasn't precisely underway, she meant to be kind and fair to the person who'd written to her. And as though she wanted to emphasize that, despite the fact that Lorcan essentially collected her from the street like so much flotsam, she did indeed have value to someone.

It both touched him and bothered him quite a lot, and he could not quite say why.

"Oh, well then. And what is marriage if not a business arrangement? Just like ours."

She fixed him with a look of strained patience. "Have you ever before been wed, Mr. St. Leger, or does your courage extend only to pantomime marriages?"

"I have thus far cleverly avoided becoming leg shackled and anticipate remaining so until the grave."

"I am *all* amazement to hear it," she murmured.

While she returned to reading her letter, he ate one of the scones in two bites. It was delicious.

She glanced up from her letter, looked at his plate, and blinked.

Not a single remaining crumb betrayed a scone had ever sat upon it.

"I only looked away for a second," she breathed. She was almost comically alarmed.

"You best eat yours now, as I'm inclined to make it disappear as well," he said. "And it was a right good scone. The best I've ever eaten."

She drew the other scone closer to her, cautiously, as if she wasn't entirely certain he wouldn't snatch it away like a wild dog who had gotten loose in the kitchen.

He watched in fascinated silence as she neatly dismantled it with her fingers and then delicately ate the pieces one by one.

She patted her lips with a napkin.

He felt a bit like he was crouching in shrubbery with a spyglass, studying the habits of wild birds.

"Does it have to be in pieces?" he asked.

"It tastes better that way," she said. "And I like to see the fluffy inside of it. I can't explain it."

"Is it everything, or just scones?"

"Mostly fluffy things," she clarified, after a moment.

"Hmmph." He was still hungry. Fortunately, they'd be fed a decent breakfast, he'd been told. He'd never really gotten into the habit of eating as an entertainment ritual. He'd learned early on to quickly devour what he could beg, borrow, or steal. At least he'd acquired over the years more-than-acceptable table manners.

"Before we go down to mingle with other guests as the rules require, perhaps we ought to decide how we mean to go on. I suspect the weather and the house rules will compel us to act like Mr. and Mrs. St. Leger for at least a few days."

"Very well," she said resignedly. She neatly folded her letter and set it aside, then looked up at him expectantly.

"I expect you will need to accustom yourself to calling me Lorcan. If you find such an intimacy excruciating, St. Leger will do, I suppose. I suppose you should endeavor not to flinch when I call you Daphne. Because I intend to, during the spirited discourse or what have you that goes on in the sitting room."

She took this in. "I am not very good at lying."

"And yet you managed it so well last night."

"I lied by *not* lying," she pointed out. Somewhat weakly.

"True enough." He was somewhat amused. "I'm genuinely curious. What do you think will happen to you if you outright lie? Will you go straight to hell? Or do you get a number of dismissals, a bit like cricket, before you're done for?"

Faint distaste flickered over her features. "I imagine you do it whenever it suits you."

"It all depends on what you fear more, the wrath of God or starvation, I suppose. And if a lie is what it takes to get food or shelter when one has no hope of getting it any other way, then a lie it is. Otherwise, I'm partial to the truth. But I deal honestly with people. It's why I've so many friends. And more than a few enemies."

It was an attempt to disconcert her and she knew it because she merely eyed him ironically.

"I feel as though one ought to live by a code," she explained patiently. "Something that sort of defines your truest self. A moral true north to turn to when you're at a loss for how to proceed. Or to let you know when . . . you might be about to take a wrong turn."

"Mine is 'take what you can get when you can get it.'"

"Charming."

"But useful. I wonder if your code would hold up to a real test?"

She regarded him coldly for a long wordless moment. "You know nothing about me."

"Fair point. Why don't you start with not lying to me about why someone with a lofty title has taken a j-o-b."

She appeared to silently dither. "I don't see why that is necessary for you to know."

"Consider it a gift to me in exchange for lying on your behalf to one of your old friends."

It was a slightly bastardly thing to say.

And it caused her some clear discomfort. She cleared her throat. "Our family has a bit of a financial difficulty. I am doing my part to alleviate it. Surely that's sufficient information."

"Your family?"

"My father, the Earl of Worth. My brothers are Charles and Montague. And my mother was named Elizabeth, and as you know now, she died when I was eleven years old."

"Does Charles feel jealous that his brother got the fancier name?"

This surprised a smile from her so brilliantly amused he went abruptly still with awe, as if he'd stumbled across a four-leaf clover.

He basked in it a moment.

"What are they like, your father and brothers?"

Her face went luminous. "Oh, my father is very clever and witty. I can hardly keep count of the number of languages he speaks anymore. A bit absentminded and sensitive you see, as most geniuses are. Our mother's death quite crushed him. He has spent years studying and reading and writing important papers. I suppose Charles and Montague take after him, although Monty is a bit simpler and kinder and Charles is better at sport and he's the heir and he fancies all the girls are in love with him."

Imagine being the people who made Daphne's face glow like the moon, is what Lorcan thought.

"Where are they all at this moment?"

"I don't know. On the continent somewhere, gallivanting. Paris, I think. They've been there about half a year. My father is at home. What about your parents, Mr. St. Leger?"

She asked that rather quickly. Eager for a subject change, if Lorcan had to guess.

"Oh, I sprang fully formed into the world, like Athena from Zeus's head."

She eyed him warily, as if he'd just torn away a mask.

"You should *see* your expression," he said softly. "The things I know, Daphne. I traveled with a Greek on a ship who told stories of gods and goddesses at night by the stars and taught me all about the dangers of the pox. All the knowledge a man ever needs."

She fixed him with two seconds' worth of a small, patient smile. "Thanks to Charles and

Montague, I know how amusing little boys find it to attempt to be shocking."

He liked this, too, but he was a bit disappointed he couldn't shock her. "Very well. My father was a right bastard. I suppose you don't need to know that, but do feel free to say so if the subject arises in company. My mother died when I was young. I suspect all of my finer qualities I got from her. His name was George and he was some mix of French and God knows what else, and my mother was Irish and her name was Siobhan. I'm named for her father. I get my sweet nature from her and I got my brutish looks from him. I am not quite certain how old I am, although I like to tell people I'm thirty-five, give or take a year."

She'd gone visibly tense from the word "bastard" on. And then her face went fully troubled.

And this made him set his teeth. He could sound downright posh, if he put his back into it. He'd sneaked into the King's Theater when he was a boy to cadge scraps of food from the vendors, and absorbed the lofty language of the actors prowling the stage. Later, he'd further refined his speaking through exposure to secret business dealings with earls and their ilk.

But out that word "bastard" had come, because it was the way he normally spoke and the only way he ever thought about his father, and he was unaccustomed to censoring himself. Sharing a suite with her was going to work nerves he hadn't suspected he possessed.

"What do you remember about your mother?"

He had never been asked this. He was disconcerted, a feeling that rarely visited him as an adult.

"She had a pretty voice," he said shortly. He hesitated for a time. Gruffly he said, "I remember she called me *a thaisce*. It means 'my treasure' in Gaelic."

He found that he'd gone quite still. As if to hold himself apart from any feelings he might have about those words.

"How lovely," she said gently. "My mother called me Daphne."

He grinned at that.

"I lived with my father until he died when I was about ten and then I fended for meself," he said.

"In St. Giles."

"Aye."

"When you were ten? But . . . how . . . how did you . . ."

"Oh, any way I could, luv," he said simply. "The details will only appall you."

He could tell she did *not* take to being called "luv," which only made him want to do it again.

There ensued a long silence, during which he could almost hear the questions milling about in her head, and during which he wore an expression designed to discourage them.

"When do you celebrate your birthday?" was what she chose to ask finally.

"I do not celebrate my birthday. Haven't a clue when it is. When do you celebrate yours?"

She paused. "I'll be thirty years old in two days. Feel free to gasp."

He probably ought to say something like, "and you don't look a day over twenty," or "I never would have guessed," but it wasn't true. It wasn't so much about how she *looked* as how she carried herself. By the age of thirty, more people had drawn a few conclusions about life and had acquired a sort of certainty, perhaps a bit of piquant cynicism, that no twenty-year-old possessed.

So he said the unoriginal thing. "I suppose getting older is better than the alternative," he said.

Even he knew that thirty years old was considered well on the shelf for a woman. He wondered what it was about her that kept her at home with her father and brothers.

He found himself relieved she had a marriage proposal. Women like her ought to be safely sorted into the categories to which they belonged. He'd witnessed the suffering of too many desperate tag ends of society.

"What is your favorite thing to eat?" she asked.

Into his mind flashed an outrageous and prurient, and, frankly, true, response, and if he'd said it aloud a man would have laughed. But the point would have been to confuse and horrify her, and he disliked himself for the impulse to constantly poke at her like an anemone, simply to see what she would do. Simply because she was pristine and blushed easily.

"I'm merely grateful for food well-prepared. You may have noticed that I like scones."

Her eyes were full of questions, all of which he was prepared to bat sharply down. He did not want to see the pity, speculation, revulsion, or sympathy reflected in her eyes. He needed none of it from the likes of her. The past was the past. He was here now and he was well fed and getting hungrier by the minute.

"I am grateful if you now regularly find enough to eat."

He gave a single, slow, forbidding nod. "What is your favorite thing to eat?"

She hesitated.

"Oranges," she said, somewhat shyly.

She was still studying him with an uncomfortable curiosity.

"A fine choice," he said crisply. "Has your family an orangery, Lady Worth?"

"We haven't."

"Why oranges? And not blancmange, or cheddar, or a turkey leg?"

She cleared her throat. "Because it's like the sun, in the form of a fruit." She said this almost resignedly, as if this was an embarrassing secret she'd harbored. "And that's how it feels when you eat one, too. As if all the joy the sun takes in shining is in one slice. And I love how the peel smells when you dig your nails into it—it's like orange, only times a thousand, with a bit of an an edge. And when you bite into it it's taut at first and then the juice sort of explodes in your mouth and it's . . ."

He realized he was frowning faintly and got control of his face. He was unsettled. More specifically, he was unsettled because he was a trifle aroused. He was at once tempted to hand all sorts of things to her to hear how she felt about them.

Was Lady Worth a secret sensualist? One

would never have guessed. He wondered why it was something which embarrassed her.

Awkwardly, he said nothing.

"What are your interests and pursuits?" she asked politely.

"Embroidery, pianoforte, and watercolors," he said at once.

She sighed impatiently.

"Oh, *my* interests and pursuits. Mine are fighting and fu—"

She looked so *braced* for more brutishness that he felt a fresh wave of self-dislike both for himself for wanting to ruffle her, and for her for providing the inspiration to ruffle her.

The truth was, he had never parsed his life into interests and pursuits. His interest was living and his pursuit was thriving, and all of it was all of a piece.

"I actually don't mind a good fight, now and again. The kind with fists. I like to win, and I like to make a point about crossing me. And that point is: don't do it. But I seldom need to, see. I like a good dark ale and the foam of it on my tongue. I like to sail. Wind in my hair, sun in my eyes, spray on my face. I like to become better and better at things, everything, I try. I love to organize and command men, because I think I'm bloody good at it. I like to invest my plunder in clever ways and it thrills me to my *core* when I make a sou or two or more on it. I like a smart wager and a hard negotiation and a good cigar and the sound a woman makes when I . . ."

Her expression throughout was some variation

of shock, alarm, fascination, and martyred patience.

He paused. "How long will we say we've been married, if we're asked?"

"We can say that it feels like forever," she said.

His short laugh became a sigh. "One year?"

"Very well."

An awkward pause ensued.

She cleared her throat.

"As for my interest and pursuits . . . I do like embroidery, watercolors, and pianoforte," she said with great dignity. "And I'm good at them. Possibly as good as you are at . . ." she sighed ". . . fighting. I like to dance. And walking in the country. I love finding tiny errors in balance sheets and creating exquisite budgets." She opened her mouth, as if she seemed about to say something else. Then changed her mind.

He frowned faintly.

Finally, she said, "And I like stars."

And then said nothing more.

He was bemused. "What do you like about them?"

"Everything."

He stared at her.

Wondering why she was tight-lipped about this, of all things.

She cleared her throat, and then confessed, in a low voice, as if relating a crime, "They seem like magic, to me. I mean, aren't they? When you look up, and when you think about it, how remarkable and almost outlandish it is that twinkling things are just . . . suspended there in the sky. Imagine a night sky without them. How shocking that would be. I like the lore around them. I love how they are so far away and so beautiful that merely to see them is to yearn, because you can never reach them, and I think maybe that's why we associate them with wishes. Particularly for things we think we cannot have. I like that they're everywhere, so that someone a continent away might now be looking up at the same stars we look at here. I like that we've learned to navigate by them. That they were used to portend events. I just . . ." She waved a hand. Somewhat overcome.

He could not imagine why she was blushing. He was, in fact, somewhat peculiarly enthralled by this recitation.

"Stars are all of those things and more," he agreed cautiously. "Stars are my friends. I've learned to navigate by them. Once you know them that way, you can feel at home anywhere in the world."

Suddenly he wanted to go outside and look at stars with her words running through his head, to see what she saw and feel what she felt.

His life had been a whole pageant: adventure, violence, subterfuge, tragedy and triumph, lust and hunger. He was beginning to feel that the speed and urgency of living might have deprived him of properly savoring textures. And nuances. It made him restless. He realized he'd been assuming a certain superiority of experience a moment ago. It was disconcerting to feel that the world, in fact, might have some dimension he'd overlooked. That she might have something to teach him.

He was tempted to ask her why talking about it seemed to bring her no joy. And yet that seemed to diverge from their current mission, which was to acquire just enough information to be able to perpetuate their little ruse so they could continue enjoying the hospitality of The Grand Palace on the Thames.

And besides the stars were not going to be showing themselves over the next few nights.

She looked relieved at his answer, regardless. "Do you like to read?"

He read slowly. He wrote simply. He'd learned to do both only about a decade ago. He'd paid someone to teach him. It wasn't yet anything he associated with recreation. Though he did quite enjoy *listening* to stories.

He was disinclined to admit any of this to her.

He said, "I've a book by the explorer Mr. Miles Redmond I've been trying to get through."

"Mr. Miles Redmond isn't for everybody," she sympathized. "But I enjoy his work. It's very thorough."

Thoroughly boring, he was tempted to say, but did not. "I've traveled to a number of exciting places," he volunteered. "The Orient, the south seas."

"I've traveled to London, Brighton, Sussex, Dover, and points in-between."

"All thrilling places." Especially when one was a smuggler.

She smiled ruefully at this.

"Do *you* like to read?" He suddenly wanted to hear what she had to say about it.

"Oh, yes. A bit of everything, really. Do you have a favorite story?" she tried.

"Oh, I like myths. Lust, murder, kidnapping, revenge, jealousy, obsession, creatures with snakes for hair, blokes getting their livers pecked out, nymphs. The story of my life."

She took this in with a somber expression. "Mine, too."

He wasn't sure whether she was taking the piss. Or if she was just indulging his efforts to rattle her. He smiled, slowly, regardless.

"Go ahead and ask the question you've been wanting to ask," he said.

"The how did you get your scar question, or the what did you do that so upset Captain Hardy question?"

He went still. Impressed, and somewhat wary.

Her gaze was very steady and a bit ironic.

He pointed to his face. "He was aiming for my heart and I knocked his sword up just in time. Seconds later he was dead." He smiled slightly. "And Captain Hardy is nothing you need to concern yourself about."

Her gaze didn't flicker. But she'd gone noticeably still, and eventually her expression went inscrutable, and then she turned slightly toward the window again. Away from him and his bare arms and his wild ways.

He wasn't entirely certain why he'd said it so unnecessarily bluntly. Or why he'd felt the need to share he'd killed the man who'd marked him for life. Some instinct had urged him to swiftly draw a sharp line between what she was and what he was.

What unnerved him was that he recognized it as a defensive response akin to piercing a pirate in the gut.

She returned her gaze to him. He had the strangest sense that she'd understood why he'd done it.

"I think we will be able to lie convincingly enough about marital bliss for the duration of a breakfast," he said finally. "Shall we go down now?"

"I think the scone will do for me for now. I believe I'll spend the morning considering my response to my letter." She gestured to the alleged marriage proposal, folded next to her elbow.

"Very well. I've business in town I must attend to before the roads flood. You won't see me again until this evening."

"Until the hour of spirited discourse is upon us, then." She offered him a small, polite placate-the-rogue smile.

She was still reading her letter when he went out the door a minute or so later, his shirtsleeves rolled down beneath his coat.

Chapter Seven

❦

My dear Lady Worth,

I hope this letter finds you in good health.
I have undertaken a good deal of reflection
since the pleasant hours recently passed in
the company of you and your father. As such,
it became clear to me that in addition to an
appreciation for literature and a fondness
for the countryside in common, we two face
similarly daunting seasons of our lives: I am
fifty-six years old, widowed for the second
time, and a father to five children, several
still in the schoolroom. You are a well-bred,
titled but unmarried woman of advancing
years who finds herself without a dowry and
facing an uncertain future.

I presume to write today with a proposal
to which I believe you may be amenable.

You struck me as a pragmatic person,
and as such I hoped you would forgive me
if I forego the superfluous frivolities of
courtship, which are rightly the province of
the young and naive.

I should like to propose that we marry.

As my wife, you would oversee the
management of household matters, including

the hiring of servants, such as you were trained to do. You will have assistance from the housekeeper, butler, and my Man of Affairs. You would also assist me in raising and guiding the children with affection and wisdom and making decisions regarding their welfare, and I will expect you to dutifully participate in the more intimate features of marriage that occur in private between a husband and wife as well as attend to my comfort in other wifely ways.

I am certain you would be a credit to me as a hostess and in all other public functions requiring our mutual attendance.

In exchange you will enjoy a grand family name and title and all the comforts afforded by my fortune, lifelong security for yourself and any future issue that may result from our union.

I have an income of fifteen thousand pounds per annum, an estate in Sussex, and homes in London and Richmond. I will be happy to negotiate an allowance for you, and to provide a suitable settlement to your father.

I enclose a list of assets and sources of income, information which may help you to come to your decision.

Given a foundation of friendship, breeding, and interests, I am optimistic that affection will arise between us over the course of years.

I expect you shall need a period of reflection, and I believe a fortnight should

*be sufficient. Should I not hear from you by
letter post haste, I shall call upon you at
your father's home in Hampshire at the end of
the month to hear your decision. I will send a
messenger ahead of my arrival.*

*I am certain you comprehend that I do not
take lightly the conferring of the honor of my
good name. Rest assured, Lady Worth, that I
believe you are deserving of it.*

*Yours sincerely,
Alfred, Earl of Athelboro*

HE HAD indeed enclosed numerous other pages
methodically listing his property holdings, his
investments, the yearly incomes from his estates,
and the names and ages of his children.

The letter was a masterpiece of delicacy,
kindness, pomposity, brutal pragmatism, and
entitlement. He saw her as a fixed set of pre-
dictable qualities which would suit his pur-
poses. He did her the honor of assuming she
possessed the intelligence to see her predicament in the same light he saw it. It solved every
problem she had, and negated her completely.

And who was to say he was wrong about any
of it?

Her father must have alerted the earl to the bargain she presented, given that she no longer had a
dowry. It had been gambled away.

"Uncertain future." "Advancing years." He'd
written these things with such authority that

her breathing had gone shallow with terror
when she'd read it. Did *everyone* believe her
circumstances dire? Was this how all men saw
her? He was fifty-six; he'd had two wives. He
ought to be reluctant to get attached to another
one, given his experiences. Doubtless any sentiment he'd ever laid claim to had been burned
away.

And perhaps that was why he'd chosen her.
For what about her would arouse undue sentiment?

He was wealthy. He would pay her father's
obscene five-hundred-pound debt. The marriage settlements would likely restore her father
to some form of solvency, too. Wasn't it her duty,
then, as a daughter, to seize the opportunity?

She would have no worries at all.

But then, neither, of course, did the chair she
sat upon. And after a fashion, furniture is what
she would be.

*I will expect you to dutifully participate in the more
intimate features of marriage that occur in private between a husband and wife, as well as attend to my comfort in other wifely ways.*

Her cheeks went hot and her stomach roiled.

She imagined the scorn with which Lorcan St.
Leger would greet such a sterile sentence.

Lorcan was a disturbingly vital creature.
Utterly foreign to her experience. He still
frightened—maybe even repelled—her a little.
And yet—she could not explain it—talking to
him this morning had been like taking that first

bite of an orange. That first sip of black, black coffee. He listened as though she mattered precisely as much as he did.

How disorienting this quality was to encounter in a man. She'd felt as if she were in a fast ship moving over water, sea spray in her face.

And she was ironically surprised to realize that of all the men she'd ever known, he alone had helped her when she'd needed it and had so far asked for nothing in return.

She ought to fall on her knees in gratitude to the Earl of Athelboro. She ought to be soaring with relief. She'd once experienced the "frivolity of courtship" and had somehow botched it, and perhaps once was all one got in a lifetime.

She could be a countess, and all she had to do was give up her pride and all hope.

But the earl was right: it was an honor.

So it was this, or perhaps a lifetime of serving as a companion to the Mrs. Leggetts of the world. She was a dutiful person, but she felt not one twinge of guilt when she imagined Mrs. Leggett discovering a bedsheet dangling from the window and her not-yet-paid paid companion missing. The weather was on her side, in that carriage travel would be nearly impossible over the next few days. She only hoped she could return to Hampshire before word somehow reached her father of her escape.

And therein lay Daphne's answer. So she set out to write a reply.

But no matter how hard she stared out the

window at the rain, she could not quite get past
"Dear Lord Athelboro."

She read a book instead.

"I THINK WE'RE lucky to get out of that alive,"
Lorcan said to Daphne about dinner.

Which had been simple, hearty, and tasty—
fish stew and root vegetables and bread and
butter—but had featured a frenzy of reaching
and devouring and several midair near colli-
sions of sloshing tureens. Three strapping boys,
curly of hair, long of leg, rosy of cheek, German
of accent, ate like sharks thrown chum, which
was fomenting the general eating panic. Daphne
and Lorcan had been introduced to all of them,
as well as to Mr. Angus McDonald, who sported
close-cropped hair so flaming red he resembled
a lit match. Delilah and Captain Hardy and Angelique and Lucien were present, too. Chewing
and swallowing took precedence over conversation.

They were told that a few other guests had
apparently opted to take dinner in their rooms
that evening, as the rules allowed, and that Mr.
Delacorte's stomach was a bit unsettled, but they
would all be joining them in the sitting room.

All the diners eventually staggered, a few at a
time, from the table, full and a trifle frazzled, and
into the sitting room.

Lorcan and Daphne both hesitated. And then
Lorcan extended an only slightly mockingly
chivalrous arm. "Time for charades, missus," he
murmured.

She stared at his arm. Then drew in a sustaining breath and delicately, gingerly, rested her hand on it. It was easily twice the width of Henry's arm. It felt a bit as though she'd just been given a cannon to fire.

He escorted her in.

The first person they saw in the sitting room was an extraordinarily picturesque young man leaning indolently against the mantel, as though he'd been propped there. One of the guests who had dined in his room, no doubt.

Daphne knew at once he was wealthy and titled. The details were all there: the ebony gloss of his Hoby boots; the coat so exquisitely tailored he might well have been sewn into it; the plum-colored striped waistcoat with silver buttons. His dark hair was just the perfect amount of floppy. His features were sculpted; his chin was dimpled. He was clearly accustomed to gawks and one got the sense he languished if he wasn't the recipient of them. This was someone who very much enjoyed being exactly who he was.

He took in the two of them in a glance, then returned his gaze to Daphne and straightened alertly. He gifted her with a slow and brilliant smile, warm and inviting, meant to bewitch. Likely every new woman he saw was treated to one of those smiles, and as there wasn't a younger or more beautiful female in view, Daphne thought wryly, she would have to do.

It wasn't ineffective. She wasn't unmoved. But it was wildly inappropriate, given that her hand rested on the arm of a man who was hard to miss.

She just wasn't certain what to do apart from smile uncertainly in return.

Lorcan was eyeing the young man speculatively.

"How do you do, sir," he said politely. "I am Lorcan St. Leger. Allow me to present my wife, Daphne St. Leger."

Hearing her name linked with his in such a fashion was a jolt.

"Lord St. John Vaughn." Unsurprisingly, the young man's enunciation was as refined as cut glass.

Bows and a curtsy were exchanged.

"And what do you do, Lord Vaughn?" Lorcan asked. Somewhat idly.

"Do? Ah, it's in the name, rather," St. John replied pleasantly. "The 'lord' part. I'm the heir to an earl." He said this meaningfully to Daphne.

"I see," Lorcan said gravely. "In other words, you mainly do what you're doing now." He gestured to the mantel against which St. John was leaning.

"More or less," St. John replied.

A tense little pause ensued while they studied each other, and something St. John saw in Lorcan's expression transformed his into something much tenser rather rapidly.

"You're something to do with violence, I would guess," St. John said to Lorcan. "Something vigorous."

"Aye," Lorcan said agreeably. "Killing. Maiming. Things of that nature."

St. John blinked.

"I've a few interests. Chess. Fencing. Horses,"

St. John offered carefully. His eyes darted toward Daphne nervously.

"Just as long as none of them are my wife we'll get along just fine." Lorcan smiled terrifyingly.

Daphne's breath stopped.

This was about as frank as things got between men before seconds were named, and Lorcan had done it in an offhand eyeblink.

"Perhaps you and I could practice fencing if you get bored during your stay." Lorcan trailed a meaningful look behind him as he escorted Daphne away from the wide-eyed St. John.

She felt Lorcan's arm tense beneath her hand.

And then she realized it was because she had gripped his arm tightly.

He looked down at her hand. His eyes met hers, somewhat uncertainly. "I'm sorry," he said quietly. "Did I frighten you?"

She wasn't certain how to answer. More accurately, the answer was "no" and she suspected it should be. Instead, a sort of darkly brilliant thrill glowed in her chest. She understood two things: what the word "my" meant to Lorcan. And a shocking sort of primitive exhilaration of being boldly, unequivocally claimed: *my wife.*

That this realization should occur within the confines of a sham marriage made her throat tight.

"No," she managed finally. "He's probably harmless but he was indeed a bit disrespectful. I suppose I'm simply unaccustomed to such . . ." She searched for words. ". . . thrilling dialogue."

He gave a soft laugh. "I see. I expect an actual

gentleman might have used a few dozen more words to convey his meaning, but I find it's best to be efficient about letting that sort know where I stand." He paused. "And he clearly made you uncomfortable, which I could not possibly let stand."

It seemed an astonishing thing to say. "Thank you," she said, humbly.

"I wouldn't really kill him, when it came right down to it," he reassured her. "Perhaps just trim off his eyebrow with the tip of me rapier."

With the sense that she was walking arm in arm with chaos disguised by a beautifully fitted black suit, they abandoned St. John as she allowed him to lead her deeper into the room.

He steered her toward where Delilah and Angelique had claimed chairs among Dot, who was wearing a stubborn expression, and a woman sporting dashing white streaks in her dark, upswept hair who was gesturing emphatically with the book she held. Cheerful bickering about how to pass the evening was clearly underway and words flying about included Spillikins, Whist, ghosts, attics, charades, pirates, and myths.

The German musicians had gathered at little tables toward the back of the room to chuckle amongst themselves, and Mr. McDonald had claimed a table for himself and opened a book.

Outside of church, where her family had its own pew, or crammed into a coaching inn, Daphne had never been thrust into a room so full of people she could not easily identify by station or rank, all of whom seemed unrelated to, quite familiar with, and even fond of, each other. It was as vibrant as an orchestra, somehow; everyone was different but contributed to the whole. And while none of the furniture and none of the people quite matched, for that reason, it all somehow paradoxically did. The room itself—the furniture, the wallpaper, the curtains, the pianoforte—had a soft, warm, gently worn charm. It was liberally lit by the blazing fire and a scattering of oil lamps, which flattered everyone's complexions.

Captain Hardy and Lord Bolt had yet to appear, she noted.

Delilah stood to greet them. "Mr. and Mrs. St. Leger, may I introduce to you to our treasured guest Mrs. Pariseau? She is a widow and well-traveled, and she knows so many interesting things."

Mrs. Pariseau, the woman who sported white stripes in her dark hair, was compact and curvy and she sprang to her feet to curtsy with a warm smile, which she aimed first at Daphne.

Then turned and looked up what seemed like miles into Lorcan's face.

Her gaze lingered there, thoughtfully.

She returned it to Daphne. Then swung it back to Lorcan, clearly increasingly bemused.

"Well. My goodness. There's certainly a story *here*," she finally concluded, with relish. Her dark eyes crackled with mischief. "I would love to know how the two of you managed to meet."

Daphne's heart gave a lurch.

Lorcan said somberly, "Well, Mrs. Pariseau, I shall tell you. Like Daphne in the Greek myth, I met her when she was in need of some urgent assistance. But instead of a tree I saved her by turning her into my wife."

Daphne was stunned to realize this was actually true, metaphorically speaking.

There was a chorus of "awwws" while Mrs. Pariseau gasped and clasped her hands to her bosom in pure delight. "We *love* our myths here at The Grand Palace on the Thames! Do you *see*, Dot?"

"Do I see what?" Dot said stubbornly. She actually liked myths well enough. It was just that she *preferred* ghosts.

They all turned when a man built a bit like a Welsh pony strode into the room. "I feel *much* better now!" he announced cheerily. "Those parsnips worked a treat to rush everything on out!"

Suddenly his face lit up like a firework with happy astonishment. "Is it . . . could it be . . . St. Leger?"

"Delacorte?" Lorcan sounded amazed.

Daphne was shocked when Mr. Delacorte whumped her fearsome fake husband on the back. "I'll be daa-a—" He came to a halt before the word became an official epithet, and Mr. Delacorte and Lorcan launched into the mutual backslaps and handshakes of men who have clearly shared some meaningful experience, while everyone else looked on in bemusement.

"I'll never forget that night at the Crown and Crow in Brighton, St. Leger. I like to tell the story about how you bought a round for all the lads and then dared that lass to dance on the bar! Ha ha! And then she fell and you caught her in your—"

"Delacorte, allow me to introduce my wife, Daphne," Lorcan said smoothly.

Delacorte's mouth froze midlaugh. He turned to her.

Daphne smiled patiently at him. Very amused, despite herself.

"*You've* a wife? St. Leger. You've a *wife*, St. Leger," Delacorte amended quickly. "What an aston . . ." He cleared his throat. ". . . er, astonishingly fine thing. Congratulations to you both. What a pleasure and honor to meet you, Mrs. St. Leger."

He bowed very elegantly to Daphne. His suit was handsomely tailored and beautifully kept, and the arc of his stomach taxed the top buttons of his waistcoat. His eyes were a rather lovely dreamy shade of blue, and his hair, a trifle too long, tufted out from behind his ears.

"Please do not leave me in suspense, Mr. Delacorte. I'm wondering how your Crown and Crow story ends," she prompted. Mischievously.

Delacorte flicked a hunted look at Lorcan, who returned it with a warning one.

Delacorte tipped his head back, face abstracted, as if he were flipping through a long sequence of events to get to the last one.

"We put out the fire just in time, and managed to find the rightful owner of the goat."

Daphne couldn't help but smile slowly at Lorcan's obvious discomfort.

"You'll have to imagine what went on in between, my dear, because you won't be getting the story out of me. I'm quite domesticated now," he told Delacorte.

"Of *course* you are." Delacorte not-so-subtly winked. "I think the two of you will be very happy here for however long you decide to stay," he added confidently. "But *you'll* want to have a care with the Epithet Jar, St. Leger." He elbowed Lorcan in the ribs and gestured to the jar standing sentry over the room. "It could bankrupt a man."

"Oh, I shouldn't worry about me, anymore, Delacorte. I'm as tame as a kitten. My *wife*, on the other hand . . . you should hear how she goes on. I'll need to carry about a pocket full of pennies for her sake." He winked.

Daphne's mouth dropped open.

"I jest of course. She only curses a blue streak when she's excited. Or thoroughly enjoying something."

"Oh my," Mrs. Pariseau said faintly.

Delilah and Angelique had gone very still and wide-eyed.

"*No* one knows how to enjoy something like my wife," he added wickedly.

Mrs. Pariseau surreptitiously fanned her bodice with her hand.

"Scones, for instance," Lorcan continued, innocently. "She enjoys them a good deal."

Daphne locked gazes with him. Hers was scathingly amazed.

His glinted wickedly.

There was a little silence.

She ought to disapprove. She hated to admit it, but she found it both very funny and exhilarating. Seldom had anyone bothered to tease her, not even Henry. Her earnestness and brisk efficiency hardly invited it, she supposed.

"Lorcan enjoys saying things like that because he likes to be scolded like a little boy." She managed to say it fondly. She suspected this was also true.

There flashed in his eyes a blend of surprise, warning, and amused approval. As though he was unaccustomed to being challenged and yet she continued to surprise him. And as long as she did, he was going to try to find ways to test her.

She found this disconcerted her less than it ought. It felt peculiarly like a relief.

"Nay, in truth sometimes I say things just to make her blush," he said softly. "For do you see how pretty it is when she does?"

And now she was certain she was scarlet, judging from the heat of her cheeks, and everyone was looking at the two of them meltingly, charmed by the unpredictable menace that was her fake husband.

"She does have a gift for appreciating things," he added more gently. Sounding conciliatory. Apologizing, just a little, for teasing her.

She stared at him, surprised. He had robbed her of words. Primarily because it was something she secretly appreciated about herself that no one had ever before thought to point out.

"We . . . both do," she told the little group around them. Her voice was faint. Because it was the fair thing to say. And because she realized it was true. For different reasons, but they did.

She suddenly wanted a moment alone to ponder this realization.

"Daphne and I knew each other when we were younger," Delilah told the little group nearest them. "I remember the picnic with garlands and little lanterns in the trees for her father's fortieth birthday. It was magical. There was a picnic nearly every year for his birthday," Delilah told Lorcan.

"Sounds enchanting." Lorcan only sounded a little ironic. "Were there picnics for your birthday, too, Daphne?" He turned an expression of cheerful expectation toward her.

She felt her face heating again. She wasn't quite certain how to reply. "My birthdays were quieter affairs." Mainly because they were seldom remembered until long after the fact.

"Ah," he said pleasantly, after a little beat of silence. There remained a little puzzled dent between his formidable brows.

Daphne was tense now. She didn't want to discuss the home she'd all but lost. It would only lead to questions about whether Lorcan had ever visited there, and what her family thought of him, and the lies would need to fly as thick and fast as . . . gnats at a picnic.

Lorcan was studying her with that thoughtful furrow between his eyes. Suddenly he turned away. "Delacorte, are you still traveling about with your case of magic powders and whatnot? It was how the two of us managed to meet," Lorcan explained to the group. "He travels a fair bit selling medicines and remedies and the like up and down the coast."

Daphne recognized it as a deft change of subject.

"Oh, indeed. And I've joined Hardy and Bolt in their Triton Group endeavor, as well."

"Have you, indeed," Lorcan mused, sounding somewhat amused, somewhat ironic.

"I'm given to understand you've been a privateer, Mr. St. Leger. You must be very well traveled," Mrs. Pariseau remarked.

"Oh, I'm certain Mr. St. Leger has been to a lot of England's more intriguing points of interest. Coves at midnight. Secret tunnels. Sea caves. Abandoned cart tracks. Dark alleys."

Thusly Captain Hardy announced his entrance, followed by Lord Bolt.

Hardy strode casually over to where their little group stood, while Bolt strode over to Mr. McDonald, as Angelique had asked him earlier to make a bit of an effort to get the dour Scot to play chess.

Daphne noted that Delilah was staring a caution at her husband.

Captain Hardy didn't seem to notice.

Once again he and Lorcan were fixedly regarding each other.

Lorcan was smiling in what appeared to be genuine, if unsettling, amusement.

"I expect you greatly regret we never encountered one another in any of those places," Lorcan said. "In another coincidence, Captain Hardy and I knew each other as boys in St. Giles," Lorcan informed the group.

Mr. Delacorte's expression went at once mistily contented. One of his favorite things in the world was to be in a room where everyone knew and liked each other.

"Oh! I'm certain the two of you were ador . . . adorable . . . together . . ." Mrs. Pariseau faltered as she realized that no one really said "adorable" with reference to St. Giles. And that the men in question had probably been dangerous looking even as babies.

That, and Captain Hardy's lips had all but vanished in a grim line.

Daphne's stomach clenched again. She almost preferred they would get it over with and fight with swords instead of innuendo.

"We were, indeed," Lorcan continued. "Hardy disappeared one day when I was about nine years old, and the next time I saw him was decades later, in a pub in Cornwall. Bought him a round, in fact. He was a blockade commander and a hero. I was right proud to know him."

Daphne studied his face for evidence of irony, and saw none.

"And what were *you* by then, Mr. St. Leger?" Mrs. Pariseau asked with genuine interest.

He paused. "Mainly I was clever," Lorcan said, with a remote little smile.

"And lucky," Hardy added.

"Aye, surely you're correct," Lorcan said humbly. "I imagine a boy rescued from St. Giles at the age of ten to spend a lifetime within the cozy structure of the navy would know a thing or two about luck."

"I suppose a boy who never left St. Giles would

learn a lot about getting away with things," Captain Hardy mused.

"I imagine so." Lorcan was amused, but not in a heartwarming way.

"Funny, but everyone seemed to know St. Leger when I met him," Captain Hardy said lightly. "Everyone. But no one would say why."

"Even *I* know St. Leger," Delacorte contributed. "Have we got a story for you, Hardy."

"Save it for the smoking room, Mr. Delacorte," Lorcan said hurriedly.

"The Triton Group's ship has been delayed nigh on a fortnight," Delilah shared with Lorcan. "*The Zephyr.* We're all a bit concerned, as you can imagine."

It sounded a bit like an explanation. Perhaps even an apology for her husband's terseness.

There ensued a little pause.

"Hard luck," Lorcan sympathized. Quietly. Genuinely.

Hardy stiffly nodded his acknowledgment.

"Do you travel with your husband, Mrs. St. Leger?" Mrs. Pariseau asked this.

She cast a worried look up at Lorcan. "I have traveled with him a little," she said carefully.

"But it's a difficult life for a woman, aye?" Lorcan said, smoothly metaphorically scooping her out of the path of the question. "And so when we miss each other . . ." He turned to her.

"We can look up at the night sky and know we're both watching the same stars, and we don't feel alone." Daphne said this slowly.

It didn't feel like a lie, somehow.

Lorcan smiled somewhat slowly, with some surprise, as if he was proud of her.

Daphne was surprised to feel touched that he'd tried to rescue her from the need to outright lie.

"Perhaps we ought to decide what we'd like to read this evening," Angelique interjected. "Mrs. Pariseau is in favor of a few Greek myths. Dot would like to read *The Ghost in the Scullery*. Shall we take a vote?"

"I find I'm in the mood for ghosts. Something about the reappearance of a past long buried, I suppose," Lorcan said, and raised his hand.

Daphne raised her hand. "I want to know if they vanquish the ghosts."

Lorcan looked at her curiously.

The ultimate vote count showed that the ghosts won the evening. Mrs. Pariseau shrugged good-naturedly. "I'll read it, if you like." She was very good at reading aloud. She glanced about the room. "Dot, where did you leave the book? It's not in our usual place."

Dot's expression was suddenly stricken. "I'm afraid I . . . well, I left it in the scullery."

"The scullery?" Angelique asked. "Why the scullery? Oh . . . wait, never mind. I think I know."

Although she and Delilah knew the run of Dot's thinking well enough by now to suspect she'd been in the midst of a daydream and had absently filed it there because the word "Scullery" appeared on it, the way she might have put flour in the bin labeled "flour."

"Well, why don't you go and fetch the book,

Dot, and Mrs. Pariseau will read to us?" Delilah said before Dot could answer.

Dot's eyes flared with alarm.

"It was only the wind, Dot," Angelique said kindly but firmly.

"And we *know* you're brave," Delilah added encouragingly, as if saying it with conviction could make it true.

Chapter Eight

❧

Dot SUPPOSED she had only herself to blame. She had advocated for reading *The Ghost in the Scullery*, and now here she was on the way to the scullery, which at this time of night would be quiet, dark, and empty. Surely ghosts lay in wait for such opportunities to steal the souls of the unwary.

As she descended the stairs, she contemplated whether ghosts could also sense fear. Particularly *her* fear—she was, after all the heroine of her own story. On the off chance that this was true, she decided to distract herself from her nerves by silently singing the cheerful song that opera singer Miss Mariana Wylde had made up on the spot in their sitting room some months ago. *I've a stick up me bum and gray in me hair!* So the chorus went. So infectious! So witty!

Down the stairs she went, singing it over and over, silently, the way one might whisper prayers. Slowly, at first. But her shadow was thrown ominously large against the wall by the candle she held, and the sound of her own feet began to unnerve her, so she decided to tiptoe, and to do it quickly.

It was right about then she realized she'd left

her shawl in the sitting room and she really wished for it. She felt chilled clear through.

She at last reached the bottom step. The kitchen was empty. Helga and the maids had finished their work there for the evening.

She was almost there!

Suddenly, from everywhere and nowhere, it seemed, a soft, low, keening sound froze her in her tracks.

Terror erased her thoughts for an instant.

She stopped breathing.

She was certain all of the hair on her arms and her neck stood on end, though she of course couldn't see the hair on the back of her neck.

She stifled a whimper.

"It's just the wind it's just the wind it's just the wind it's just the wind," she whispered. Mrs. Durand had said so, and she'd been a governess, and knew so many things. And *surely* she wouldn't send Dot into danger? Both Mrs. Durand and Mrs. Hardy cared about her, she knew. They cared about everyone.

This made her feel a little better, and she proceeded more confidently, even as her heart was pounding so hard she thought it might crack her ribs. She could hear it in her ears, mingling with the lyrics of the song. *Whoosh Whoosh Whoosh. I've a stick up me bum . . .*

Thusly she crept across the kitchen, one foot in front of the other, as if on a narrow fence rail, either side of which was water filled with crocodiles, heart pounding.

She exhaled in relief when she saw the book,

The Ghost in the Scullery, sitting neatly right next to the pump, precisely where she'd left it. Snatch it and run like the devil back up the stairs—that's what she would do.

She stretched out an arm to seize it.

Just as the tip of an icy finger pressed the back of her bare arm.

"*BOLLOCKS!*" she roared, and shot straight up in the air, spun around, and hurled her fist like a shot put.

It connected with the granite jaw of Mr. Pike.

His arms swung in wide loops as he staggered backward, fighting for balance. He careened into the wall, slid down it.

And lay still.

Dot stared down at him. Mouth agape.

Riveted in absolute horror.

Then dropped to her knees.

"Mr. Pike!" she moaned. "I'm so sorry I'm so sorry I'm so sorry. *Speak* to me, Mr. Pike. Please." She clapped her hands to her face and moaned. "*Ohhhh,* I killed him. I'm going to Newgate. I'm going to the gallows! I'm going to hell! I'm going to *cast my accounts!*"

The prospect of being vomited upon after being nearly knocked out cold reanimated Mr. Pike, who groaned in abject horror and rolled to his side.

"Oh, thank *God*! Mr. Pike, you're alive." She sat back and clasped her hands over her heart.

He sat up with some effort, and gave his head a shake. He gingerly touched his jaw where she'd connected. "I'm fine, Dot. Don't you *dare* cast your accounts."

"I'll try not to. But I feel *ill* over hurting you! I'm so terribly sorry. I didn't mean to hit you, let alone knock you down."

"It's *my* fault," he said grimly. "I tried to scare you and obviously I failed. *I'm* sorry."

"You did scare me! I thought you were a ghost touching me and I'm ever so afraid of ghosts!"

"*Afraid?* You thought I was a ghost and you nearly knocked me out cold! Frightened people run and scream like banshees. They don't *attack* like Gentleman Jackson." His face was scarlet with equal parts outrage and approbation.

"Don't say banshee!" she begged.

"Oh, for *God's sake . . .*" He groaned in frustration. He rubbed his jaw delicately.

"And please, *please* don't tell Mrs. Hardy and Mrs. Durand I said 'bollocks.'" She sucked in a breath. "Oh, I said it again! What if I can't stop saying bollocks?" she said wildly. "*Help!* See what you've done!"

"Dot, *shhh*, or we'll have an audience for this debacle. Take a breath, and then take another. Let's both."

They both took long breaths.

Silently she reminded herself to ask Angelique what "debacle" meant.

"Better?" he asked.

She nodded.

They were quiet a moment.

"It's your fault I said 'bollocks,'" she accused.

"As if you've never heard that word from Mr. Delacorte in the sitting room. And by the way, you said 'hell,' too," Mr. Pike said wickedly.

Dot's eyes bulged in alarm again. "So did you!" she accused. "Just now!"

Mr. Pike sighed heavily. "It's something of a curse, knowing epithets and managing not to use them," he explained more gently. "It's a test of character, I think."

"And I *failed*," she breathed. "I am so very disappointed in myself I might swoon."

"Considering recent events, I doubt sincerely you're a swooner," he said flatly and frankly, thereby breaking Dot's Gothically romantic heart.

Although it was probably true.

She sobered.

"And besides, we can't both of us lay about on the floor. We'll get fired of a certainty." He paused. "Though I must say this might be the cleanest floor I've ever seen in a scullery." He sounded bemused.

"Everything is very clean and in good repair here. We take our jobs seriously here at The Grand Palace on the Thames. *All* of our jobs," she said meaningfully.

He sighed.

"Dot, I do, too. I *love* my job here. And I should like it if we could be friends."

Dot considered this.

"Why did you try to scare me?"

"I . . . because you stepped on me twice and it was an impulse, born of frustration. Which I confess is childish. The opportunity seemed too good to miss. I am not proud of it and I expect I only got what I deserved."

Dot considered this answer, which she rather

liked for its directness and honesty. "Very well," she conceded. "I expect I deserved it, too," she admitted bravely.

Mr. Pike exhaled in relief. He had taken a bit of a risk in being honest.

"May I ask . . . don't you think it's more appropriate for me to answer the door at night?" he asked.

"Appropriate how?" she demanded.

"Because most fine establishments have a footman to greet the guests," he explained, a trifle loftily.

"We're a fine house, and we have me," she said firmly. "Are you saying we weren't a fine establishment before you appeared?"

To her satisfaction, this brought him up short.

He sat all the way up and leaned against the wall, while she leaned against the opposite wall. She wrapped her arms around her torso. She really missed her shawl.

"Why does it mean so much to you?"

"Because I think opening the peep hatch is like getting a gift every time. Who will it be? It's ever so thrilling to be the first person to see someone who might fall in love with a duke, or be a fine lady in disguise, or discover a tunnel."

He stared at her. "What on earth are you . . . Dot, *I* was the one who got hit in the head."

"All of those things really did happen! This is a *very* special place, mind you. I opened the door to Captain Hardy, and now look, he's married to Mrs. Hardy. I opened the door to Lord Bolt! I was one of the first people to see him in years.

Everyone in all of England thought he was dead! And now Mrs. Durand is his wife. I opened the door to the King. Of. England," she added on a marveling hush. "Me. Dot. I like to feel a part of things and this is my favorite place in the world."

Mr. Pike's fine eyes had lit with a certain appreciation throughout this.

"But what if you open the door to thugs, bent on mayhem?"

"But what if it's a lady, who is running away from harm and feels more comfortable and welcome speaking with another lady?" she countered.

He pressed his lips together as he considered this. "Your point is taken."

She raised her eyebrows.

"Forgive me," he said humbly. "I did not realize there was a particular art to answering the door at a boardinghouse. And clearly there is."

Pike had kind eyes, Dot thought, but they were also very intense eyes, not dissimilar to Captain Hardy's. He was not, on the whole, a soft or very easy person, she would warrant. But he had said "forgive me," and she knew enough about men to know the ones who conceded anything at all to a woman were rare as hen's teeth.

"I *do* think about things, you know," she said. Quietly.

"It sounds rather nice, the way you put it. Answering the door. Opening the peep hatch," he said wistfully. "Being excited about the new people."

"Oh, it *is*," Dot agreed.

Mr. Pike seemed thoughtful. He sighed. "How is your hand?" he asked. "Does it hurt?"

"It does, a little," she said shyly.

"May I see?"

Dot had a powerful sense of propriety. One did not go about casually surrendering their hands to men, and touching the very handsome ones was particularly inadvisable.

But his eyes were wry and reassuring, so finally she gingerly laid her wounded hand in his outstretched palm.

He inspected her knuckles. "You ought to put cool water on it as soon as you can. The water in the basin in your room should be nice and cold now."

"All right," she said. Blushing. "How is your face?"

His face was handsome, that's how it was. This fresh realization made her own face even hotter.

"Never mind my face. I've stood up to worse than you. But don't take that as a dare!" he added, hurriedly, with a laugh. And then a wince.

He was going to be sporting a bruise.

"What if . . . we answer the door together when someone knocks after dark," he suggested, tentatively.

"Perhaps . . . every Wednesday, when there is a full moon, you can have your turn," she said magnanimously.

Mr. Pike could tell that it cost her. "Are you jesting?"

"A little," she admitted. "Or we can flip a coin."

"That is very generous of you, indeed," he said humbly. "You've a kind heart, Dot. Perhaps now that I'm working here you'll even find you have more free time to do other things you want to do."

"Like write my memoirs?" she said brightly.

He blinked.

"Perhaps you can include a chapter about the time you knocked a six-foot-tall footman to the ground."

"Maybe I will include a sentence or two about that in one of the chapters," she humored, kindly.

He stared at her. Pike had never, in all of his born days, met a more confounding female. And he'd worked with *many* different sorts of women, housemaids and the like, and he had a sister. And it was increasingly clear to him that while Dot wasn't featherbrained or witless or silly, her mind operated in unfathomable-to-him ways. Ben Pike was a serious person, dutiful and intelligent and straightforward. Following the run of Dot's thoughts, or predicting what she might say next, felt to him as futile as trying to catch hold of a sunbeam. Wherever had Mrs. Hardy and Mrs. Durand found her? he wondered.

He stood, and like a gentleman, reached down and hauled her up by the elbow, as her hand was sore.

They smoothed out their clothing and gathered their composure.

"Your cap, Dot."

He reached over and nudged it back into place with one finger.

They were on their feet just in time. They whirled at the brisk sound of feet on the clean, clean floor. Dot knew the light, swift treads of Mrs. Hardy and Mrs. Durand well.

They came into view wearing worried expressions.

How lovely to be someone they worry about, Dot thought, touched and pleased.

"Is everything all right here?" Mrs. Hardy said. "We thought we heard a terrible shriek."

"It was probably just the wind," Mr. Pike told them gravely.

Dot nodded soberly. "Definitely not a ghost."

"You're going to love the smoking room, St. Leger," Delacorte had confided with confident relish.

Lorcan, leaning against the wall, lit cheroot in hand, was forced to concede that, given time, he might indeed develop great affection for it, for a certain genius was evident in its design. The proprietresses had clearly understood men could scarcely be trusted to be civilized once out of sight of women, so they had decorated it with a thick rug, perfect should a ridiculous wager or a drunken insult result in an impromptu wrestling match, for instance. Not unheard-of in his experience. Long velvet curtains hung from the windows, the chairs were well worn and comfortable and the little table in front of the settee was handsome but battered, and everything was in attractive shades of dirt-and-blood-hiding brown.

All of the gentlemen—save Mr. McDonald, who neither smoked nor imbibed in spirits, though Delacorte secretly thought he could benefit a *lot* from both—of the house had repaired there upon listening to Mrs. Pariseau read *The Ghost in the Scullery* for a half hour or so. A cracking story, Lorcan thought. They'd left the women behind to get on with knitting or whatever it was they wished to do.

Lorcan's imagination had not extended to coming home every day to a place where the comfortable settees matched the carpet and the curtains. Or to the same woman, for that matter. He'd never even had a permanent home of his own. He'd been grateful for safe shelter wherever he'd found it.

Hardy and Bolt and Lorcan and Delacorte, like pillars, occupied the wall in corners of the room, whilst the German musicians had flopped at once onto the settee, slouched, and spread wide their legs or flung their boots up on the table, all the things they wouldn't dream of doing in front of the ladies. Before the weather eye of the older men, they were always more subdued, and nightly they quickly and quietly enjoyed the kind of good tobacco and brandy they couldn't otherwise afford before excusing themselves again.

St. John claimed a chair as though it was a throne.

Cheroots were passed around and lit and sucked into life, brandy was gurgled into snifters, and the air filled agreeably with smoke.

It would take a lot of brandy, however, to ease the tension in a room which contained both Lorcan and Captain Hardy in close quarters. Which mordantly amused Lorcan, and was the reason he'd decided to join everyone.

Lorcan gazed through the haze of smoke at

young Lord Vaughn, who looked too comfortable for Lorcan's satisfaction. The young lord was studying him somewhat sullenly.

For a moment they regarded each other as though each were exhibits in a menagerie.

"Mr. St. Leger, why do you wear an earring?" Lord Vaughn asked finally.

"Because I feel it enhances my delicate beauty." Lorcan exhaled a plume of cheroot smoke.

"Did it hurt to be pierced?"

"No more than getting shot or stabbed," Lorcan said agreeably.

Out of the corner of his eyes, he detected smiles twitching on Hardy's and Bolt's faces.

"You aren't worried you'll be robbed for it?" St. John pressed.

He smiled faintly. "Anyone is welcome to try, certainly."

St. John sank back against his chair and gloomily sucked on his cheroot.

Lorcan decided that disconcerting young Lord Vaughn would be his new favorite pastime. It was both entertaining and an act of charity. He could perhaps save him from getting killed in a duel one day for aiming sultry smiles at other men's wives.

His visceral response to that had surprised him. Because of course Daphne wasn't really his wife. "Wife" was a word he shied away from the way Mr. McDonald shied away from spirits.

It was the principle of the thing, surely.

And something to do with the way her hand had felt resting on his arm when he walked her into the sitting room. It was the oddest thing. But it was as if suddenly everything in him was marshaled in preparation to catch her should she need it.

Why hadn't a daughter of an earl married yet? At her age?

This puzzled him.

The young lord sitting across from him was the sort of man the daughter of an earl ought to marry. Titled, privileged, boring, safe, and rich.

"Will your parents be worried about you, St. John?" Bolt asked.

This made Lord Vaughn, who was just past twenty if Lorcan had to guess, sound like the veriest little boy. Lorcan shot Bolt an amused look. He wondered if Lord Vaughn had smoldered at Angelique or Delilah.

"No doubt," St. John admitted after a moment. "But they knew I was out with Delacorte. They like him."

"They were bound to, eventually," Delacorte said complacently, pleased.

"Still live with your parents, eh?" Lorcan asked dryly.

St. John shifted in his chair. "I like my parents," St. John said. "It's a big house. Barely see them some days."

"My friend Mr. Hugh Cassidy is an American who stayed here, and married St. John's sister," Delacorte told Lorcan. "He met her right here at The Grand Palace on the Thames when her family came to stay. Mr. Cassidy took her off to live in New York."

"You don't say," Lorcan reflected.

"St. Leger and I in fact met when a pirate was attempting to kill me," Bolt volunteered, apparently inspired by the talk of piercings. "It was after the war, in the sea outside of Spain. Pirates boarded our ship, and his ship came along and noticed our signals and . . . let's just say we were triumphant. And there were quite a number of piercings that day."

St. John looked both pale and enthralled.

"One evening we even all playacted pirates in the sitting room," Delacorte told Lorcan and St. John.

"Did you now?" Lorcan was wildly amused. "Even the ladies? Even Hardy?"

"All of us."

Unsmilingly, Lorcan and Hardy exchanged a glance. Hardy as a boy had been as full of willing wildness as Lorcan had been. As quick to laugh or fight. Smart. Just as frightened and feral as he was.

Lorcan hesitated.

Then said, "Do you remember, Hardy . . . what that bloke what sold apples used to say every time we tried to nick one?"

For a moment it seemed as though Hardy intended to coldly refuse to respond. And then, seemingly almost against his will, the corner of his mouth tipped up. "'I'll purple yer backsides, ye mongrels!'"

"Backside." Lorcan shook his head. "When the word 'arse' was right there and ready to be used."

Hardy clearly fought it, but he gave a short laugh.

"Funnier if you were there," Lorcan explained

to the others in the room, who were listening and smiling, clearly willing to be amused but a bit confused.

But Lorcan knew the words would viscerally conjure for Hardy the world they'd once shared: the terrors of St. Giles, the anarchic pleasures of boyhood. The proving ground for both of them until Hardy had understandably seized a way out that was serendipitously presented to him when a naval officer had taken him under his wing.

"So. How did all of you come to live in a palace by the docks with such a quality smoking room?" Lorcan mused.

"I came here because I tracked smugglers here," Hardy said. "But stayed for the beautiful woman."

"Indeed. Such noble pursuits, smuggler tracking." Lorcan exhaled smoke. "And beautiful women."

Bolt surreptitiously shot Hardy an unreadable look.

Which meant that Hardy had told Bolt exactly what he'd thought. Lorcan wasn't certain he cared. He trusted Bolt to draw his own conclusions.

"The Blue Rock Gang," Hardy said offhandedly.

"The Blue Rock Gang were nasty thugs," Lorcan said with idle contempt. "That kind of violence is for amateurs. And for men who flirt with other men's wives."

St. John choked on the lungful of smoke he was inhaling and coughed.

"Yes. They were thugs," Hardy agreed politely.

"The rest of everything else they did was still, of course, a hanging offense."

"Smuggled cigars, is what they did," Delacorte, who had been present for all the drama, explained. He added more quietly, with a degree of wistfulness, "The most remarkable cigars."

Captain Hardy looked at him askance.

"Thank goodness that military took you in hand, Hardy, to teach you right from wrong," Lorcan said pleasantly. "Otherwise, how would a bastard child from St. Giles ever know?"

"Laws are laws," Hardy said evenly. "Smuggling during wartime, with or without violence, is treason."

Lorcan gave a soft laugh. "Ah, of course. Treason. One of the few things the very poor and the very rich have in common. Because they don't care about it. The poor don't care about treason because they're desperate, and the rich don't care because they don't need to care. Just ask an earl whose mistress is pouting because she can't find French silk. The duke will always be able to get French silk, war or no war."

The very smoke in the air suddenly seemed to stop circulating, held fast by tension.

"The Earl of Brundage was recently arrested on suspicion of high treason. And he might just hang for it," Hardy remarked.

"Mmm. I'm going to guess it's not because he purchased some contraband tea," Lorcan said, pleasantly.

Both had stopped blinking and were regarding each other, expressions entirely inscrutable.

Lorcan was too aware of his own less than noble motivations for taunting Hardy. And that every other man in the room was on guard now, too.

He surreptitiously drew a breath to steady his temper.

Even when Hardy and Lorcan had met again for the first time in over a decade in a pub in Cornwall years ago and had reestablished how much they liked each other, and even when it became clear that Hardy suspected, but could not prove, that Lorcan was indeed the head of a smuggling ring he'd been tracking, Lorcan had admired him. Hardy wouldn't relish arresting him if given the chance, but damned if he wouldn't have done it anyway. Both in order to prove something to himself, and because he'd made a commitment to his men and to the crown. He was not a man who ever went back on his word or veered from duty. He would genuinely suffer if he failed.

Lorcan respected the devil out of all of that. He would never have gotten a chance to arrest Lorcan, of course. But he still, perversely, could not and would not have faulted Hardy for trying.

Still, it didn't prevent him from savoring what felt like a victory over the man who thought he had a moral high ground.

"England is safer because of you and your men, Hardy," Lorcan said shortly.

This was only true. The Blue Rock Gang and their ilk were menaces. Entire towns were grateful to Captain Hardy and his men for ending their reign.

Just as so many others had been grateful to

Lorcan and his crew for keeping them alive. And for helping them prosper.

"It's amusing to debate moral shades of gray forever, but laws exist for a reason." Hardy casually exhaled smoke.

"Thank you. I'm quite aware of the point of laws," Lorcan said, with a certain scathing tenderness. "And I expect you feel the same beholden loyalty to the military as young Lord Vaughn feels about his parents."

This was perhaps an unwise little jab. But Lorcan could feel his temper begin to simmer.

Hardy fixed him with a cold stare.

"A man ought to be able to adhere to a principle," he said flatly. "Otherwise why should any other man trust him for any reason?"

Lorcan recalled Daphne's faintly hunted expression when, a few minutes ago, she'd thought she might have to outright lie. How had she put it this morning? She'd said her code was "something that sort of defines your truest self." He'd been surprised by his instinct to throw himself in front of anything that might cause her to violate it.

He'd glibly told her that "take what he could get when he could get it" was his, and it had indeed proved a serviceable code. But he was beginning to understand that this didn't define him.

Lorcan tossed back the rest of his brandy. "Can't agree more, Hardy. Mine is, 'I take care of my own.'"

St. John and the German boys took this opportunity to excuse themselves.

Eventually Hardy's stare evolved into something

more abstracted. He turned slightly away, and drank his own brandy.

"Isn't it remarkable how two boys from St. Giles have since prospered. I own my ship outright now. I've been fortunate in my investments."

"Investments, eh?" Bolt interjected hurriedly. "What do you like these days?"

"Did well with canal shares, in particular, but I do think railroads are going to become important. And gaslight."

Bolt and Delacorte nodded. Hardy likely took little pleasure in imagining Lorcan prospering thanks to a noxious mingling of ill-gotten gains and privateer plunder.

"It's amazing to think there's probably not a thing in the world I truly want that I can't somehow get now. And I'm grateful." Lorcan said this almost piously.

It was true. Inwardly, he was just a little sardonically amused.

And he was suddenly glad for an opportunity to say it aloud in a room that contained Tristan Hardy, lest the captain think his beautiful wife and cozy home with the fine smoking room were merely the rewards of virtue.

LORCAN RETURNED TO their suite from the smoking room to discover Daphne standing by the hearth, one of her embroidered stockings dangling from her hand.

She spun about and held it sheepishly behind her back.

He paused in the doorway, bemused and diverted by her flushed cheeks.

He contemplated saying, "I saw your stockings before I ever saw your face, when the wind whipped up your skirts. You've some of the finest calves I've ever seen," just to watch her blush deepen, or see her expression change. Or to hear what acerbic, precise thing she'd say in her elegant voice.

He respected her dismay and kept his eyebrows in check, though they wanted to suggestively launch by way of teasing her.

"I wasn't expecting you just yet," she said finally. "I hope you don't mind. I rinsed my stockings and I thought I'd hang them to dry out here in the main room, since the fire is larger and hotter. I thought they would dry more quickly."

"Not at all," he said. "If you can survive the intimacy of my forearms, surely, I can endure your drying stockings. But if you don't mind, I'd like to rest here on the settee a bit."

"Of course not," she said, magnanimously, while also managing to intimate, "I can hardly stop you."

Amused, he sighed and sank down onto the comfortable settee. Every bloody thing in The Grand Palace on the Thames was comfortable.

It was like a great trap for domesticity.

A woman ought to be exempt from ogling when she was merely trying to hang up stockings, Lorcan thought. But his mind was restless and his mood remained on edge, and he rested his eyes on her the way he would watch a bird flit from tree to tree, lulled by the way her shoulder blades shifted beneath her dress as she reached toward the mantel, the sway of her skirts about her ankles, the skim and cling of the fabric over the full apple curve of her arse when she bent a little. She made performing a homely chore seem as graceful as a dance. He didn't know why he felt blessed to be in the presence of it, but he did, as though he'd suddenly walked in on a snatch of pretty music.

And he imagined her as a girl who had lost her mother, suddenly in charge of a vast house and three men. Just a wee thing, engulfed by duty in the midst of grief.

And it wasn't as though he hadn't witnessed girls scrape and struggle before.

That a man such as Daphne's father should have so many blessings, including a daughter who worshipped him, and had been so cavalier about that she'd nearly been robbed at knifepoint near the docks, struck him as somewhat despicable. It was the carelessness of it. The waste of it all. The indolence of a sort exhibited by Lord Vaughn, who could not help what he was.

"It's a shame about your father's lumbago," he said idly.

"I beg your pardon? He hasn't lumbago!" She gave a little laugh.

"His game leg, I meant. The wooden one."

"You're thinking of someone else, surely. Some pirate friend of yours."

"Oh, right, right. His *rheumatism* is the trouble."

"He hasn't that, either, Lorcan," she said crisply.

"His wasting lungs. A pity about those. Can hardly get a breath."

"Lorcan, my father might be healthier than you or I. He walks several miles every day. He used to ride but . . ."

"Then he must be getting senile."

She recoiled. "My father is a *genius*," she said with the conviction of someone who had been told this her entire life. "His mind is sharp and nimble. He reads more and faster than anyone I know. He can do calculations in his mind in an eyeblink."

"Ah! So he's *mute* then."

She paused to stare at him, her straight dark brows nearly meeting in a V. "What on earth are you running on about?" she said evenly. And with great, great patience.

"I'm just sorting through all the reasons a titled gentleman would allow his daughter to not only go out to work, but to do the sort of work that exposes her to danger and ruin and leads to her living in near sin with a fake husband. Have I missed one?"

She froze as if he was holding her at knifepoint.

Her mouth dropped in shock.

He saw her realize that she was rather cornered.

Lorcan wasn't new to getting information he wanted. And strategy was his gift.

Her eyes were enormous.

"An . . . earl can hardly take a *job*," she said faintly. She tried to give the words a frisson of disdain. Perhaps to imply that someone like him surely couldn't possibly know.

"Heaven forfend. People would talk. How embarrassing that would be. What sort of man would lose face in order to support his family?"

Her face went closed and she spun around and showed her back to him again. "You don't understand."

"That's likely true. I'm too thick to understand the curious customs of the aristocracy. It wasn't embarrassing at all for you to be chased about the place by the old dear's husband. Or frightening."

"It was *my* idea to take the job. I've never done such a thing before."

"It seems as though you've been taking *jobs* for your family since you were eleven years old. Your family was a job."

She slowed and then stopped. "That was different."

"And you helped to run your household from that point on."

"You don't understand . . . our house . . . all the things my mother used to do . . . organizing the servants . . . it was coming quite apart. I did the budget and managed the servants and arranged the shopping and cooking and entertaining for my father. I was the one who was best at it," she said, a little proudly.

"What about your brothers? Couldn't they have helped?"

She hesitated. "They were accustomed to a woman managing the house. It wasn't the sort of work for a man. They had no acumen for it."

Lorcan snorted. "You weren't a woman at all, then. You were a girl."

She turned slowly around. "My father grieved terribly. My brothers, too."

"What a fortunate thing it was, then, that you had no feelings about your mother's death at all."

She froze. And the blood drained from her face. Something flickered in her eyes.

Perhaps a comprehension she fought against.

"It made me feel better about things, you see," she said slowly. "They were so grateful and so lost. And . . . it made me feel less lost, too, to have something to do. My father was . . . well, you know how geniuses can be."

He gave a short laugh. "Surely you're not suggesting I consort with them."

"Practical things often elude or bore my father," she clarified stiffly.

"*Just* the quality we like in people who father children. Funnily enough, the same might have been said for my father."

Her eyes sparked with temper. "My father is *nothing* like yours was."

Lorcan doubted this, somehow. He'd learned over the years that all deeply selfish men were fundamentally similar.

"And rather than botch things he allows me to do them. He can be rather hapless."

"'Allows,'" Lorcan repeated neutrally.

Personally, Lorcan thought the Earl of Worth was a con man par excellence who had bartered his daughter's affection for a life of comfort and leisure, like a bloody pasha. Hats off to the gentleman.

"Are your brothers aware of your sudden change

of fortune? Are they gallivanting about Paris on credit?"

"My brothers do not know the full extent of it. They cannot be blamed. And yes, I expect they are. Staying with friends and the like. But I believe they both have some money of their own."

"Mmm. Well. What a fortunate man your father is to have someone to look after his well-being," he said gently.

She exhaled, with some apparent relief.

And then he added, idly. "Who looked after yours?"

She went still again.

"*I* did. I looked after mine by looking after them because they're what mattered to me. I had a governess . . . for a time."

Her voice trembled now.

"All I am saying, Daphne . . . if I had a fortune . . . and a title . . . and every advantage, and if I had a wife or a daughter such as you . . . I would be damned if I allowed her to carry my burdens. What is a man for if not to protect those that are his?"

She spun again, and his view once again was her back. She fumbled her stocking and nearly dropped it.

"What is it? Is your father mad?" he said gently. "Truly mad, the sort where he can make no decisions and must be watched at all times?"

"I'm beginning to think *you're* truly mad," she said tersely.

He was, a little. It suddenly seemed important to root out a truth to show to her. It seemed imperative to seek out understanding for himself.

He suspected he was taking out a little bit of his mood on her, unfairly. And yet he could not seem to stop.

"Is it melancholia?"

Her words were clipped and brittle now. "He's cheerful and witty and marvelous company. Which is more than I can say for . . ." She paused meaningfully.

"Is it drink? Did he drink his fortune away? Is that how you came to have a job?"

"Never imbibes," she bit off, angrily.

"It's gaming."

Ah, poor lass. She was a novice at this. She could not control the way her head jerked toward him or the way her eyes flared in shock and fear.

"That's it. He's gambled away his fortune and your dowry."

She took a stunned step backward into the fire screen, which rocked perilously, then dumped her stockings into the fire. She half gasped, half shrieked.

But in moments they were devoured in flames.

She stared, stunned. Then her face dropped into her hands.

He watched as her back swelled like a bellows with her breathing.

She whirled on him, face white with fury.

"How would you have any idea what it's like to sacrifice for a family? You, who have no family and can't be bothered to marry!"

Oh, *well* done, lass, he could have said. Such lashing scorn.

But for a second or two he could not speak or breathe.

"Maybe I don't," he managed quietly. "But believe it or not, I have a code, too, Daphne. I treat people accordingly. And no one recognizes a swindle better than I do."

Her face spasmed with pain for an instant.

"Oh, what can you possibly know about any of this? How could you possibly know what you would do? You're not even a gentleman. You're a . . . you're just a *heathen* from St. Giles. You have *no one*."

They stared at each other in shock.

She covered her mouth with her hand.

For a few moments the only sound was the fire, cracking and popping as it consumed the stockings.

He didn't quite slam it. But the door shook in its frame when Lorcan closed it behind him.

Chapter Nine

ୡୠୡ

*F*UMING, DAZED, a trifle surprised by the turn of events, Lorcan stalked through the passage that connected the annex to the rest of The Grand Palace on the Thames.

What the bloody hell had just happened?

He was all the way in the foyer when he realized he hadn't a key to the suite.

He swore softly.

Returning now would ruin his dramatic exit.

He would also be damned if he would go and knock on that door and beg her to let him in.

And damned if he would return with her scornful words still echoing in his ears. He simply couldn't imagine doing it. And while it wasn't as though she'd experience his absence as some terrible punishment, it would still make a point of sorts.

Although . . . he was beginning to think he deserved to be locked out.

He sighed, heavily. Swiped his hands down his face.

Why? Why couldn't he have just let it be?

He was contemplating how he was going to manage to pass the night when he noticed a shadow that resembled an egg on legs moving with impressive stealth and grace up the stairs.

"Ho, there, Delacorte," Lorcan stage-whispered.

Mr. Delacorte froze midstep. "Ho, St. Leger," he replied on a whisper, sounding pleased, and thereby revealing that Lorcan's silhouette was easily recognizable, too. "What are you doing wandering the halls? Can't sleep?"

Lorcan quietly moved over to the stairs. "A bit of to-do with me wife. I can't go back tonight. So I'm roaming like a ghost."

Delacorte made a sympathetic clucking sound.

"I expect she needs a little time without me," Lorcan said. "And I without her. What's your excuse?"

"You'll not tell Brownie or Goldie."

"I'm nay a snitch, Delacorte." He surmised Brownie and Goldie were Delilah and Angelique.

"Couldn't sleep. Went down to the kitchen. Thought a wee piece of cheese might help." He uncurled his fingers and Lorcan peered: the candle he held in the other illuminated a little wedge in Delacorte's palm.

"Often does," Lorcan said amiably.

"I usually keep a slice or two in my room, but with the roads flooded, I can't get to my favorite cheese shop. Why don't you come in and bunk with me? You can make it up to the missus in the morning."

Lorcan mulled. He was not interested in the martyrdom of huddling on a settee in a cold room or endlessly drifting through the halls like a ghost seeking vengeance in an attempt to stay warm.

And he was damned if he was going to give Daphne the satisfaction of begging at the door. His temper and his pride—and guilt—were still simmering.

"Kind of you, Delacorte," he said. "I believe I will."

He'd piled into beds with men before out of necessity when he'd lived in shabby rooms shared by multiple families. Delacorte was at least clean and there was no question that, between the two of them crammed in the bed, they would be nice and warm.

"Mind the third step. It creaks," Delacorte whispered.

Delacorte's room smelled of the herbs and powders from his case of remedies, bay rum, linseed oil, tallow, sweat, feet, tobacco, and something a little musty that Lorcan suspected was the ghost of cheeses past. All in all, a friendly, male smell.

"Make yourself at home," Delacorte said cheerfully. "Would you like a bite?" He gestured with his wedge of cheese.

"No, thank you," Lorcan said.

Delacorte ate his cheese, yanked off his boots and snatched his nightshirt off a hook. Lorcan perused the room while Delacorte got dressed for bed.

Scattered about—on the desk and a little bookshelf and in corners—were a stuffed owl on a perch, a cigar cutter, a cricket bat, a telescope, an astrolabe, a compass, a scale, a mortar and pestle, and jars of various sizes and shapes apparently filled with unguents. He'd pinned a map of the world on the wall; beside it he'd hung a poem featuring the words "jingle bang," which he'd underlined. Next to them he'd written "ha ha!" A little cluster of miniatures were arranged on the desk. A swift glance revealed all of them bore a passing resemblance to Delacorte. He noted several pairs of big blue eyes and imposing eyebrows.

Lorcan pulled off his boots and hung his coat on a hook. He dropped his trousers, folded them up, and placed them on the chair. He'd sleep in his shirt.

Thusly the two of them piled into bed and pulled up the blankets.

It was a snug fit, of a certainty, with the two of them wedged in. Not too objectionable, however. Neither of them complained.

"Thanks for the hospitality, Delacorte."

"Think nothing of it." Delacorte had taken a book to bed with him. "I like to read a bit before I sleep. Will I disturb you?"

"Not at all. I'll just be staring at the ceiling." Lorcan folded his arms behind his head and did just that.

But maybe he ought to read. He could use a distraction.

From out of nowhere he wondered if Daphne would weep tonight. Would she take advantage of his absence and sob out her grief and frustration or whatever ailed her and rail to the heavens? Or would she still ration her tears, quietly? As if she hadn't the right to do it at all?

His stomach went tight.

He felt like a damned scoundrel to add to the reasons she might be weeping.

Suddenly Delacorte went so abruptly still Lorcan turned to look worriedly at him.

A faraway look had come into Delacorte's eye.

He slowly lowered his book.

"I think it only fair to warn you, my friend, that you'll want to batten down the hatches at once," he said matter-of-factly.

Lorcan turned to him, puzzled. "Beg pardon, Delacorte?"

"Now. It's a matter of some urgency, St. Leger. Do not lift the blankets. Seal them tightly. Batten them down. I cannot put it any more plainly."

"Delacorte, what the *devil* are you . . ."

Lorcan became aware of a squeaking sound, rapidly escalating in volume. It evolved into a sort of fluttering, then terminated abruptly in what sounded like the honk of an angry mallard.

His mind blanked with astonishment.

"Delacorte . . . did you just . . . was that . . ."

Decades from now, tearing back the corner of the blanket so he could bolt out of bed would still rank as one of his worst decisions.

Because there was no escaping what he'd just set free.

He'd been warned.

He crashed back against the pillow as if felled at the knees by an ax and flung an arm over his face. "Oh. Oh no. Oh, dear God."

The arm was insufficient. He retrieved the pillow from beneath his head and covered his face with that instead.

He lay in stunned silence a moment, struggling not to inhale.

"Delacorte," he said hoarsely, finally. "My *eyes* are watering. I'm literally *weeping*, you bastard. I haven't wept since I was a boy."

"I did try to tell you," Delacorte said, with some regret, but no real shame. "I honestly thought you of all people would understand 'batten the hatches.'" He paused. "I *had* hoped to be more discreet about it."

"Fair play," Lorcan admitted through the pillow after a moment. "You did warn me."

"And the window frame is a bit stuck from all the rain, so I can't open it to get any air in. I'm afraid you'll have to wait it out. Which is why I insisted upon a seal."

"You thought of everything," Lorcan said bitterly.

He would survive this. God knows, the thing he did best was endure.

Aa Lorcan lay quietly recovering beneath the pillow, he listened to Delacorte turn a few pages of his book.

They lay like this in more or less companionable silence.

"I bet *that* will teach you to argue with your wife," Delacorte finally said.

Lorcan gave a shout of laughter.

Which set Delacorte off.

Soon the two of them were roaring with laughter, thumping the bed with their fists. Lorcan coughed and wiped his eyes, happily disgusted.

They jumped when the ceiling thundered as if someone was taking a hammer to it.

"Haud yer wheesht ye *grrrrrreat FARRRT-*

INNNNG wrrrrretch!" Angus McDonald howled through the floorboards.

"His 'r's go on forever," Delacorte said admiringly.

They took pity on Mr. McDonald and settled down.

Lorcan tentatively lifted the pillow from his face. He found the air tolerable enough to restore it to its rightful place beneath his head.

"Would you like a book?" Delacorte gestured to his little shelf.

"No, thank you. I think I shall lay here and brood until sleep takes me under."

"What was your fight with your wife about?"

"I accidentally caused her to drop her best stockings into the fire and up they went."

"Oh, you can't go and burn a woman's stockings," Delacorte said with great conviction. "But most rows are seldom about one thing, are they?"

"Not with women, apparently," Lorcan said dourly.

This was a novel experience. All of this. Discussing woman problems while in bed with a man.

"Have you any lady friends, Delacorte? A frisky widow, perhaps?"

"Oh, I've a few lady friends up and down the coast who are game for a tumble now and again." He brightened. "There's one in Devon who always gives me dinner and she knows a few saucy tricks."

"Tricks, eh?" Lorcan was instantly intrigued.

"She takes two fingers . . ." Delacorte illustrated by holding up two of his.

"Aye?"

". . . and she shoves them up my—"

Lorcan dragged the pillow over his ears just in time. There were limits to what a man could bear in one evening.

He returned the pillow to beneath his head just as Delacorte was saying, "She seems a lovely girl, your wife. A bit sad, maybe."

"Sad?" For some reason this observation bothered him a good deal.

"It's probably the weather," Delacorte said. "We're all a bit brought down by it. Even me, a bit."

"*Caged* in by it," Lorcan said. "That's the feeling, after a while. One gets to know how to endure it over the years."

"That, too. And true enough."

"She's worried about her father and her brothers."

"There, now, you see. Every little thing looks a bit bleaker when you're worried about one thing. I find lots of happy shouting takes my mind off things. Donkey races, a lively pub. Or beating Bolt in chess."

"They are good-for-nothings. Her fathers and brothers."

He was assuming a lot. But if there were three men in a family and the only daughter was exiting from a window in the middle of the night at the London docks because the father had gambled away their fortune, then as far as he was concerned no other conclusion could be drawn.

"Then it's a very good thing she has you," Delacorte said.

Damn.

Lorcan went still.

How had this happened? How did he come to feel responsible for this woman?

Because he bloody well did.

He had only himself to blame.

He closed his eyes briefly, and unbidden images flitted in. Daphne sitting in the window with the sun on her hair. Her hand resting on his arm as he led her into the sitting room. Her slim shoulder blades moving when she hung up her stockings with deft grace. There was a fragility to her at odds with her lacerating wit and crackling eyes and ramrod pride. She would fight like the devil not to break. But she was breakable. He was certain of it. No one who felt things as strongly as she did was unbreakable.

It infuriated him that the men in her life did not seem to care. Caring seemed the very least a man could do.

What a fortunate thing it was she had a marriage offer.

But then he wondered if the husband would be any better.

A bleakness that had nothing to do with the weather settled into his bones.

"She would prefer me to be different," he said quietly. He was certain this was true in about a thousand ways.

"Hmmm. Well, I shouldn't mind changing a bit for the right someone," Delacorte mused. "A cozy sort of woman, with a big laugh, who'll say, 'oh, Stanton,' very fondly quite a lot. Perhaps with a little sigh. Brownie and Goldie are angels on earth and thanks to them, I feel I'm becoming more refined by the minute. Hard not to say 'bloody' when I'm excited about something, which is most of the time, but I like a challenge. It's lovely, don't you think, finding the ways you are the same and the ways you are different. Like fitting a puzzle together."

He thought, but wisely did not say, that Brownie would have to be an angel to put up with Captain Hardy. How had a woman who seemed so gentle and kind wound up with a man that hard?

But then he was coming to realize why a man like Hardy could crave something gentle, and kind, and soft. How it could feel like respite.

He thought about what Delacorte had said about puzzles.

And how anyone looking at Lorcan St. Leger would never dream anything at all about him was soft. Would assume that not one vulnerable place on him existed.

"She called me a heathen." In truth, it was the rest of what she'd said which had landed on the raw. *You have no one.* As if it was the worst indictment she could conjure.

Delacorte hissed in a sympathetic breath. "That's a hard one, especially when it's true."

"Ho there, now!"

"It's true. We're all of us men bloody heathens under the skin. If it weren't for women's efforts we'd run amuck, scratching, swearing, farting, fucking, chewing with our mouths open, and throwing our bones down on the floor. Even St. John. And there's something about the fussing of a womanly woman that makes me feel more like a man and I quite like it, bless 'em. It makes me feel cared for."

It was quite a vivid point of view. Lorcan wasn't sure he concurred entirely.

He hated to admit to himself that some tiny part of him, in fact, yearned toward Daphne's refinement, her delicacy, and her otherness. It was the same small part of him he'd hoped was dead forever. If he was Achilles, it was the part of him that hadn't been dipped.

He sighed. "So, you want to be a husband, eh, Delacorte?"

"Oh, yes, indeed. I expect I shall be soon enough. I'm in the prime of my life. I've time," Delacorte said comfortably. "And people always seem to leave The Grand Palace on the Thames with a wife. Although maybe she'd like to live here, too," he added hopefully.

They lay quietly for a moment, listening to the rain.

"Do you worry about the ship not coming in?" Lorcan asked.

Delacorte pondered this. "Oh, aye, I do. A bit. But worrying won't make it get here any faster. I worry more about Hardy and Bolt taking it to heart. They'll feel guilty about me but I went into the endeavor with my eyes open and I'm proud to be a part of the Triton Group. Those blokes are the best friends I've ever had. As long as we have The Grand Palace on the Thames, we'll all be fine, no matter what."

"Well, I'm glad you have it, then, Delacorte."

He thought of Daphne, who had her father and her brothers, fat lot of good it did her.

"Shall we go to sleep now?"

"Why not? Good night, Delacorte."

"Good night, St. Leger."

They each settled into their pillows.

"Fair warning, I snore a bit," Delacorte told him, as he turned down the lamp.

LIKE MOST NIGHTS during the previous few busy weeks, Angelique's beloved husband crawled into bed smelling of cheroots and brandy a good half hour after he normally did.

She reflexively scooted over to touch her bottom to him, her typical way of helping to warm him whenever business kept him up late. He draped his hand absently, affectionately, over her hip. Lucien usually liked to sleep naked, which she usually counted as just one of the delicious bonuses of being married to him. They kept the fire burning high and hot in the room and indulged in lots of blankets.

They lay for a moment in familiar and contented silence.

"Lucien . . . do you ever think you married beneath you?"

He gracefully rolled over, propping himself on his arms over her, and gazed smolderingly down. "What's that you said about wanting to be beneath me?"

Normally, she might have laughed.

But without warning, her temper ignited. She went rigid instead.

"Lucien, you've hardly spoken to me for days." She gave his chest a little shove.

He was surprised. "You know we've been busy. Sandbags at the warehouses in preparation for the storm. Meetings with Lloyd's. With investors. With merchants."

"I understand. But I'm not like Mr. Delacorte's midnight cheese. You might have to talk to me a little before you . . . partake."

"Partake?" he quoted incredulously.

"Hike my night rail, then."

He rolled over again and lay flat on his back. He looked stunned. He lay there, clearly speechless.

"You're the son of a duke," she continued.

"Oh, we're still on the 'beneath you' question. This is what you want to talk about before we sleep, Angelique? Yes. I'm the bastard son of the worst possible duke who is wholly disinterested in me. No, I don't feel as though I married beneath me. What does that even mean?"

She could not quite articulate what she meant. Or rather, she felt a little too unsettled and raw to explain it to Lucien, and a little too tired to find the proper words.

Before Angelique had met Delilah, and well before she'd met Lucien, she'd been a governess. But she'd left in disgrace after the gentleman of the house had taken advantage of her. Thus had begun a terrifying descent from decent society until she found herself the mistress of an earl who'd left her—and his wife, Delilah—destitute. She and Delilah had seized upon The Grand Palace on the Thames as a lifeline.

Until Lucien, every man she'd ever known had preyed upon her beauty, used her, and discarded her. She'd endured it, in order to survive.

"You're thinking about the governess that Havelstock married," he hazarded, slowly. "And the fact that Lady Worth married a privateer."

"I was. A little."

"Is it because you were once a governess?"

She was silent. In truth, though Lucien knew the entire truth of her past, and was fiercely protective of her and had never once judged her, she had never fully explained to him some of the things she'd felt or experienced.

In part because she could still feel the shame of it when she was tired or vulnerable. And in part because he would suffer enormously on her behalf.

"I never thought of marrying anyone at all until I laid eyes on you, Angelique," he said quietly. But she could hear a bit of impatience in his voice. It was something he felt she should understand implicitly.

"And I married you, didn't I?" she asked. "What do you suppose that says about my judgment?"

"What the devil?" Lucien was bewildered now.

"Both you and Captain Hardy saw fit to not only question our judgment with regards to Daphne and Mr. St. Leger. Does that apply to my judgment in *general*, or with regards only to that St. Leger?"

Lucien had gone rigid now. "Is that what this is about? St. Leger? Suddenly I'm too busy to give you the kind of attention you want so your thoughts have wandered off to a behemoth with an earring?"

"What on earth?" She was aghast. "My thoughts are not *wandering*. Is that what you think of me? That I'm just that bloody fickle? That I'll dream about any man in your absence?"

She'd propped herself on her elbow to stare down at him in outrage.

"No. But how about this?" Lucien said brightly. "We make love tonight and you pretend I'm St. Leger."

"ARRRRRRRGH!" She flounced herself out of bed, seized her pelisse from the wardrobe, threw it on, and stalked out the door.

USUALLY, THEY PERFORMED their little bedtime rituals together. Tristan would sit on the bed to pull off his boots while she brushed and plaited her hair at her dressing table, because he found it soothing to watch her tame all that silky darkness. And they would have a cozy, meandering chat. Nonsense and seriousness all entwined with the coded language of marriage and love—little jokes, endearments, the details of the world they'd created between them when they'd wed.

Then they would tumble into bed and into each other's arms.

The *bliss* of it all.

But tonight he was late again to bed. For a fortnight now he'd been lingering of nights in the smoking room with Lucien and Delacorte, when business didn't keep him out late.

And Delilah was beginning to realize that it

was because he was, in fact, avoiding her specifically.

And her heart squeezed like an icy fist.

Delilah was already in her night rail, her hair
brushed one hundred times and plaited, before
the doorknob turned and he quietly entered the
room.

He shook himself out of his coat.

He hadn't yet bothered to look at her.

When he sat down to remove his boots and still
hadn't said anything or looked at her, her heart
lurched portentously.

She'd had enough.

"So. We married for better or for worse, Tristan.
I believe that's what the vicar said when we were
wed." She said it conversationally.

He went still. He'd already gotten his shirt off.

He turned slowly to her, shirt in hand. "And?"

And?

Oh God.

That tone.

Just like that—*Foosh.* The flame of her temper
leaped up like a bonfire.

Oh, she was ready to throw her hairbrush at
her gorgeous, beloved husband.

"*And* the trouble is, I married a man who spoke
in complete sentences and respectful tones and
who actually enjoyed speaking with me. Not one
who communicates in monosyllables and grunts.
'*And.*' What ruddy nonsense is 'and'?"

With satisfaction, she saw his whole body tense
and his eyes go narrow and flinty.

Good, be angry, Tristan, she thought. She was

ready for an argument. They clearly needed to have one.

"All right, Delilah," he said evenly, slowly. "Speaking of words unspoken. Here are a few you never said to me: 'I believe you, Tristan.'"

She went still, confused.

"Bolt said it. About St. Leger. But you never did, Delilah."

She was stunned. "Is *that* what is bothering you?"

She immediately realized her terrible mistake in emphasis. She'd trivialized it.

"Tristan—"

"My entire career was made upon identifying, tracking, and putting a stop to smugglers terrorizing towns across England, because smuggling is both treason and criminal. I was so bloody good at it the *king* agreed to make an appearance here. He skillfully managed a smuggling organization that stretched along the coast of England for nearly two years. My word on that should be good enough for you."

"And my word about who should stay here at The Grand Palace on the Thames should be good enough for *you*."

"And yet there you were, cozily having tea with a former criminal out of a sentiment for your old friend. So tell me again why I should blindly trust your judgment."

Delilah nearly soared up out of her body with fury. "*That's* what you think of my judgment? Tristan . . . what if for some reason you weren't *meant* to catch him? Do you think people can

never change? You yourself said he did no terrorizing. When you were a little boy, would you
steal to eat or starve? Two different roads were
offered to the two of you. He's been working on
behalf of the crown for a few years now. Does
that count for nothing? Are people not allowed
redemption?"

He stared at her.

"Sometimes I feel as though you don't understand me at all," he said finally.

Delilah was speechless.

"I—need to sleep somewhere else tonight."

And to her absolute astonishment, he dragged
his shirt back on and flung open the door.

She flinched when it slammed behind him.

CAPTAIN HARDY COULD hear his own furious
breath as he stalked down the hall.

He stopped abruptly in surprise when he encountered a stalking Angelique, who was wearing a pelisse over her night rail and much the
same expression he expected he sported.

"There's a vacancy with Lucien if you need
a place to sleep, Captain Hardy," she told him
coolly.

"Likewise with Delilah," he said bluntly.

They passed each other in righteous huffs.

HARDY PAUSED OUTSIDE the room Angelique and
Lucien shared. Their door was wide open. Quite
as though it had been flung dramatically so.

He found Bolt was sitting upright in bed, wearing a stunned expression. The lamps were still lit.

Lucien took one look at Captain Hardy. Read his face correctly.

And then wordlessly, shifted over and patted the pillow next to his.

Captain Hardy shut the door, rapidly shucked his trousers, then plucked them up off the floor. He stood motionless for a moment clutching them in his fist.

And then he whirled and hurled them in a very uncharacteristic fit of pique across the room.

Lucien snorted.

Hardy got into bed in just his shirt and pulled the covers up.

They lay there in absolute silence for quite some time.

And then Captain Hardy sighed, got out of bed, fetched his trousers, folded them neatly, laid them on the desk, and got back into bed.

Military training really never released its hold.

"Are you ever going to share with anyone the nature of the particular stick you've got lodged in your arse lately, Hardy?"

It was Captain Hardy's turn to snort.

"I know how you feel about St. Leger is complicated," Lucien continued. "But it's more than that, I would warrant. And whatever it is, if you won't tell me, you *have* to tell her."

Captain Hardy lay still, eyes on the ceiling, arms crossed behind his head. He took a few deep breaths to settle his temper.

"I know. I don't know why it's so bloody hard to do that," he said finally. Softly. Genuinely pained.

"Because something in you believes she'll find

some fatal flaw in you and just stop loving you. But she won't."

Captain Hardy turned to Lucien in amazement.

And then after a moment he said, "Are you *naked*, Bolt?"

Lucien sighed, got out of bed, snatched his nightshirt from the back of his chair and threw it on over his head.

"I'll sleep imprisoned in this thing for your sake." He climbed back into bed.

"What did you and Angelique argue about?" Hardy asked.

"Something very stupid. And the fault belongs to us both. But mostly to me, I think. I think I know where I went awry and now I want to kick myself. But it's not as though I do not have a point."

"I'm beginning to think there are no stupid arguments in a marriage," Hardy said dryly. After a moment he asked, "Would you like me to kick you?"

"Kind of you to offer, but I think I'll save that pleasure for Angelique," Lucien said.

Captain Hardy smiled.

Lucien blew out a long breath. "Bloody hell, it's been a very trying few weeks."

"We'll get through it," Captain Hardy said shortly. After a moment.

The two of them had already talked so much about potentialities there was no point in going over them again.

"I do have something to confess," Hardy said so somberly that Lucien turned to him in concern.

"I've fantasized about throttling the German trio."

"They're really inordinately *merry*," Lucien said darkly.

"Too bloody merry," Hardy agreed. "I'm so close to batting Hans gently on the snout like a hound to keep him from flirting with the maids."

"They're just boys."

"I'm sure some woman will bat him on the snout sooner or later, metaphorically or not," Captain Hardy said, somewhat morosely.

"No doubt. Good night, Hardy. Try to sleep."

Lucien doused the lamp.

Chapter Ten

࿇

$\mathcal{D}$ELILAH GAVE a start when she heard the knock on her door and her heart leaped both in hope and dread.

"It's me," Angelique said.

Her heart didn't precisely sink. At least now she had a sense of where her husband was going to spend the night. Which was all to the good.

"Come in," Delilah called to her.

Angelique came in and shut the door quietly behind her. "I saw Tristan in the hall. Are you all right?"

"No," Delilah said. Miserably.

Angelique sat down on the bed and pulled Delilah into a hug.

Delilah sighed. "Remind me why we thought we wanted to marry these men?"

Angelique gave a short, pained laugh. "Lust clouded our brains."

Delilah laughed shortly. "Tristan is usually so *reasonable*. You would think bullets would glance right off of his hide. Well, you know. He's usually an island of calm and certainty. We can talk about things rationally, even when we disagree.

And we *do* talk, about everything. We seemed to have reached some sort of philosophical impasse and I can't seem to untangle it. There's something troubling him that he won't tell me. My stomach hurts."

"For better or for worse," Angelique mused. "It's almost as though whoever wrote those vows was married. They must have known it could get bad."

"I hate it so much, Angelique," Delilah said bleakly. "I wish he would talk to me. And I can't help but feel guilty because we've accidentally managed to cram the house with, er, challenging guests, during the worst possible time."

"We'll call it a lesson learned," Angelique said.

Delilah twisted her mouth wryly. "Why are *you* here?"

Angelique hesitated. "I'm not entirely certain, only it ended up being incredibly stupid, but I'm angry and Lucien is angry."

"Something to do with St. Leger?"

"A little. How did you know?"

Delilah just sighed.

"I know Lucien has a jealous streak," Angelique said. "I think a lot of it has to do with his father, who never properly loved him. But this is . . ." She bit her lip.

Delilah lowered her voice. "*Do* you think he's attractive, Angelique? St. Leger."

"Oh, yes. I mean, wish to God I hadn't blurted that. And God only knows I'd hate it if Lucien ever blurted something similar. And it's not like there's anything I'd ever want to do about it, but . . . don't you think he is? Attractive?"

"Yes." Delilah whispered it. "We're allowed to think that, aren't we? It doesn't mean anything."

"Certainly. It's probably best to keep those thoughts in our heads, though," Angelique said dryly.

"What is it that we like?"

"Competence. Confidence. He's enormous, as Dot says. He's a little scary, which is rather exciting, but with Daphne he seems so . . ."

Delilah said softly, "I have to say . . . I love the way he looked at her."

"Like she's this wondrous thing and he's still struggling to decipher her."

"Like a bear with a butterfly on its nose."

Angelique laughed. "Didn't a bear almost eat Mr. Hugh Cassidy and his dog?"

"Imagine all the stories we'll hear from guests over the years," Delilah yawned.

Angelique shrugged off her pelisse, draped it over the chair, and crawled into bed next to Delilah.

"I sleep on my side," she said.

"I once peered in on Dot and she was all the way under her covers, somewhere in the middle of the bed, in a little hump," Delilah said.

Angelique sighed. "She's so odd, our Dot."

"I sleep on my back. And in the morning usually find Tristan's head right about here." Delilah pointed to a place on her pillow, near her shoulder. Her throat had gone thick.

After a moment, Angelique gently, sympathetically patted Delilah's shoulder where her husband's head usually rested.

They turned down the lamps.

DAPHNE FELT INCANDESCENT with rage. She hadn't known she was capable of it; she hadn't realized such exhilaration could be had in such an indulgence in temper.

She relived—she savored!—the sound of Lorcan nearly slamming the door behind him.

He'd realize soon enough he hadn't the key. Ha! She wasn't going to open the door if he returned and begged. The *cheek* of him. *I know when I've been swindled* indeed. What was he implying? That *she'd* been swindled? She, the daughter of an earl?

What could *he* possibly know, a man who didn't have anyone at *all*? A man who had been raised without obligations or ties or . . . the Gordian knot of familial love?

And in this heightened state of righteous indignation, she seized up the fireplace poker and prodded at the remnants of her best stockings and it stirred up her anger even more.

Then she sat down on the settee with a great sigh to mourn them and wallow in the intoxication of fury.

And it was very good.

For a while.

But anger receded, bit by bit. And bit by bit she was left feeling muzzy and deflated and abashed, the way one felt the morning after too much ratafia at a ball. She was unused to indulging challenging emotions. They were so *unseemly.* There simply wasn't time for them in her home.

Or at least, she'd learned early on that no one had any use for hers.

Steady, steady Daphne.

When she was anything other than steady and kind, her father was cold and her brothers confused and Daphne was distressed. She had learned how to *be.* They had taught her to be.

She was coming to realize how they'd taught her to be bore only a passing resemblance to who she in fact truly *was.*

This little fissure that allowed in reason also allowed in a little voice. It said: Lorcan probably understands families the way a man missing an arm understands the point of arms.

She sighed and dropped her face into her hands.

Damn Lorcan.

Because when her anger receded, what was left behind was a terrible, seething grief.

For herself, or for her mother, she did not know. Perhaps both. She felt that, along with a sort of hollow panic. Her birthday was the day after tomorrow. She wondered if her father or her brothers would even remember.

She allowed her mind to flow to where it wished.

Doing only this was a luxury and a little unnerving. She was not accustomed to facing swaths of time uninterrupted by responsibility. And because guilt was also second nature to her, her thoughts almost immediately lit upon the expression on Lorcan's face when she'd called him a heathen. She had perpetuated a cruelty, with relish, to defend herself, and it shocked her. She could not recall ever before doing such a thing.

She sucked in a breath, leaped up, and restlessly poked at the fire again, feeling strangely now as if the crime of burning the stockings had been hers, not his.

When she paused this pointless task, the room seemed to echo with emptiness.

Lorcan's life force was immense. His presence hummed the way a ceaselessly flowing river did.

How could she miss someone she'd scarcely known a day?

More specifically, how could she miss a man like *that*?

She returned to curl up on the settee with her feet beneath her. Where had he gone in the dark, cold house? Was he angry? Was he grieving, as she was, some old wound? Was he tired and uncomfortable?

She gave a start when she heard a little scratching sound at the door. She leaped up and cautiously creaked open the peep hatch.

She saw no one.

The hair prickled at the back of her neck.

She opened the door a crack. She peered down the hall. She saw, and heard, no one. No Lorcan.

But then the sconces had been doused for the night.

And then:

"Prrrp!" Gordon the cat said cheerily.

She nearly leaped clean out of her dress, so startled was she.

"You gave me a fright." She knelt and offered her hand to him to sniff. "Well, good evening. So kind of you to knock. Would you like to come in? I'd be grateful for your company."

He rubbed his cheek once on her hand and sauntered in as if he owned the suite, which, after a fashion, he did. She supposed it was his job to patrol the entirety of The Grand Palace on the Thames, the way the watch and the Charlies roamed the streets of London.

Except they weren't tonight, of course. No one was going anywhere tonight.

Because outside, the rain fell and fell.

The next morning . . .

THE RAIN AND wind had eased a bit, but no one was fooled. The storm was clearly pacing itself for the marathon it intended. The clouds were fat, low, lead-gray and juicy, and in the distance, thunder grumbled. The Thames was the same gray as the sky; wind chopped it into restless swells and foam.

Together St. Leger, Bolt, Hardy, and Delacorte walked in near silence to the docks. Their moods were the collective equivalent of the weather.

True to his word, Delacorte had intermittently snored like someone sawing away at a rusty anchor. And Lorcan dreamed of Daphne's stricken face when she'd seen the ashes of her stockings.

As if she'd seen the remains of her hope go up in flames.

Bloody hell. The guilt. Over *stockings*.

He wondered if she'd slept. Or if she was spending the morning hurriedly dashing off an acceptance to her marriage proposal, begging her swain to come and fetch her at once lest she endure one more moment with a *heathen*.

The streets were surprisingly milling with people, all of whom had bolted from their hidey-holes to run an errand or stretch their legs before the next battering onslaught.

He'd been away from this area for some years. There had been a time when he'd been quite familiar with it. The docks, after all, were a prime place to move smuggled goods.

And yet quite a few hats were surreptitiously tipped as he passed; heads nodded; eyes flared in surprised recognition.

Lorcan nodded in return.

And one or two men immediately crossed to the far side of the road. Far, far away from him.

Finally, the four men reached the harbor and stared out at the vast collection of ships, none of which were charred ruins. It was a relief to discover that lightning had spared them.

"Your Lordship."

The woman's quiet voice came from the right of Lorcan. On her hip rested a child with bright blond hair whose entire fist was shoved into his mouth and whose other arm was around his mother's neck. He regarded Lorcan solemnly.

"I'm Mrs. Brown. Perhaps you'll remember. I

cannot thank you enough for what you did for me Davey."

"I remember, Mrs. Brown. Twas naught," he said shortly. Very aware that three other men were listening.

"It wasn't," she insisted softly. "It was a miracle for us. Kept us alive, dint it? He's on a ship now, Davey. 'as a good job. 'e keeps us well."

"I am very glad to hear it."

"I'd 'oped to 'ave a chance to one day thank you," she said shyly.

Lorcan merely nodded.

"This is wee Michael," she told him.

"Fine little chap," he said.

Michael pulled his fist from his mouth with a wet suctiony sound and beamed at him.

"We be waitin' for 'is da," the woman told him. "He's to meet us here." And then she curtsied and backed away, as if she knew her audience with him was concluded.

Michael craned his head over his shoulder to stare unabashedly at Lorcan. When he beamed, his entire little face seemed to fold in two.

Lorcan found children that age hilarious, on the whole.

"What did you do for Davey?"

Of course it was Delacorte who asked.

"I gave him a job, and paid him well, when his family was hungry."

He said this evenly, for the benefit of Hardy.

Upon whom he knew it would grate.

Hardy would never know the specifics, but the job he'd given Davey had to do with moving contraband silks into London. Davey had been one of many decoys Lorcan had used to confuse and diffuse the blockade runners.

"You seem to know everybody, St. Leger." Delacorte was pleased with this. A salesman at heart, more friends meant more people to spread the word of his wares, and possibly more people he could talk into going to donkey races with him.

"Aye, well, who can forget me pretty face?"

He'd rather hoped a few would, in fact. A slight beard only partially obscured his scar. It was more difficult to begin a new life when his old life was so vividly carved into him.

When his old life was everywhere underfoot in London.

When his old life was striding next to him, looking every bit of what he was, which was a former blockade captain who regretted not catching him.

"Reminds me a bit of Hawkes," Delacorte said. "He seemed to have friends of all sorts, too. Dukes, hack drivers, chaps on the street."

"Hawkes." Lorcan was surprised. "You can't mean Christian Hawkes?"

"You know Hawkes?" Delacorte was thrilled. "He stayed with us at The Grand Palace on the Thames. I miss him."

"Of course I know Hawkes," Lorcan said, as if it went without saying. "Hawkes is how I got a charter from the king to be a privateer."

Hardy shot him a searching, penetrating sidelong look.

Hardy could well imagine how Lorcan had come to know a legendary British spymaster.

But he didn't know the whole truth, and probably never would.

Lorcan would have been a spectacularly well-placed informant. Hawkes would have sussed that out straightaway. And Hawkes was the sort of negotiator who would be willing to overlook a good deal if the information at stake was critical enough.

"Very good man, Hawkes," Lorcan said. He was. He'd been damned sorry he'd been caught by the French.

"He's out of prison and a viscount now," Lucien said. "Lord Redvers."

"I'll be damned. Everybody's a bloody viscount now, aren't they," Lorcan muttered.

Lucien looked at him askance.

Delacorte had wandered away a moment to speak to someone he knew. He returned to them.

"The end of the Barking Road is flooded," he told them. "Seems no one can get in or out. Well, not with anything like ease or safety. No hacks are on the roads, of a certainty."

The Barking Road is what linked this part of the docks with the rest of London.

"Bloody fucking hell," Lucien said on behalf of all of them.

More grim news.

"We'll be fine," Hardy said calmly. "We're prepared to feed our guests for a couple of weeks if it comes to that. But it won't. St. John will likely be climbing the walls, however."

"Whereas you'll be a bastion of tranquility," Bolt said to him.

Hardy shot him a wry, weary look.

"Your ship should have been in a fortnight ago?" Lorcan asked Hardy.

"It's been nigh on three weeks now," he said grimly.

Lorcan said nothing. They all knew what that meant.

"There's my ship," he said absently. "See her, way out next to the clipper? A converted merchant."

Bolt whistled in approval.

"She's bonnie," Hardy said shortly.

"Aye," Lorcan agreed.

So odd, the outsized affection one felt for those crafts. They were enormous when viewed moored next to humans. Tiny as corks when seen at a distance bobbing on the indifferent ocean. Mankind was purely mad to attempt it at all. Though of course, this had never stopped a man from doing anything. Madness, arguably, perpetuated the species.

Far off in the distance lightning slashed the sky. A reminder that they were at the mercy of the elements.

For a moment they all stood and stared, as if that way they could will the ship into appearing in port.

Later, he remembered what came next as a sequence of sounds:

The slaps of little running feet on the damp dock.

A splash, as though someone had tossed something small, perhaps a brick, into the water.

Then a scream that split the heavens like the end of time.

Lorcan saw Michael's bright blond head bobbing in the slate water, his little arms thrashing it into foam.

The sea was already coming for him, ready to do what it did so well, bear him under and away.

Lorcan ripped off his coats and plunged in.

The icy water nearly punched his breath from him. The weight of it shocked him as it shoved him sideways. He was purely mad, but in madness was strength.

In two strokes he was near the bright hair just as it was about to bob beneath a swell.

He lunged and caught hold of a fistful of his little shirt, then a soft, plump little arm, and he managed to hoist the boy, who weighed no more than Lorcan's boots, it seemed, over his head. He took a face full of water and nearly went under. He threw his head back and saw the gray sky, and he turned it toward the sound of screaming and shouting.

He saw that Hardy was stretched out over the water like a ladder, Delacorte and Bolt holding on to his legs. With an awkward one-armed stroke and treading kicks, he managed to get close enough to lever the boy up and into Hardy's reaching hands. Hardy caught the sobbing child by the trousers and pulled him into his body.

Relief nearly sank Lorcan. His boots felt like anchors as heavy gray curls of water assaulted him and pulled him backward again. He struggled to get closer to the dock using overarm strokes. The cold and the weight of the water and his clothes wanted to take him under. How odd would it be to die so close to land, after all this time.

And he thought, of all the ways he could have died over the years, perhaps he'd merely been waiting for the one most worthy. The one which, like the other chances he'd been given, would get him at least a shot at the pearly gates.

And then a rope slapped him in the face.

Delacorte had found it and hurled it with admirable aim. Lorcan caught hold of it and gripped it hand over fist. The three men towed him in until he was level with the pier. Then a half-dozen hands were hard in his armpits, arms, legs, as they hoisted his sopping bulk out of the sea and onto the dock.

He crouched on his hands and knees as those hands came down hard on his back. He hacked and vomited a stream of water.

Then turned over and collapsed on his back.

Sobbing for breath he managed, "Is . . . he . . ."

"The boy's fine, he's alive." He wasn't certain who said it.

He collapsed, heaving, on his back, and looked up to see the boy's mother's face, radiating light like an angel, her son sobbing in her arms. *You have no one*, Daphne had said. And then he closed his eyes and wondered what it would be like to have anyone scream for him.

Chapter Eleven

✦✦✦

DAPHNE PENSIVELY took apart her scone and ate it with sips of black coffee while Lorcan's uneaten scone rested accusingly on the plate across from her.

Eventually she covered it gently and carefully with a napkin.

She thought about him as a boy, grateful for any scrap he could get, and her stomach tensed miserably.

She hoped he'd gone down to breakfast.

She hadn't. And she'd slept poorly. Last night's argument and the ensuing cascade of realizations went round and round in her head all night until it ached dully, and it still did. She wasn't in the mood yet to eat competitively with the German boys.

By eleven o'clock in the morning, Lorcan still hadn't returned to the suite.

She sighed, then curled up on the settee with a book, Gordon the cat purring against her thigh, and drank tea and desultorily read a few pages.

BAM BAM BAM.

She shot to her feet, sending Gordon flying through the air in shock. He landed neatly on all four feet, cat-fashion, by the hearth, and raced to the door.

She peered through the little peep window.

"It's Mr. Delacorte. I've got your husband. Hurry! It's a matter of utmost urgency!"

Daphne's heart at once was an icy block. She clawed the bolt and swung open the door to find Mr. Delacorte and Mr. St. Leger.

She gasped.

The latter was soaked to the skin. His shirt and trousers were glued to him, his hair was flattened against his skull, his skin was stark white and his lips were blueish, and his boots and coat were missing.

Lorcan's shivering, stoic abjectness flipped her stomach in upon itself.

She whirled about, snatched the coverlet from the settee and flung it over him, as if he were a fire needing putting out.

"Oh my goodness. Come," she said gently. She got him by the arm and steered him gently toward the hearth. He objected to none of this. She could feel him shivering violently beneath her hand.

"We got his boots off downstairs, but he's frozen near stiff. You'll need to get him out of those clothes straightaway," Mr. Delacorte said matter-of-factly.

Oh, God.

This was merely true.

And naturally it was a thing a wife would have done many times before.

"Aye, you'll want to get me out of me c-clothes, missus." Lorcan's joke was punctuated by the chatter of his teeth.

"What *happened*?" she demanded.

"You ought to know he's a right blood . . . he's a right hero!" Delacorte said fervently. "He jumped right in and plucked that child from under the water like he was a wee cork and handed him out to Hardy. Like it was nothing at all. Nothing! Cor, never seen such a thing in my life and I have seen a *lot* of things."

"A *child*?" She turned to Lorcan, stunned. "You saved . . . you jumped . . . what on . . ." She recollected her wits. "Mr. Delacorte, will you kindly ask the maids to fetch us some coffee and a tisane for fever, if Helga has one." She issued those orders crisply. "Some brandy, too."

Taking grown men in hand was her bailiwick, after all. For better or worse.

"It would be my honor. I would have done that right off but I thought you'd want him brought straight to you. You could have lost him for good," he added with something that sounded ever-so-slightly like gentle reproach. Delacorte shut the door.

She and Lorcan regarded each other.

He looked no more pleased about these developments than she felt.

She was being thrust into too many new experiences over and over, and each one a fresh shock, a bit like his dip in the Thames.

But she was hardly a child.

So then. Time to rapidly strip naked the big, strange man she'd locked out of the suite the night before.

"Do you mind if I . . . ?" she asked shortly. She knew she was already blushing.

"B-b-believe me, if I'd a choice . . ." he said grimly.

She shifted the coverlet she'd flung over him to hang off his back like a cape. He clutched it in one hand.

She pulled in a long breath, as if she was about to enter an airless cave, and got right to it. Her fingers clumsy with nerves, she peeled up the long tails of his shirt from where it clung like seaweed to his trousers. She could feel him quaking. Sympathy knotted her stomach.

Submitting to her help was probably well nigh unendurable for him.

From there she was compelled to pluck the shirt free from where it clung transparently to muscles which, from the looks of things, were as hard and precisely hewn as the ruby in his earring. He quivered where her fingers brushed his chilled flesh. His skin was shockingly soft over all of that hard muscle.

Her breath snagged at the contrast. Her eyes burned with peculiar emotion, not all of which was embarrassment.

Her heart clenched.

It seemed wrong. By rights he ought to have been made of iron.

And just like that, her hands were like leaves in a windstorm. Visibly trembling.

Moreover, there was no way he wouldn't notice. She wished she could transfer some of the heat in her cheeks into the huge shivering man. The fact that she could not speed through the whole affair, and was compelled instead to painstakingly peel his shirt upward like a venetian blind, gave the whole thing an absurd air of ceremony, as if she was unveiling a statue.

She tried crossing her eyes to spare him any ogling she was tempted to do while he was in this vulnerable state. She succeeded only in moderately blurring the gradual reveal of great curving mounds of chest lightly furred with the manliest of black, curly hair. More of which, dear God, trailed up from the band of his trousers.

It was all searingly new and almost wholly unanticipated to her. Unnervingly, primitively magnificent, equal parts beautiful and ugly, intimidating in its implicit raw power. It flooded her senses; she braced herself against it, tensing every muscle, clenching her teeth.

She couldn't repress her sigh of relief once she got the shirt up around his clavicle.

"Lorcan, can you raise your arms?" Her voice sounded strange in her own ears.

He tried. They were stiff; he needed help.

Together they levered his big arms up as if they were pump handles.

The massive gleaming mounds of his shoulders were revealed. Her head officially went as light as if she'd been punched.

She cleared her throat. "All right, that's done. Let's have this all the way off." She'd tried for brisk and jocular.

But her voice emerged at a flutelike pitch.

She took a fortifying breath. And then another. As if she was preparing to rescue him from the Thames.

She averted her eyes from the vast, stunning bareness of his torso as she pulled up his shirt only to meet the gaze of Gordon the cat, who was unabashedly staring at her.

For a fraught moment Lorcan's face vanished in the wet, white folds of linen, like a mummy or a ghost. Dot might have indeed fainted clean away if she'd gotten a look at him.

"Help," he said through the shroud.

After a harrowing moment of struggle, Daphne was able to reach up and pull the shirt over the back of his head, where it swung damply. Briefly he resembled a large hairy nun before it dropped to the floor.

His cravat was quickly dispensed with, as well.

"Very good. Here now," she said gently, and tucked the coverlet all the way around him. "Hold on to this." She seized one of his chilled hands and closed his fingers over a blue knit corner.

She glanced up at him, to discover some expression she could not interpret fleeing from his face.

For a moment their gazes locked.

His eyes were glinting with unholy amusement. "Trousers now," the wretched man said.

"Thank you. Yes. I know," she said tersely.

She pulled in a sustaining breath.

And went to reach under the coverlet for the fall of his trousers.

He stopped her hand with his.

"Nay, Daphne. I was jesting. I'll do it." He sounded amused, but gentle.

His hand was still icy on her wrist and it oddly made her nearly frantic to help him.

But he'd noticed her distress. She was grateful, even as she felt ashamed, like the veriest virgin, and useless. Imagine feeling shame at *not* unbuttoning a man's trousers.

Then again, in all likelihood, she was very nearly the last woman on earth he'd want to undress for.

His hand vanished beneath the coverlet for a time.

"There. I've got the buttons," he said. "I may need you to t-t-ug just the legs of them a little."

His voice sounded somewhat strangled, too.

She was certain he was hardly savoring the need to be undressed like a helpless child. All the better to hurry this along.

She squeezed her eyes closed briefly, reached under the coverlet, and managed to pinch the nankeen between her fingers and tug. But the fabric hugged the great cannons of his thighs with as much loving tenacity as his shirt had hugged his torso, and ridiculously, she had to fight to drag them down. Her fingers brushed hard, hard, furred muscle and she felt it tense like iron.

Oh God oh God oh God.

When they finally collapsed in a heap at his ankles, she was envious. She wanted to collapse into a mortified, scorchingly blushing heap, too.

"So I'm nearly naked," he announced, superfluously. "Our ordeal is almost over."

She gave a short, strained little laugh.

She nudged the settee closer to the fire and gave him a little shove. He sat down, drawing the coverlet around him, huddled there while she whipped the blankets from her bed and covered him in layers like papier-mâché.

She dropped to her knees before him. "Hold out your hands. Keep the coverlet over them, the way you would mittens."

Without question, he obeyed.

And one at a time, she took his hands between hers and chafed vigorously.

And this, and the crack of the fire, was the only sound in the room for a good long time.

She looked up when she sensed in his body an easing of his shivering tension.

She looked up at him. His eyelids had gone a little heavy. Likely he was exhausted.

"Thank you," he said, after a moment. Quietly.

She paused. "How are they?"

"I can feel them again." Beneath the coverlet, he flexed his fingers. "They ache a bit. Coming back to life will do that to a body. I'll live to use them to catch women flying off of crates."

More color had returned to his face and to his lips.

She hadn't fully realized how desperately worried she'd been until relief nearly made her dizzy.

He continued chafing his own hands. Suddenly he stopped.

"Who is that?"

She followed the direction of his gaze. "Oh. That's Gordon."

"We have a cat now?"

He sounded so surprised she gave a short laugh. The word "we" landed strangely on her ears. For some reason, it was a relief to hear it. "He visited last night and I let him in. Then I let him back out. He returned today. He seems to like it here. Probably we have the juiciest mice in all The Grand Palace on the Thames."

"So you let the *cat* stay last night. I see. I take it the cat isn't a right bast—"

Very surprisingly, he stopped just short of using the whole objectionable word.

Gordon stared benignly back at the two of them as if he'd never seen anything more interesting in his life.

"Do you mind having him here?" she asked, somewhat carefully.

"No. Clearly you missed having a homely hairy beast about the place."

She snorted softly. "Where did you sleep?"

"With Delacorte."

"I imagine he's twice as good as a heated brick."

"Aye. But there were a few drawbacks," he said shortly.

She blew out a breath.

"All right. You ought to be able to chafe your arms a bit on your own now. You do that while I do—"

She stood and reached for a shawl and dropped it down over his head as if he were a parakeet in a cage. And perhaps a little too vigorously rubbed his hair.

He squawked a little.

"Sorry," she said insincerely.

More gently, she wound the shawl around his head, turbanlike.

He ought to have looked absurd, and any other man might have. Instead, he resembled a stern sheik, awaiting the arrival of his harem.

"Stockings now," she said valiantly. "Or can you do them?"

"I'll do them," he said.

She watched to make certain he could.

He bent and peeled his wet wool stockings from exquisitely shaped, huge, hairy calves. She tried not to stare at his big bare feet, tufted in hair. Like the rest of him, they were profoundly, aggressively masculine.

He pulled his feet up into his nest of blankets and rubbed them with his hands.

She collapsed in a weary heap on the opposite end of the settee. Who knew relieving men of their clothes could be so thoroughly draining?

"I know it was difficult for you," he said somewhat stiffly. "So thank you," he said, finally. Then added, more amused, "for helping me out of my clothes.

"I would have done the same for you," he added.

She gave a little shout of laughter. She had the pleasure of seeing his eyes light like fireworks.

DELILAH WAS IN her room searching for the

proper color of thread to mend the hem on one
of her gowns when her husband appeared, grim-
faced and far wetter than the rain ought to have
made him.

Her heart gave a jolt.

They briefly, silently stared at each other. He
didn't look well-rested. She certainly wasn't.

"Tristan, are you all right? What happened?"

"We went down to the docks. St. Leger saved a
child from drowning. He could have died. He *and*
the child. Neither did."

Delilah felt the blood leave her skin.

Her hand went over her heart. "Oh . . . my
goodness. Are they . . . are you . . ."

"Child and St. Leger will both live to tell the
tale. St. Leger is with his wife. I'm fine."

Delilah sat down hard on her bed.

She watched her husband strip off his damp
shirt.

The words were out of her before she realized
she was even forming them.

"Tristan. Stop it."

He turned to her. "Stop what?"

"The cold, short, curt answers. The not looking
at me when you speak. *Stop it*."

His eyes flared in shock. Her last words were
pitched in near hysteria.

"The worst thing in the world I can imagine is
to be without you. Worse than death." Her voice
was trembling now.

"Aye," he said hoarsely, stunned. After a moment. "And that goes for me losing you, too."

"When you go . . . cold and hard and remote . . .

it feels like I've lost you, Tristan. Like you've died. Like you never loved me at all."

And just like that Captain Hardy was breathing swiftly in horror.

"I can't feel *you* at all when you're like that. I imagine it's how it would feel if you ever stopped loving me. And if you do that, you'll win every argument, because I'd do anything to make it stop. But do you want to win that way? Tristan, it *terrifies* me."

And she covered her face with her hands and burst into tears.

She might as well have run him through with a sword.

"Christ, Delilah. Oh God. My love. Sweetheart. I'm sorry. I'm sorry. I didn't know. I'm so sorry, love." He wrapped his arms around her and pulled her tightly into his body. He fanned the back of his hand against her hair and buried his face in her throat. She was shaking with sobs.

"I never meant to . . . Delilah, I would die rather than hurt you." His voice was a desperate rasp.

"Then why? Why do you do it?" she demanded. Her tears were both angry and heartbroken as she pulled her hands away from her face. "What is *wrong*?"

"I just . . ." His words clogged jaggedly in his throat.

"Tristan. Talk to me. Please. *Please.*"

"Because I'm afraid." He said the words in a low rush.

She went still. "Why are you afraid?" She stopped crying nearly at once.

He took a shuddering breath. Hers was held.

"It's fear that makes me a bastard. Fear and shame. Because I'm ashamed of being afraid." His voice was gruff. "And then I'm ashamed of being a bastard. Delilah, what bloody good am I if I cannot keep and protect you? What is the *point* of me?"

She was stunned. "Tristan . . ." she breathed. "Oh my God. What on . . ."

He took a breath. "If we lose the ship, we're insured, but it will take us over a year to catch up to where we are now, and that's income that Bolt and I aren't bringing in. And we *all* will feel the effects. Delacorte, too. It was *years* of work to buy the ship in the first place. I'm feeling a little helpless, and I honestly can't remember the last time I felt helpless at all. Probably because I've *never* felt that way. At least since I was a child. I was *really* bloody good at my job and you know it. It was who I am. Perhaps it is still who I am. And then St. Leger shows up, reminding me of a failure, and . . . I do not like being reminded that I am fallible." He gave a short laugh. "In the past, if I was fallible, people could die."

He tenderly drew a strand of hair away from her wet cheeks with a single finger and tucked it behind her ear.

"I do not know how to reconcile being afraid with the man I thought I was. The man I want to be for you. I understand now that I never felt helpless because there was never as much at stake. I love my life with you more than anything. And I love you more than life."

"Oh, my heart," she said softly. She gently kissed his chilled cheeks, his eyelids, his mouth. "I don't love you for your ability to slam the heads of intruders on tables." Which was, in fact, something he had once done in order to save her from a man who had intended to harm her. "Or because you make love like a demon. I love you because you fell completely apart and showed me your heart and wrote me a poem. The fact that you can slam heads and bark orders is a useful feature. I love *this* part of you. I love what you're telling me now. You are safe with me, do you hear?"

She sat down hard on the bed.

He sat down next to her.

Then they lay down together, stretched out, loosely wrapped around each other.

She stroked his hair while he rested his head on her chest, soothed by the reassuring rise and fall of it. The very fact of her.

"A terrible poem," he murmured.

"The best poem I've ever heard," she sniffed.

"I trust you implicitly, you know. I do. There are two of us now, and you have enough bravery for a whole continent but even the sun can't always shine through clouds, Tristan. When you cannot be brave, I will be brave for you. Don't you see, there's nothing we can't face together? We can fight about anything you like, but you cannot use . . . taking yourself away from me . . . as a weapon. Or as a way to protect yourself. Do you understand? You can't. I cannot bear it. You must talk to me."

He drew in a long breath, then exhaled at

length. "You have my word. I won't do it again.
I'm sorry."

Already the tension he'd been carrying for
weeks had left his body. She could feel it, and she
rejoiced.

She knew his word was as good as his wed-
ding vows. And she knew how tremendously difficult it was for him to be open and soft. It was too
close to surrender. Life had trained him to be so
very hard.

"Thank you for telling me how you felt, Delilah."

"We're still learning how to be married," she
said.

He gave a short, pained laugh. "Humbling as
hell to not be perfect at it."

She laughed softly.

For a long time they merely lay in peaceful silence.

"He's a good man, Delilah," he said after a moment. "Years of commanding men, and I think I
can discern a man who acts the part and a man
who fundamentally *is*. I think I've always thought
he was a good man. Even a fine man. He's certainly
a singular man. It's not about diving in and saving
babies. God only knows why he did that. But that's
what has eaten at me. I saw who he could have
been, and then there was what he did, and . . ."

"He probably doesn't think of it as a waste,
Tristan. He probably sees it as the reason he's
alive."

She said this very carefully, delicately. She
knew honor was an ironclad notion for him;
it was as much a part of him as his spine. He'd

been saved from St. Giles in a way that Lorcan St. Leger had not. He owed his life and loyalty to the navy. But the military had gotten lucky when they'd saved the ten-year-old Tristan Hardy. He'd been as brilliant and dedicated an officer as ever walked. His men would walk through fire for him. As would Delilah.

"I am struggling with whether . . . accepting this . . . is a betrayal of everything I have stood for in my life."

"What if what you stood for . . . is all that is good in the world? Maybe he is good, and the path to good was simply different for him. Maybe he's meant to do better in the world. Maybe he was meant to save that child today. Maybe . . . something in you never really wanted to catch him."

He was quiet. But she knew he was listening.

"I don't know if I can change who I am this late in my life," he finally said.

"Maybe it isn't a change. Maybe it's sort of like . . . trees. Nobody says trees are changing when they sprout new leaves. They're merely . . . oh, fully expressing what they are."

This awkward analogy made him smile. "Like me with my terrible poem."

"Like you with your brilliant poem."

DAPHNE GAVE A start when a sharp rap sounded at the door.

Funny, she thought, how knocks had personalities. The maid's knocks were polite and deferential, Mr. Delacorte's was loud and cheerful. This one sounded like the *law* was at the door.

She was unsurprised to find Captain Hardy on the other side when she opened it.

Behind him, Dot was holding a tray bearing coffee and what must be a tisane.

She stepped aside so this little delegation could enter.

Lorcan immediately straightened warily.

And from out of nowhere a wayward sense of protection surged in her. As though she wanted to put herself between the man on the settee and Captain Hardy.

Captain Hardy said, "I brought whiskey."

He gestured with a flask in his hand.

Lorcan jerked his chin in her direction. "Give it to her first. She's had quite a shock."

He winked at her, very subtly.

Both men were looking at her, eyebrows upraised in a question at her now.

She'd never tasted anything stronger than champagne. "Perhaps a little splash," she said.

Dot settled the tray and departed, and Daphne poured coffee into the cups. Captain Hardy sprinkled a few drops from the flask in hers and tipped a torrent into Lorcan's.

They all sipped.

Daphne's eyes widened. It was at once clear that ratafia had nothing on whiskey.

Lorcan closed his hands around his cup, gulped, and closed his eyes in apparent ecstasy.

Nobody said anything for a while.

Gordon apparently found this lull so uninteresting he plunked down, hoisted his leg, and began urgently licking his privates.

"Fetching bonnet," Hardy said to Lorcan, finally. He gestured.

Lorcan reached up and touched his shawl turban. "Thank you. My wife made it for me," he said somberly.

Captain Hardy said to Daphne, "Did he tell you what he did?"

"Mr. Delacorte told me. It was an extraordinarily brave thing to do."

There was a pause.

"Yes," Captain Hardy said.

Lorcan and Captain Hardy were still staring at each other from across the room, having one of those complicated silent conversations.

"But it's just like him. He is always doing brave things," Daphne said softly.

Even somewhat defiantly.

Lorcan looked at her swiftly.

Maybe it was the two drops of whiskey she'd just sipped. It was odd how little this seemed like a lie. As though something within her, beneath her defenses, understood this to be essentially true.

Captain Hardy merely nodded.

"You'll take care of him?" Captain Hardy said finally. Gruffly.

She had a feeling he wanted to say a good deal more, but his very presence, the whiskey gift, a little jest and a taciturn compliment, somehow said what a thousand fancier words couldn't.

"Of course," she said softly.

"I'll leave you to it, then," he said.

He departed.

Daphne and Lorcan stared at the closed door.

She thought she was beginning to more clearly understand a few things. "Captain Hardy was a blockade captain," Daphne said carefully.

It wasn't quite a question.

"Yes, a brilliant one. But not a perfect one. And that's what he is struggling with."

She turned to Lorcan.

"Blockade captains are charged with capturing smugglers?"

He looked at her at length.

"Yes," Lorcan said finally, gently.

Clearly, he was not going to guide her to conclusions that she was about to make on her own.

She was suddenly certain he would answer her questions if she mustered the nerve to ask them. She did not want to ask them. She wanted to remain suspended in this moment for a little while, spent, warm, a trifle tipsy, a condition in which judgment would glide right off her. A rare, pure state of just being, which allowed truths to surface, unfettered by breeding, manners, or assumptions.

FROM HIS NEST of coverlets, from beneath eyelids at half-mast, Lorcan watched Daphne as she watched the fire. He liked the lines of her profile—the soft swell of her lips, her sharp little nose. The valiant Lady Worth, he thought, bemused. She'd leaped to help him today before she'd known he was an alleged hero. Within her was a fundamental decency and sense of fairness. She had taken care to thank him for her window rescue, even as it must have scraped against her pride.

Your truest self was what sprang forth when you were tested, Lorcan had come to know over the years. Challenge any man, or, he supposed, woman, and you'll discover their wounds and weaknesses as surely as you'll discover their strengths.

He wondered what it said about him that he'd dived in to save a child. He hadn't known that he would. It had simply seemed unthinkable not to.

More accurately, he hadn't thought at all.

"That sound."

She lifted her head. "I beg your pardon?"

He was surprised to realize he'd said those words aloud.

He cleared his throat. "She screamed when he fell in the water. His mother. It was as if . . . it was the sound of someone's heart being sliced out. It nearly peeled the skin from me body. I have heard screams before, mind you. But I've never heard a sound like that before and I never want to hear a sound like that again."

Daphne's breath left her in a gust and she squeezed her eyes closed. As if she could see it all too clearly.

He was suddenly very glad he'd told her, because it was so very clear she understood.

When she opened them again, her eyes were haunted and weary and wry. "Love is terrifying."

He went still.

He understood something with uncomfortable clarity then.

She probably knew her father and her brothers loved themselves more than they loved her. It didn't matter. She did what she did because she loved them. And it caused her pain.

He felt a peculiar weight on his chest.

"How did it happen?" she asked.

"He did what children do, and ran impulsively out onto the dock and slipped and into the water he went. I went in after him at once. Dragged him out by his wee arm. Handed him off to Hardy. Delacorte threw the rope in and they fished me back out, like a big eel."

"You could have died."

"I might have died any number of times before. I'd have been just one of thousands of men who've drowned in the Thames."

Her expression was a picture of incredulity at his relative nonchalance.

"I'm glad you were there. I cannot even imagine what his mother must have felt."

They were quiet a moment.

"Everyone thinks you're my wife. You would have inherited all of my worldly goods." He was amused by this.

"I could always use a few pairs of gigantic stockings."

He laughed.

And then silence again, apart from Gordon making snorkeling grooming sounds into his striped flanks.

"Daphne . . ."

She looked up at him.

"I should like to apologize for upsetting you so terribly yesterday. And for the loss of your stockings. I was . . . I overstepped."

She fixed him with a deep, steady, measuring look. Surprisingly it was not at all discomfiting to gaze back at her. He liked seeing what she thought of him reflected in her eyes, regardless of whether it was flattering.

"You think I'm ridiculous," was what she said finally.

It wasn't the beginning of an argument. It wasn't an accusation. It sounded as though she was not going to let him off with a rote apology. She was going to *solve* this.

"No. It isn't the word I would choose."

"You cannot sympathize with the way I was raised, because you were not so much raised as born and then let loose to fend for yourself like a wolf cub. And you succeeded against enormous odds."

He coughed in astonishment. "Christ. No wonder everyone in your village thought you were clever."

She snorted softly.

"Very well then . . . it doesn't give me the right to disdain the things that are precious to you. For I do not, in fact, disdain them. I think they merely remind me of what I am not and cannot be."

He began to realize he was a little drunk. Something about the cocoon of coverlets, the whiskey, the near death, had stripped a layer of reticence from him.

Her eyes flared in shock.

"And whatever you think of me—and odds are even the worst you can imagine would not be *far* wrong—I know the value of things. I know the value of people. I do not ever take the things I value for granted."

Her eyes flickered as her expression reflected amazement.

And then she ducked her head.

He could no longer read her expression.

After a moment she lifted it again. "I don't really think you are a heathen. It was about the worst thing I could think to call you, so I said it."

"You struck bone."

"I'm sorry."

"I don't think you are *very* sorry, however."

And now she was clearly suppressing a smile.

"And may I introduce you to the very useful word 'bastard'?"

Damned if she didn't laugh. What a lovely laugh she had. A happy, cascading, shouty sort that made him laugh, too.

How bright the gray day seemed, for an instant.

"I am not so sheltered or ignorant as you might think, Lorcan. Not in all the ways you think."

He nodded, humbly acknowledging that he realized this.

"Perhaps I should not have said those things about your father and your brothers. Perhaps it is not any of my business, after all."

"No," she agreed softly. "But there is something to be said for a person who sees a truth so clearly and so swiftly he knows where to insert the sword. And that is how *you* are clever, Lorcan." She paused. And then surprised him again. "I don't completely dislike it."

She'd said it hesitantly.

He was still, silently taking her words in, turning them about in his mind. And as he did, he felt a peculiar pinprick of light in his chest. He did not know what to call it. Almost like excitement. Perhaps happiness. It was like that first sliver of sun you see in the morning on the horizon, when you don't know what the day will bring. Anything at all could happen.

"And . . . you weren't completely wrong," she said more hoarsely.

And for a moment her expression slipped and the shame and grief she'd never faced was revealed. And it was like a knife through him: she knew she was not valued as she ought to be.

Perhaps she'd always known it.

He wanted very much to speak to her more. He wanted very much to hear her thoughts and watch her expressions shift and to see the light in her eyes change with them.

But the whiskey, the fire, the exertion, the blankets, the soothing presence of a woman and a cat . . . all of it was conspiring to knock him out for a good long sleep.

"I think I canna stay awake, Daphne."

"Drink the tisane first, will you please?" she said. "It's only willow bark. You shouldn't want to get a fever. And then you can have a nap right where you are."

He sniffed it. He was familiar with willow bark tisanes. So he drank it.

He closed his eyes.

The falling rain, the crackling fire, the grooming cat, the breathing man.

Daphne watched him unabashedly, the way one would if they stole across a sleeping satyr in the forest. His thick, dark lashes brushed his stern cheekbones.

Somehow, he did not look any more innocent asleep than awake.

Her heart squeezed, oddly, for the boy who had never been allowed to be innocent.

She thought someone somewhere must have loved him, probably his mother, for him to dive into the water. Some corner of his soul had understood that mother's scream for what it was.

How odd it was that she, Lady Daphne Worth, of all people, found it difficult to care that she was sharing a settee with a naked criminal. For if he'd been a smuggler, he'd been a criminal. He wasn't one now. Privateers go out on the seas with a charter from the crown, after all.

But she suspected he'd been some sort of rather grand criminal, too, if Captain Hardy remained so put out by him.

She was beginning to understand what people would be willing to do to survive. And to think, she could have gone a lifetime without knowing. Possibly it never would have mattered. But if her own life was the only bargaining chip with which she'd entered the world, she might ruthlessly, craftily barter and gamble and buy her way into something better, too. She'd learned quite a bit about herself in just a few days.

Even in sleep, Lorcan somehow exuded power and authority in the truest sense of each word. Earned. Not the sort conferred by a title. He had vanquished terrible odds to be here now. He seemed to know precisely what he was capable of. He was a man who had done difficult things.

And yet she'd still been able to wound him with her words.

She stood to allow him to stretch out his legs. He gave a great sigh and did that. She rearranged his blankets to cover his toes.

And in seconds his breathing was even and his face utterly slack.

She collected his clothes—the wet shirt, the trousers, the stockings, his cravat—smoothed from them the wrinkles, carefully arranged them over the fire screen to dry, and then fashioned a makeshift clothesline from a strand of yarn. She could probably ask a maid for assistance with this sort of thing. But she found it meditative. It was how she cared—through service.

She turned around.

Lorcan did not quite properly fit on the settee.

One of his big furry calves had trailed off the side a bit. Very stealthily, she lifted a corner of the coverlet and draped it back over the bareness.

She hesitated.

Then lightly she laid her palm on his forehead but he was warm, not feverish. She was glad.

Chapter Twelve

_{ও⁂}

THE MOMENT she heard from Dot what had happened at the docks, Angelique dropped her mending and raced to find a wet Lucien in their room, standing in front of their clothing press.

He fixed her with a searching, careful look as he pulled open a drawer in search of a dry shirt.

"St. Leger dove into the Thames to save a child and then we all pulled St. Leger out." He sounded subdued. "We all got wet. St. Leger got the wettest, of course."

Angelique's hand went to her throat. "I heard. Lucien, are you . . . ? And is he . . . ? And the child . . . ?"

"St. Leger and the child are both fine. As am I."

An awkward little lull ensued, to be expected in the aftermath of an unresolved argument. The two people involved were taking each other's emotional temperature.

Lucien tried for levity. "I've a little experience, as you know, with being tossed in the drink so it was a good thing I was there to advise."

When he'd been an angry young bastard son of a neglectful duke, someone in his life had a selfish reason to want him dead. He'd been set upon and tossed into the Thames late one night and assumed drowned. Fate had intervened in the form of a rescue; he'd disappeared from London. A resurrected Lucien had gone on to shock the *ton* nearly a decade later.

Angelique was quiet a moment.

"Lucien, when you joke about being tossed into the drink . . ."

"Yes?" He pulled off his shirt.

"I've never told you this . . . but I've had nightmares about it. About what you told me about the night you were kidnapped and thrown into the Thames and how you could have drowned."

He froze.

Good God, was he beautiful. She'd been married for more than a year, but when confronted by her husband's bare torso, Angelique still felt a spasm of stunned longing.

"I dream of you sinking, alone in the water . . . and I wake up and I stifle my screams with my pillow so I don't wake you."

He stared at her.

"Holy Christ," he breathed.

"Do you have nightmares about it, too?" she asked.

He tossed his wet shirt across a chair. He was quiet for a long moment. "I do," he confessed. "And then I jolt awake. And turn over. And when I see you, I decide that it doesn't matter whether I'm alive or dead. If you're there, I'm in heaven, either way."

She exhaled a stunned laugh. He did this, always: brought her close to tears by saying something beautiful as if it were a cardinal truth.

This side of Lucien was for her only.

She looped her arms around his bare waist and pulled him closer. She laid her warm cheek against his hard abdomen. "Lucien, I love you. You're so chilly," she murmured. "Sit with me."

He sat.

She tugged the coverlet up to cover the two of them and put her arms around him, so she could warm him.

"Did you enjoy sleeping with Captain Hardy?" she murmured.

"I did not. It's like sleeping next to a plank. He made me wear a nightshirt."

She smiled.

"Did you like sleeping next to Delilah?"

"I did, at that. She smells nice and we had a good chat."

Lucien laughed.

They sat quietly. "I don't ever have to joke about it again, Angelique, if you don't want me to."

"I know that humor is what you do with painful things. We both do it. Joke if you must, in company. I mean that sincerely. I just wanted you to know that I have never once thought of it lightly. The notion that anyone could hurt you . . ."

He nodded, silently, very moved.

For a moment they sat together wordlessly.

"Angelique . . ." The word sounded hesitant.

She turned to him.

"I think I know what was bothering you last night. About the governess." He took a breath. "It's to do with Derring. And the others before. Or rather . . . is it?"

"It was," she said, stiltedly. "Yes. In a way."

Lucien closed his eyes. "I'm devastated if even for an instant I made you feel like . . . something to *partake* of. You are so indescribably precious to me."

"I knew you would suffer over it, Lucien, and I . . . I really cannot bear the idea of you suffering."

"I understand. But Angelique . . . I need you to understand this, too: for you I would bear anything."

She drew in a long, shuddering breath.

"Thank you," she whispered.

He gently brushed her tears from her eyes.

"And Lucien, last night . . . you did nothing wrong. You always make me feel cherished. I was just very tired, as we all are, and feeling a little raw, and . . . somehow your playfulness found that vulnerable place in me and it hurt quite a bit. I'm sorry, too. I should have been able to tell you."

Thusly, two slightly battered people with old wounds destined to every now and then ache held each other fast and forgave.

"St. Leger is a brave man, Angelique. You have my permission to make love to him if the two of you are the last humans standing in an apocalypse."

She gave a shout of laughter.

And she kissed him, lingeringly. He sighed, with pleasure, against her lips.

"Do I have permission to make love to my husband right now?" she murmured.

"Permission granted," he growled, and he tugged her down with him onto the bed.

Chapter Thirteen

❧❧❧

Two days later ...

DELILAH HAD become attuned to the usual daily music of The Grand Palace on the Thames. There were the main themes—the clatter of dishes and the thwack of knives on wood in the kitchen; Mr. Delacorte snoring at night; Gordon's little cat feet galloping up and down the halls. Then there were the melodies new guests brought with them— thundering footsteps and giggling maids for the German trio, for instance.

There came a point about midday when she realized the house had gotten strangely quiet. No big feet galloping up and down the stairs. No hearty, echoing laughter, German chatter, or giggling maids.

What was one more layer of dread and portent? Delilah thought.

She thought it best to investigate.

Two of the maids were in the kitchen, doing their jobs and following Helga's orders like little angels. She'd count that as a blessing. She found Rose diligently dusting one of the rooms. This brought another rush of relief.

She found Dot dusting the mantel in the pink sitting room.

Mr. Pike was on the second floor, trimming candles. He likely would have seen guests coming and going. "Have you seen young Lord Vaughn this morning, Mr. Pike?"

"Not since breakfast, Mrs. Hardy. I don't believe he went back up to his room, nor did I see them go out. Mr. Delacorte is in his room, I believe, and Mr. St. Leger went out very early this morning and hasn't yet returned."

No ghostly strains of violin or violoncello wafted through the passage. They were diligent about practicing, their guests. So this was very unusual, too.

It was entirely possible the Germans, Mr. McDonald, and St. John had all gone on an expedition into the relentlessly wet world, which was within their rights, of course. It seemed improbable, as St. John was so fond of comfort, and it would have involved a lot of damp effort, and Mr. McDonald was so very easily irritated.

"Does it seem quiet to you?" Delilah asked from the foyer when her husband appeared at the top of the stairs.

"Yes," he said fervently and gratefully.

"It's *too* quiet."

He listened. Then sighed. "You're right. Let's go on a little expedition."

He said this just as Angelique appeared on the landing, too. "Does it seem quiet in here to you two?" she asked.

"Come with us. We're off to investigate." Captain Hardy took Delilah's hand and the three of them headed downstairs for the little passage that connected The Grand Palace on the Thames to the Annex, where the ballroom and all the suites were located.

Voices as they approached the ballroom. The door was open, as usual.

Captain Hardy put his finger to his lips.

Hans, Otto, Friedreich, St. John, and, startlingly, Angus McDonald, were crouched in a circle around something in the middle of the ballroom floor.

"What on . . ." Delilah mouthed. "Is it a séance?" she whispered.

And then they heard a rattling sound, almost as if a little ball were being shaken around the rim of a wheel.

But surely not?

They stealthily crept toward their wayward guests, who were wholly absorbed and as tense as runners at a starting line, excitedly poised over a makeshift roulette wheel.

Angelique, Delilah, and Captain Hardy watched them, unnoticed, for a few seconds.

And then: "Whose idea was this?" Captain Hardy said conversationally.

Years later they would still talk about how all five men shot straight up in the air simultaneously, their eyes as white as cue balls, as it was one of the funniest things they'd ever seen.

They were still furious about it, of course.

And no one was surprised when four frantic arms thrust out and aimed accusatory fingers at Lord Vaughn.

"I see. And who's been winning most often?"

Four arms pointed at St. John again. In front of whom a few pence were piled.

Captain Hardy reached down, got St. John by the earlobe, and pulled.

Needless to say, St. John was outraged. "Ow ow ow let go ow I'm standing! I'm standing!"

"You turned our ballroom into a *gaming hell*?"

Delilah said this. She and Angelique were equal parts incensed and wounded, which was a devastating combination for all of the men present.

It appeared to have rendered them speechless.

St. John regarded them wordlessly, his face warring between defiance and abject contrition.

"It's not a *hell*, per se," St. John finally said quietly.

St. John blanched at their expressions after that.

"Shame on all of you! Shame on you. We are so disappointed! *Wir sind so enttäuscht!*" Angelique scolded.

Hans, Otto, and Friedreich were scarlet with rue. Mr. McDonald's face was nearly as flaming as his hair.

They peered down at the roulette wheel, a clever little makeshift construction cobbled together from what appeared to be a scrap of wood left over from when Mr. Hugh Cassidy built the stage, foolscap carefully cut and inked, and various little bolts and screws. They wondered if it was a team effort or if St. John had methodically put it all together himself.

"'Do not fashion roulette wheels' is not in our rules because we all assumed you were gentlemen, and that it would be not only unnecessary but *insulting* to spell out such a thing. I cannot believe grown men cannot find another way to pass the time." Delilah's incredulity was scathing.

"Imagine what you could do with your life if you applied your ingenuity to almost literally anything else, St. John," Captain Hardy added.

Never mind that St. John, as a gentleman and heir to a viscount, was not obliged to do anything with his life but enjoy it.

"We are going to discuss your fate," Delilah said. "Please meet us in the reception room in exactly one hour to hear it. You may all wish to pack your bags just in case. You may recall we locked you out once before, St. John, and we have no compunctions about barring you permanently. Forever. *Shame* on all of you."

All the men flinched again at her forceful "shame."

It was Angelique who had arrived at an almost poetically brilliantly solution, which they presented to the pale and chagrined men squeezed together on one of the pink settees an hour later. Mr. McDonald had opted to stand.

"We've decided not to evict any of you. Instead, you, St. John, will learn to play the cello. You, Otto, will teach it to him."

"I—" St. John squeaked.

"But—" Otto protested.

"You are not yet invited to speak," Angelique said politely. "You will learn to play at least one very simple song competently within the next few days or we will tell your parents, the earl and the countess, what you've done and insist that they pay not only the fees for your room, but room and board for our German friends here as well. We know your father and he will *not* be pleased. I expect unfortunate things might happen to your allowance."

She turned to Angus McDonald.

"Mr. McDonald. *You* will learn to play the violin. Hans will teach it you. Hans, do you comprehend?"

Hans slowly nodded, the very picture of rue.

Mr. McDonald, however, actually looked somewhat intrigued.

"We think Mozart's variations on '*Ah, vous dirai-je, Maman*' might be a suitably simple place for all of you to start. You, along with Mrs. Pariseau, will give a recital at the end of the week, so you're going to need to practice a good deal. At which point we will have a party in the ballroom, and we will all dance and celebrate and drink and eat because we know this weather has been *very* trying for everyone and we like and value all of you *so* much. We are truly grateful to have you with us."

They beamed beatifically upon them.

All of them, even Mr. McDonald, melted.

"And you can stay," Angelique said sweetly, "if your performance goes well."

Their smiles slowly faded.

St. John cleared his throat. "If I may . . ."

Delilah nodded regally.

"We were just bored," he said quietly.

Angelique and Delilah exchanged a look. If ever a handsome young man needed his ears boxed . . .

"Mr. Delacorte taught you how to play chess, and look at how close you are to one day winning against him. Now you'll have an opportunity to become adept in an instrument. You're in grave danger of becoming interesting, St. John. And if you become interesting, you might just become genuinely devastating. Imagine that."

Angelique and Delilah stood, and all the men on the settee leaped to their feet immediately and respectfully, and exited the room, chastened and charged with purpose.

ON THE MORNING of her thirtieth birthday, Daphne awoke to coffee, one scone, and an otherwise resoundingly empty suite.

Next to Lorcan's empty plate was a note that read simply:

I will return this afternoon.

She studied his handwriting. The letters were large and bold, neat and careful. She supposed it was kind of him to alert her at all. Certainly he wasn't obligated to do it.

Surely it was absurd to feel somewhat forlorn.

Or worse . . . relieved that he intended to return.

But in her experience men never remembered birthdays or other sorts of anniversaries. That was the point of women, as far as they were concerned. To remember the things they deemed not important enough to store in their own brains.

Lorcan had slept stretched out on the settee

for most of the previous afternoon. She'd crept around the place, feeling as though she'd been given a sleeping dragon to tend. Every now and then he shifted with a sigh, or a snort, and part of a great hairy limb emerged from his cocoon of blankets. She quickly covered him back up, lest something more startling than a calf or an elbow break loose.

She'd sat at the chair near the window and watched him for a time, a little furrow between her eyes, and a pair of gradually dawning realizations unsettled her: sleeping with such abandon must mean he trusted her.

The fact that she hadn't really minded at all that he was sleeping in the middle of the room told her she trusted him, too.

She didn't know why his trust should feel like a prize she had won. Or why this notion should settle like a glow in her chest.

He'd been awake and hungry by dinnertime but he hadn't lingered in the sitting room. He'd gone up to bed early, well before she did. Perhaps because he'd known, but hadn't told her, that he'd be out the door before dawn.

The rain still fell in sheets against a flat gray sky.

Her birthday choices seemed to be pensive self-pity, something in which she seldom indulged, or breakfast with the rest of the guests. She finally decided to go down to breakfast, where she found only straggler Mrs. Pariseau, munching on fried bread.

"If you're at loose ends while your husband is out, dear, perhaps you can ask Hans for violin lessons. I've paid him a shilling and I've made marvelous progress. Isn't it a pleasure to learn new things? One never gets bored!" she said happily, as she pushed herself away from the table.

Daphne wistfully somewhat envied Mrs. Pariseau, who as a widow had gotten her marriage over with and was now free to do as she wished.

The day yawned before her, both empty and fraught.

To remind herself that she was in some way wanted, she read again the letter that was somehow tantamount to both signing her own death warrant while receiving a stay of execution. Perhaps there was something she'd missed.

Particularly the part that haunted her.

I will expect you to dutifully participate in the more intimate features of marriage that occur in private between a husband and wife as well as attend to my comfort in other wifely ways.

Well. What was she if not "dutiful"? She was proud, that's what she was. But she would naturally be expected to share a bed—and her body—with the earl. And while her pride balked against the notion of submitting to anything he wanted, it also shied away from the notion of fleeing duty simply because it was distasteful.

In other words, she couldn't see herself going out the window on a bedsheet again.

If she married the earl, perhaps she could take refuge in . . . gratitude.

She had less than a fortnight to decide the rest of her life.

An icy mist pooled in her gut. Her hands were suddenly clammy.

Given how thorough a man he seemed to be, the earl had no doubt imagined what she looked like under her clothes, and included that in his calculus before he'd written that letter.

She ought to wonder what Athelboro looked like under *his* clothes.

She pressed her cold hands against her scorching cheeks and closed her eyes, like a child attempting to hide. But waiting for her there in the dark was the indelible image of Lorcan's abdomen as she'd peeled up his wet shirt.

Clearly there was no safety in the dark.

She was a pragmatist above all, was she not?

She forced her eyes open again, and willed her mind to practical matters. She drew in a long, shuddering breath, and brought her hands down to her thighs. But her fingers curled there, remembering the jump of Lorcan's cool skin against them.

AFTER ANOTHER FRENZIED (thanks to the German boys) yet satisfying dinner, Daphne returned to their suite rather than joining the gathering in the sitting room, which meant she'd miss the next installment of *The Ghost in the Scullery*. She regretted this. But it seemed the best way to forestall questions about her husband's whereabouts.

Because Lorcan hadn't yet reappeared.

Eventually she braided her hair and slipped into her night rail and climbed into bed.

She waited in vain for sleep. She felt oddly weighted and desolate, yet uncomfortably restless. The combination finally drove her out of bed.

She swathed herself in a coverlet and paced over to the blue settee, curled her legs up beneath her, and stared into the fire, contemplating her future. Fancying she could see the ghost of her stockings.

She didn't know why she should feel so haunted and bleak.

Or why, when the knob finally turned on the suite door at some time past ten o'clock, her heart should so painfully leap.

Lorcan entered quietly.

She watched as he hung his hat and coat on the little rack near the door.

He froze when he saw her on the settee.

After a moment he said, "Good evening, missus."

"Good evening, Lorcan."

"Were you . . . waiting up for me?" He sounded surprised.

And in truth, pleased.

If a little wary.

"I found I couldn't sleep. I thought pacing a bit might help, and I paced all the way over to the settee, and got no farther."

It wasn't quite an answer to his question.

He approached her slowly. Surely the fact that she was swathed in a coverlet and clad only in her night rail had not escaped his notice.

"I apologize for not returning much earlier. I intended to. Some travel challenges prevented it."

"You do not have to apologize to me," she

said, truthfully. "I suppose I'm glad you're not soaking wet."

There was a little beat of quiet.

"Are ye glad, now?" he said softly.

Her heart gave a little skip.

For a moment she thought he was poised to go to his room. He hovered indecisively before her.

"Daphne . . . close your eyes and hold out your hand."

"Oh, I think not. I have brothers, Lorcan. I know that trick."

After a moment he said, "I'm not your brother, lass."

Something about the way he said that started an interesting tingle at the back of her neck.

And suddenly, her breath came just a little shorter.

She settled her shoulders, and closed her eyes.

Then tentatively, with a little smile, she extended her hand.

She felt the heat of one of his hands move gently beneath as a sort of support before something with a pleasing heft dropped into her palm.

"Open them," he said.

She did, and beheld an orange.

She stared at it as if he'd just handed her the sun.

And from the place it sat on her palm a warmth stole through her limbs, fanned out into her entire being, and settled around her heart.

Her mouth dropped open. She could only stare, riveted, wholly flooded with happiness.

She looked up at him.

"Happy Birthday, Daphne," he said.

She'd lost the ability to speak.

"I am tempted to hand oranges to you over and over just to see that expression on your face again."

Her face was ablaze with heat. "How did you . . ."

"I swam to Cadiz, you see, which is why I was gone all day."

"I see."

"I've an old acquaintance who has an orangery."

She was mute. The only sort of acquaintance who might have an orangery within the confines of London would have to be a duke or an earl or some such. She could only imagine how they'd met.

"It must be my good influence, Lorcan. You couldn't adhere to that lie for more than two seconds. Still, you must have done some swimming to get to him."

"A bloke with a wee boat was selling rides across the bridge for a couple of pence. Then there was another boat ride, and a . . . well, let's call it a wade . . . of sorts. There really are no limits to what a man who regrets burnt stockings will do, Daphne. Now hold out your other hand."

"More?" she breathed.

"Are you complaining?"

She laughed, softly, wonderingly, and obediently held out her other hand. Her heart was, in fact, hammering with suspense.

Something cool and metallic was settled into it. Larger than a guinea, though she wouldn't have minded a bit if that were her present.

She peered down at a little brass instrument of some sort that resembled a compass.

"Do you have one?" he asked.

"I do now," she hedged.

On a little laugh, he said, "It's an astrolabe."

"For stars," he clarified. When she said nothing. She stared, momentarily absolutely mindless with happiness.

And then she gasped like a child with delight and goose bumps rained over her arms. She actually gave a little hop.

He laughed, delightedly.

"Put those stars to use for something other than wishes. For showing them you can harness them to steer to a location. And master your destiny. You can do all sorts of calculations if the mood takes you. After a fashion, the whole universe is right there in your palm, Daphne."

She was breathless.

"Lorcan . . . where did you . . . it's . . ."

"All this is just to say I could not find stockings."

"I'll hurl the rest of my stockings into the fire if you keep handing me gifts."

He laughed.

She felt a trifle raw and shy and positively aglow. She had little experience with just sitting and receiving. She felt she hadn't said enough to thank him. And yet he appeared to be basking in her happiness all the same.

"I haven't any gifts for you. I would offer to engage you in a knife fight because I know you'd enjoy it but you'd find me no challenge at all."

"I doubt that sincerely. I think the depths of your wiliness have yet to be fully explored, Lady Worth."

She laughed. "I don't know what to say. 'Thank you' feels inadequate."

"I'm honored, indeed. Usually you have many, many words," he teased. More gently he said, "It's your birthday. You must endure the celebration."

"Thank you for my presents. They are perfect."

He looked even more pleased than she felt, and she felt positively airborne.

Trailing the coverlets like a cape, she gently placed her astrolabe in pride of place on the mantel, then returned to sit on the settee.

He produced a knife from out of nowhere on his person, because of course he carried about a knife, then snapped open a clean white handkerchief like a tiny tablecloth over the little game table. "Shall I?"

She surrendered her orange to him, and she watched, fascinated, as he dragged the glinting point of the knife in a precise, careful pattern across its skin.

And then he slowly pulled it loose.

He handed the curly peel to her, ceremoniously. She held it to her nose and inhaled with her eyes closed.

She opened her eyes to find an interesting expression fleeing from his.

"May I?" he asked.

She handed the spirally peel over to him and he lifted it to his nose and breathed it in.

She watched, riveted, and quite touched, as his eyes closed. This, too, felt like another gift.

He placed the naked fruit on his handkerchief. "Would you like to . . ."

She separated it neatly into little segments, and he watched, silently. She handed one to him.

"Cheers, Daphne. To your health." He held out his segment so she could bump it with hers in a toast.

She put it up to her lips. And oh, the heaven of it. The snap of the taut outer skin between her teeth. The squirt of the juice. The squish of the pulp.

She opened her eyes to find him watching her. He seemed absolutely riveted.

Wordlessly, ceremoniously, they ate the whole thing. He honored her by going slowly, savoring it just the same way she'd savored it. As if he truly wanted to understand what she was experiencing. As if in so doing he'd accepted a gift from her, too.

Chapter Fourteen

⌒⌒⌒

*A*FTERWARDS THEY cleaned their fingers on his handkerchief.

"May I—again?" he asked. He gestured to the spiral of peel. She nodded.

He reached for the peel. The triumph Lorcan felt over the success of his gifts was nearly as unprecedented as the impulse to get them and the odd nerves he'd had about delivering them.

He'd talked Delacorte into selling him the astrolabe.

And while he was out tracking down an orange, he'd taken it upon himself to conduct another effort on her behalf. It was, in truth, more of an inquiry, delivered in a strategic ear, with a request to pass the message on through appropriate channels. Specifically the English Channel. Had she known about what he'd done, she might feel considerably less charitable toward him right now. Or perhaps not.

He didn't know yet whether he'd been successful in his endeavor. He might never know. But he'd been driven to try.

He held the peel to his nose again and inhaled deeply again. "It helps to have a great large beak with which to sniff," he told her. "Thank you."

He handed it back to her.

She accepted it, put it gently down again, and studied him curiously. "Lorcan . . . have you been laboring under the delusion that symmetry is equal to beauty?"

"Laboring under the delusion that symmetry is equal to beauty," he repeated slowly. "You do say the *filthiest* things, Miss Worth."

How she fought it. But it was a joy to watch her lose a battle with a smile. "What I *mean* is—"

"Oh, for heaven's sake, lass, I know what it means. I always know what you mean. I was just taking a moment to savor that sentence. Every word so precise and glittering and perfectly chosen, like a diamond. And probably capable of flaying lesser men to ribbons. I've come to quite like it."

Daphne gave a stunned little laugh.

"Mind you, it's an acquired taste. A bit like how blowfish—the Japanese call it fugu—are a delicacy but they can also kill you if you don't prepare it exactly perfectly."

"First I'm a diamond, now I'm a blowfish?"

"Only the properly cooked sort."

She gave a little shout of laughter, then covered her mouth with her hands, as if loath to wake the house. "And here I was so close to being charmed."

The firelight laid a burnished path along her hair, along her smooth throat. The tips of her thick eyelashes were gold, the rest chestnut.

He found her beautiful.

The realization arrived less like a bolt from the

blue and more like a feather he'd been watching drift to a landing for days now.

"Oh, you're charmed," he said quietly.

She went abruptly silent.

But she did not deny it.

He absently reached over and tugged the hem of her night rail over her bare toes, which were peeping out.

"Aye, Daphne, you see, I am not Hardy or Bolt. When a woman imagines a prince coming to their rescue, those are the kinds of faces they picture, aye? But I know full well the nature of my appeal to a woman, and it's this. Have you ever stood at the edge of a cliff and looked down at the ocean crashing and foaming against it, and some mad little inner voice urges you to jump in, just to be part of something bigger and wilder and more dangerous than you are? Some mad part of you wants to know what it's like to just . . . surrender."

She was watching him in something like a thrall.

"It's the appeal of a night by the docks, inky black and danger in every corner. It's the appeal of shinnying out of a window on knotted bed-sheets, even though you have no idea what might await you out there in the dark."

He realized his voice had dropped to a mes-merist's cadence.

She took this in. "Be that as it may . . ."

He smiled slowly at this.

". . . objectively you are not."

During the rather long wordless interval that

followed, neither one of them blinked, and neither one of them shifted their gaze.

"Are you flirting with me, Daphne Worth?"

"I'm correcting a misapprehension." She said it
gravely.

"I *see.*"

A strange, unmistakable thrill was banking in
him. In her way, with her honesty and precision,
she was as relentless as he was. He'd never realized how erotic it could be.

"Lorcan . . . who first told you that you were
ugly?"

And for a moment he pretended he hadn't
heard her.

His expression—a little smile, the relaxed
crinkle at the corners of his eyes—he was certain
none of it changed.

But his beat of hesitation surely revealed to her
that some inner mark had been hit.

She'd surprised him.

"What makes you think anyone told me I was
ugly?" he finally said. Pleasantly enough.

"The way you use the word . . . I'm reminded
it's after a fashion a sort of shield. It's a bit like . . .
oh, if someone throws a stick at you, you snatch it
up and say 'thank you for the weapon.'"

He was so stunned for a moment he couldn't
answer. It was not a question he'd ever before
been posed.

"Oh, I first heard it from me da. 'Git up, ye ugly
little git.' 'That ugly wee bastard will amount to
nothing.' 'Twas part of my name. Ugly Wee Lorcan. Till the day he died. Didna see myself in a

mirror until I was nine years old, and do you know . . . I learned something important that day. And it was that my father was wrong, for damned if I could see anything to complain about."

She smiled at that. "So you had an epiphany."

"Oh, certainly. If you say so."

Her left eyebrow lifted.

"You are dying to tell me what it means, Daphne, so tell me."

"It means a revelation, of sorts. An insight."

"And a pretty word it is, too. Feel better now?"

She mimed mopping her brow, and he smiled.

"And an epiphany indeed it was. For if me da was wrong about that, then what manner of other things might he be wrong about? From that day forward I questioned all authority. And when I was big enough, I resisted all authority. And then . . . I made damned sure I became all authority. And then . . . I made my own laws."

He paused, then huffed a short laugh.

"So I suppose you're right, Daphne: every time he said that word, he handed me a weapon."

She was quiet a moment.

"I should like to say . . ." she began carefully, "that I'm very sorry you were compelled to endure such unkindness. I imagine it was like being pelted with sharp little rocks all the time."

Lorcan had, in fact, been pelted with sharp little rocks before as a child, because he grew up among little heathens like himself, and it was just one of the many things they did both for fun and for defense.

But the analogy disarmed him. It was apt. But

he found himself hoping she'd said it because her imagination could not extend to worse violence. He wanted to shelter her naivete about such things in the way he'd never been able to protect the hopeful child he'd so briefly been.

And her eyes were haunted.

"Aye, but I warrant few of us get through life without needing to *endure* something, lass," he said gently. "Or lots of somethings. Endurance builds muscle, aye? Until your very soul is brawny." By way of illustration, he languidly curled his forearm.

Gratifyingly, her eyes fixed on the rising bulge of his bicep as if she were present for the birth of a mountain range.

"I'll wager there's naught I can't endure now." He shrugged.

She rested her cheek against her knees a moment and considered this. Then lifted her head.

"I have wondered . . ." She hesitated. Her voice lowered. "Is it muscle . . . or is it scar?"

She turned to him.

He went still. Suddenly he was wary.

"Both are useful," he said shortly. "After a fashion."

She flicked her eyes over his features. Then she gave a short nod—agreeing with him or merely taking in his words, he could not say—and turned back toward the fire. He felt, oddly, that she'd been seeking an answer to a question that had dogged her, and had not yet found the right person to ask.

He wondered if she was disappointed in his answer.

He was disconcerted to realize he found the notion of disappointing her distasteful.

Even cowardly.

It was a new way to feel about himself, and he didn't like it.

And yet. These exchanges of little intimacies formed a mesh from which it was difficult to escape. His entire life so far had been predicated on knowing the routes of escape. He did not see any advantage to letting Daphne Worth take a look at his fluffy insides, so to speak.

A log languidly tipped in the fire, succumbing to its fate: consumed in flames.

He gave a short, not entirely amused laugh. "You're not a restful woman, are you, Daphne?"

Her head whipped back toward him. Her eyes went wide and alarmed as if he'd caught her in the midst of picking his pocket.

She settled her shoulders resolutely.

"No," she admitted, on a frayed hush. She sounded resigned, almost sorrowful. Perhaps a little bemused. As if this was some cardinal truth, something which simply could not be helped.

But she didn't sound sorry.

And for some reason this both amused him and made him powerfully glad.

He leaned forward and suddenly, almost before he knew he was doing it, slowly drew a fingertip along the gleaming, clean line of her jaw. It was a reflex; it seemed necessary to touch the source of his confusion, his fascination, his restless irritation. The way he might attempt to puzzle out any mysterious found treasure.

She went abruptly still. As though her breath had ceased in her lungs.

But she didn't flinch away.

Her eyes remained fixed on him.

And as his fingertips slowly glided along her skin he felt a jolt in the vicinity of his heart. Like someone had kicked in a rusty door. He was assailed by a strange, sudden rush of emotion. He could not sort out whether it was anger or impatience or yearning; it felt like a blend of all of those. It was pure and brilliant and new to him.

He curved his hand, slid it back until his fingers threaded into her hair.

And because her breath was suddenly swift and warm against his palm, and because she ever so slightly tipped her head to better fit against the cradle of it, he kissed her.

What the bloody hell are you doing, you daft cove, St. Leger thought.

He truly didn't know. He knew how to kiss a woman senseless when their mutual goal was to be naked with her legs hooked over his shoulders within minutes.

He'd never kissed a woman in order to express something he did not know how to put into words.

Her lips felt like innocence and decadence. Crushable as petals, seductive as a feather bed. The contradiction did his head in. He felt at once like a common thief. As though this rare pleasure, like so many others before, was not meant for him.

And then her eyes fluttered closed. And at that sweet, primal signal of complicity, of desire, anticipation tensed his every muscle.

Hadn't his credo always been "take what you can get when you can get it"?

He eased her deeper into that kiss as if it were a bath of honey and cognac. Slow, slow. So she could pull away, if she chose. So he could come to his senses, if he chose.

So that it seemed like the most natural thing in the world when her lips softly parted beneath his. And when his tongue touched hers for the first time, that little sound she made, that helpless catch in her throat—he knew it was lust hitting her blood like a drug.

That sound went straight to his cock.

He kept the pace slow. Punishingly, maddeningly—for him—so. He could not ever before remember *luxuriating* in a kiss, of deliberately teasing his desire to a fine, stiletto point. His cock was soon painfully hard, and this seemed an exquisite torment. They both shifted, restlessly, on the settee, accommodating ramping need. Soon their breaths mingled in swift, rough gusts, as their lips touched, and slid, and nipped and met and parted, met again.

And when her head fell back into his hands and her fingers curled into his shirt he made a thorough, lascivious plunder of the hot, wet satin of her mouth.

She met him with devastating instinct.

Every stroke of their tongues danced him closer

to the very ends of his control. Until he found himself at the edge of what he sensed was a deep shocking seam of need.

That's when his survival instincts burned through the fog of lust. Something told him if they plummeted into that there would be no getting out.

He ended the kiss as he started it: gently.

Pulled his fingers free of the silky net of her hair.

Astounded to realize his hand was trembling a little. Such were the rough tides of his blood.

He sat all the way back against the settee.

And stared at her while the room spun in lazy circles.

He watched her shoulders rise and fall as she pulled in a long breath.

Which audibly shuddered as she released it.

Like water settling when the kettle is taken off the boil.

Oh, you felt me, lass. You felt me in your body the same as I felt you.

He drew in a breath against a fresh wave of lust.

Tentatively, she rested her fingers against her lips.

Her eyes were hazed and huge, and somber, and intent.

For a second or two, they adapted to this new world. One in which, improbably and inadvisably, the two of them now knew the taste of each other.

"It will perhaps come as no surprise to you that no one finds me a restful man," he said finally. His voice was a husk.

She didn't reply. But her mouth did curve a very little.

And she didn't turn away.

By now he knew she wasn't the sort to turn away from what undid her, even if she wanted the respite.

This was the thing he'd sensed in her from the beginning, he realized. That shone from her eyes. She fair pulsed with passion. So far, her life hadn't required any of it from her. Or perhaps life had stifled it.

He remained still so she could study him.

"Should I apologize?" He said this quietly.

Or perhaps it merely seemed quiet over the rushing of blood in his ears.

She seemed to consider this. Then she shook her head very slowly. He suspected the room was spinning for her, too.

"But I think I shall go to bed now. Good night, Lorcan."

"Good night, Daphne," he said politely.

He would have stood, but his cock was currently tenting his trousers.

She stood gracefully, and she moved past him toward her room, trailing the knitted coverlet like a queen in an ermine robe.

He fancied that her walk was a trifle less steady than usual.

DAPHNE CLOSED THE bedroom behind her.

She moved very slowly across the room, then gingerly, in stages, lowered herself to the bed as though she'd just been given a brand-new body and was still familiarizing herself with its ways of locomotion.

The kiss wasn't done with her.

Her blood was lava and champagne. She ached—throbbed—between her legs. Her nipples were so hard it felt as though she were smuggling pearls beneath her night rail, and the whole of her night rail was suddenly an erotic caress against her humming skin. Her stomach was unsettled. She was beset by a sense of incompletion. Her entire body felt now like a treasure map to seduction: *touch me here, and here, and here,* it was saying. *Glory awaits.*

What "glory" entailed . . . well, she remained in the dark about that.

The very thought of Lorcan touching all of those parts sent such a rush of blood to her head she nearly swayed.

Imagine that. All this time, her quiet disdain for the notion of swooning had really only been ignorance. She just hadn't been properly kissed before.

She had an even greater respect for the dangers impressed upon women now. One taste of this and a weaker woman might see ruin as a perfectly reasonable risk.

Henry had kissed her the day he'd proposed. Time and again over the years she had conjured the feeling of his lips against hers.

But his kiss had not made her feel . . . combustible. Or as though a dozen different dungeon doors hidden inside her had just been flung open.

She'd never once thought of Henry in terms of danger at all. And still he had destroyed her.

She could not, would not now imagine the Earl of Athelboro kissing her.

Lorcan might well be a former criminal from St. Giles. They were indeed different species. He was alarming and fierce both inside and outside of his clothes.

But that kiss had hardly been inevitable. She was not naturally coy. She'd had the option at any point to remove herself from the risk. She realized she had stayed awake tonight, deliberately waiting.

She'd simply wanted to be kissed by him.

And so seldom did she take what she wanted that she'd scarcely noticed that this was precisely what she'd been doing.

He had brought her an orange and an astrolabe. And he'd gently, absently, tucked her night rail over her bare toes.

Somehow this last thing seemed far more dangerous than the kiss.

THE FOLLOWING MORNING, almost without thinking, Daphne spooned a little sugar into Lorcan's cup and poured his coffee.

"Thank you," he said. He silently gestured with a little knife that apparently practically was one of his appendages, so easily was he able to access it, and she nodded, and he cut her scone into little pieces so she could see its fluffy insides.

His scone vanished apace while hers was carefully enjoyed. Perhaps more slowly than usual, because he'd come to the table with his sleeves rolled. She was riveted by the dark hairs curling at the wrists. The glint of copper in them.

She recalled his fingers sliding along her jaw, lacing through her hair. She had to force herself not to brush her own fingers against her cheek, to relive the sensation.

They'd each had an evening to more or less soberly reflect upon the advisability of kissing each other. The answer was, of course: not advisable at all.

And because she wanted to be brave, she met his eyes, to see what she might discover there.

His gaze kindled and his lips turned up just a little at the corners. His eyes flickered to her mouth, and lingered, and his pupils flared.

He didn't free her from his gaze until she dropped her eyes.

Heat moved into her cheeks.

And finally she stood and wandered to the window to gaze out at the ceaseless wall of rain.

She didn't turn when he came to stand behind her. He was very close, but was careful not to touch her at all.

He was in many ways a surprisingly subtle man. As not touching her was perhaps more powerfully seductive than seizing her in his arms.

"Are you concerned about your father?" he asked.

"I suppose I am. He expected me home two days ago. Doubtless he knows the roads are impassable. But I shouldn't want him to worry. He's there alone, with just two servants."

"Only two," Lorcan mourned. Not entirely unsympathetically. Gently teasing.

By now she knew this. She quirked the corner of her mouth. The way she thought about her father was in the process of uncomfortably, irrevocably transforming. But he was still her father.

"I need to try to go out into that weather again," he said. "A bit of legal business regarding getting paid for our last ship seized. It might be a long day."

"Perhaps you'll be careful about diving into any more bodies of water?"

She found that she meant it.

There was a little pause. "Would it be such a trial to remove my clothes again?"

He said it softly, conversationally. He sounded deadly serious.

She tried a laugh. It emerged somewhere between a wheeze and a sigh.

Her senses were engulfed by him. The heat of his body sank into her skin. She felt as though she echoed with longing, like struck crystal.

They stood like that in absolutely absorbed silence, their bodies silently communicating.

She heard him inhale. Slowly, at length. As if he were breathing her in.

As he went out the door, she knew it was not a question of if he kissed her again.

It was a question of when.

Chapter Fifteen

❧✦❧

"You've finished drinking and smoking and cursing and . . . the other mysterious things you do in the smoking room . . . for the evening?"

Daphne had never watched a doorknob turning with as much breathless anticipation as she had a moment ago.

She'd excused herself after dinner, quietly demurred regarding gathering in the sitting room, as the rules allowed a few times a week, and gone up to the suite just a few minutes ago.

And not more than ten minutes later Lorcan had appeared.

"A bit crowded in the smoking room, what with the size of Lord Vaughn's head.

"But I'll gladly endure his company if you'd like to be alone," he offered, after a moment.

"No," she said quickly. "That is, you don't have to leave."

He stood at the end of the room, restlessly shifting from foot to foot, watching her knitting needles flash in and out of the coverlet she was knitting.

"I could read to you," she offered. "Or you could hold my yarn while I knit."

This particular menu of entertainments made him snort, which made her laugh.

"I could draw a target on a piece of foolscap and practice knife throwing while you read to me," he countered.

"Is your knife arm growing rusty while we're cooped up, then?"

His smile started crooked, then spread and became a soft laugh. "It's just that I'm not a lazy man, Daphne. I'm not meant to be confined. I'm always after besting myself at . . . everything I do."

Well.

And those words throbbed with unmistakable meaning in the room.

"We can play Spillikins," she suggested shyly.

The suggestion took him almost comically aback.

And then he went very still.

She watched another inspiration dawn across his face, and one of his eyebrows crept upward. "Very well. Spillikins . . . but with stakes."

"Stakes?"

"Yes," he said as if this went without saying. "Indulge me in one of my favorite things, if you would: a good wager."

"I haven't any pennies to spare. My most valuable pair of stockings went up in smoke. You can't have my astrolabe back. I like it."

"A kiss if I win."

Her hands stilled on her yarn. She stared at her fingers as if she'd never seen them before.

What a talent he had for erasing all of her thoughts and replacing them with nothing but sensation.

She contemplated saying, "But what if that's what I want, too?" For the pleasure of watching his expression change.

She didn't know if it was what she wanted.

Or rather: she wanted to kiss him again. He likely knew it.

She *didn't* want consequences.

She could not have it both ways.

And then she understood his strategy: he wanted it. And very much.

This was his way of allowing her to choose it.

"Done," she said.

She had the pleasure of watching the most carnal of satisfactions darken his eyes.

"And when I win . . ." She gathered the nerve to say it. And inspiration was upon her. "I want your earring."

He went absolutely still, his face, for an instant went almost cold and speculative.

And then his expression evolved into one of rank respect.

That earring was worth hundreds of pounds. And it would change her life.

And for an instant Daphne was afraid that she had overshot her mark. That he might not want to kiss her several hundred pounds' worth.

"Well played," he finally conceded, quietly. "We'll make a sporting woman of you yet. I agree to your terms."

Her breath hitched.

"Though, of course, you can't win." He held his hand out flat over the floor. "Do you see this? No board was ever steadier. I can slice the gizzard of a pirate with the tip of my rapier in the dark of night on the deck of a ship listing in a storm. I can shoot the eye out of a mosquito at fifty paces."

"Impressive. No wonder the South Sea is populated by little mosquitos wearing eye patches."

His little shout of delighted laughter lit her clear through like a sunburst.

"Have you *seen* my embroidery, Lorcan? Absolutely flawless. I can patiently render the most tedious of inspirational phrases on any pillow as smoothly as the finest calligraphy. My mending? Every stitch exquisitely straight and tiny. My knitting? Tell me whether you can see any light through these rows."

She held up the beginnings of the coverlet she was knitting and he peered at it. "I see a hole big enough for a mosquito wearing an eyepatch to fit through."

"Lies," she said indignantly.

He laughed softly.

Surprisingly, she thoroughly enjoyed the mutual bragging. In his presence, unanticipated corners of her character seemed to be unfolding like a secret letter written long ago.

"And furthermore, I had the extraordinary nerve to leap from a crate into the dark right into the arms of a man I couldn't even clearly see."

"Seldom have I such a worthy opponent," humored the man who dove into the water to save a child and fought pirates, somberly.

He pulled the little table in front of the settee.

And sat down next to her.

"Let the slaughter begin."

She hesitated, but only because the moment she set her knitting aside the clock would start ticking on when her next kiss could very well occur.

Or when a fortune that could restore her choices and save her family would be hers.

The moment she did set it aside, her heart leaped, then began a sort of skittering, rabbit-kick rhythm.

He lifted the Spillikins from their tin.

"You see, Daphne," he began, as if continuing a conversation already in progress, "I think you have come to think of me as something like a large pet."

She stared at him, astonished. "What on—I most *definitely* do not think of you as a pet."

"Hairy, a little unpredictable, occasionally barks but mostly manageable."

"Ah. I see your point."

"This is all just to remind you that I am absolutely ruthless. And I know that rules make you feel safe. To you, they're like the rungs in a ladder, aye? Or like a net below you that will catch you. Whereas I look at the rules, and like a mosquito wearing an eye patch, I see how I can maneuver through them."

"Mmm. Are you going to natter and bluff your way through this, or are we going to play?"

"In a hurry to be kissed, are you?"

She clapped her mouth closed.

"Do you want to do the honors?" he asked.

She gathered the sticks into her fist and let them fall with a satisfying clatter.

She stared at the complicated little heap.

She hadn't been lying: she had a precise and critical eye, honed from years of poking thread through needles and finding the flaw or the missing penny in a household budget or the dust in a corner.

With exquisite care she chose and withdrew a stick. Not a single other stick so much as moved a hair.

She showed her prize to him, eyebrows arched, and gently laid it down.

He immediately ducked his head and squinted, making a rather entertaining show of examining the pile.

"Do you know why I love these kinds of searches, Daphne?" His voice was abstracted, almost a murmur, so apparently seriously did he take his stick inspection. ". . . it's because that feeling when you find just the right stick . . . the one you can slide with ease from the pile without disturbing any of the others . . ." His hand reached, hovered, then retracted, as he shook his head, changing his mind. ". . . it's a bit like discovering those secret places on a woman's body. The ones that will . . . no, not that one, either . . ." He rejected another stick. ". . . the ones that will make her sob and cry out with pleasure."

Daphne went rigid.

Her mouth dropped open.

She closed it quickly.

He wasn't looking at her. He tipped his head to inspect the pile from another angle. "I like to start by trailing my fingers along the curve of her calf . . ." and suddenly his was a mesmerist's voice as he tipped his head to investigate yet another angle ". . . just my fingertips, you see, like feathers, lightly, so softly, drawn over her skin . . ."

His voice trailed like feathers over her senses.

All the tiny hairs on the back of her neck went erect.

Followed by her nipples.

". . . until I reach the hollow behind her knee. And then I linger there with my lips, and my tongue and my fingers . . . oops, not that one . . ." He retracted his outstretched hand from a choice.

He hadn't so much as glanced up at her through this entire little soliloquy.

Daphne realized her lips had dropped open a little. She was now breathing in swift little gusts.

"And then with my lips I continue on their leisurely way . . . up . . . and up and up . . . until I reach that tender place inside her thigh. And *oh*, that place, it's like satin, so sweet, so hidden, so secret . . ." he paused and squinted at the stack ". . . and by the time my tongue and my lips and my fingers have reached that destination her quim is so wet . . . and so hot . . . that I can just slide my finger right into—ah, here's the one."

And as he slowly, triumphantly, flawlessly withdrew his chosen stick, Daphne all but went up in flames.

Heat engulfed her, head to ankle. And from her ankle to her . . . her . . . word that began with "Q" . . . a trail of skin tingled as surely as though she'd been sprinkled with cinders.

She had never considered her leg as a sort of sensual road leading to one particular destination.

Of course, that only implied her entire body was a sensual road.

With *words* only he'd done this.

Imagine what actual fingers . . . and lips . . . and tongues would do.

She stared at Lorcan, dumbstruck. Absolutely livid.

Shockingly aroused.

Thoroughly impressed.

He stared back.

"Your turn," he reminded her politely.

He wasn't blinking.

All of her blood seemed pooled between her legs. Which meant there was none left available to her brain with which to formulate thoughts, let alone words, let alone to surgically choose a stick from an increasingly precarious Spillikins pile.

He gazed back at her sympathetically. "Perhaps it will help if you remember how precisely you knit."

Which made her imagine driving a sharpened Spillikins javelin-style right through his forehead.

She ducked her head. She blindly regarded the Spillikins.

Inhaling deeply, in the hopes it would clear her head like a good breeze clears cobwebs, she reached for the stick.

The blood simmering in her veins made her hand visibly tremble. It was all but useless.

Short of taking a moment to put her head out the window, there wasn't much she could do about it. She reached for a stick. Closed two fingers over it. And as she lifted it brushed the one next to it and suddenly all was chaos.

They stared at the little collapsed pile.

"Oh, what a pity," he said kindly.

She was torn like a wishbone between regret that the word "bastard" had sprung to mind so swiftly, since surely this was emblematic of her plummet into iniquity, and a new appreciation of its power.

"Hallelujah" was another word that came to mind, and it was equally troubling, given the circumstances.

Surely, he could see her heart pounding in her throat.

It wasn't fair. But she of course couldn't say that aloud. She would sound like a petulant child. She was naive, and she hadn't anything equivalent in her arsenal with which to combat him, and he likely knew it.

Just as he'd somehow known precisely how she would respond.

Well, he'd warned her.

"Two out of three." Her voice was an embarrassing near croak.

They stared at each other across the table.

Firelight had turned his skin to copper, and his eyes to gold.

He appeared to be considering this.

"If the price is too high, I'll release you from the bargain, Daphne. And I shall not bear a grudge."

His voice was calm and nearly uninflected. The voice of a man who had gambled and won countless times. A tone that could mask a million emotions.

She could see herself reflected in his pupils. She could read nothing of his thoughts. But there was something watchful, perhaps even braced, about him. As if so very much hinged on her answer.

And exultation slowly bloomed in her. He *powerfully* wanted to kiss her again.

All of this was a way to arrange it so that she could if she wanted to.

She could blame a wager and a sense of honor for kissing him, rather than her own clearly lustful, newly discovered animal nature.

"It's not too high," she almost whispered. "It's a fair wager."

His pupils flared hot and black.

There was an outrageous answering throb between her legs.

She did not think she'd ever before factored into a man's appetites.

She'd never dreamed *she* possessed appetites.

Both of these things were like discovering powers she did not fully understand and was uncertain yet how to control, like fire-breathing, or flight.

She had never wanted and feared something in such desperate and equal measure, something that was reckless and mad, purely hedonistic.

If she kissed him once, she could call it an experience.

Twice and she suspected there would be no return to the person she was supposed to be. Twice and she was a person who wanted to kiss rogues.

There he sat, clearly brimming like a pirate's treasure chest with sensual knowledge.

"I very much want the earring." This was also true.

He studied her for a long, silent moment with his formidable brows drawn together.

"Very well." He paused. "I'll agree to your change of the rules. But the forfeit is now two kisses."

A tiny indignant sound escaped her.

"You will be offered a choice of locations for the second kiss, neither of which will be the lips."

Now she was shocked silent.

"Those are my terms. You can pay now. Or you can pay twice in a few minutes, when I win again."

His expression was implacable.

She knew she could refuse. It would be easy enough to open her mouth, form the words, "No, thank you." Part of her wanted to do it to watch how his expression changed, if it would.

Panic and lust and good sense warred in her.

Panic that she would never again have this opportunity.

"Do you want to do the honors?" she said. Her voice was a thread.

Wholly masculine satisfaction blazed fleetingly in his eyes before he re-donned his game face.

He seized the sticks in his fist and let them haphazardly clatter to the table.

"Why don't you draw first, Daphne? Just to get a head start on your losing."

She tried for some of his composure by fixing him with a steady look of absolute indifference.

Then pulled in a long, steadying breath.

Her palms were damp.

She eyed the stack of sticks, identified three likely, easy prospects, and then, despite the fact that her hand wasn't yet entirely steady, delicately freed one of them from the stack.

She held it aloft like Joan of Arc with a torch. Then laid it down in front of her.

Unperturbed, Lorcan assumed his peering position. He scanned the pile and took up his mesmerist's tone. "Now, Lady Worth, you might want to . . . take this opportunity to begin thinking about where you'd like me to ki—what are you doing?"

The change in tone was almost comical. Swift, sharp, wary. His head jerked up.

"It's a bit warm in here. I thought I'd loosen my laces a little."

And she'd done exactly that. It was the most wanton thing she'd ever done in her life, that one little deft reach behind her back. The tug.

He narrowed his eyes speculatively.

"Carry on," he said silkily, finally. Calling her bluff.

He resumed his search.

She ever-so-slightly tugged her bodice. He flicked his eyes up and he briefly froze to see what might happen next.

She didn't think her nerve extended to anything beyond what she'd already done.

". . . and forgive me if this is information you already possess, Lady Worth, but when a woman is . . ." He adroitly tweezed his stick flawlessly up and laid it on the table before him ". . . ah, your turn . . ."

Daphne surreptitiously pulled in a few, long shuddering breaths.

She was startled when the exhale made her bodice list a little. Not for the first time did she feel as though she were an aghast onlooker on her life. What on earth was she doing?

She fanned and wriggled her tense fingers as if she were about to attack a particularly aggressive Beethoven passage, then let them hover over the pile for a time. As if her hand was a creature that could sniff out just the right stick.

". . . as I was saying," Lorcan continued idly, into the prolonged silence ". . . when a woman is aroused, her nipples go erect . . ."

Every part of her seized. Her lungs, her heart. Her muscles. Her hand froze midair.

". . . in fact, sometimes you can even see them through the fabric of her gown."

How had her life led to sitting across from an . . . *incorrigible*—she was suddenly furious she'd never learned more pungent adjectives—man who possessed no pedigree whatsoever, who was the filthiest, cleverest of all competitors.

This must be how her stocking felt after having been dropped into the fire.

She longed for the protective camouflage of experience or indifference. Surely the jaded did not turn magenta. She was certain she had, judging by her temperature.

She craved this indifference nearly as much as she craved another kiss.

The tension was well-nigh unendurable.

Her hand, still hovering over the pile of sticks, began to tremble.

His voice lowered to a confiding murmur. "This

is all just to say that I can see your nipples through the fabric of your gown, Daphne."

A tsunami of arousal and horror roared through her, obliterating thought.

The universe narrowed to her nipples.

The brush of her gown over them caused her to bite the inside of her lip.

Now. Now was when he would move in for the kill, surely.

But he said nothing else.

He'd gone, in fact, quiet. Perhaps, at last, taking pity. Perhaps he did possess a conscience. And this, too, embarrassed her: perhaps he'd come to realize he could only push a spinster so far before she combusted before his eyes.

Perhaps he'd exhausted inspiration.

She risked a glance at him; his face was inscrutable. But his eyes were soft.

She took advantage of this apparent moment of weakness to commit to closing two fingers over a stick. With the delicacy of a surgeon splinting a dragonfly's wing, she commenced freeing it.

"I think when nipples go erect . . ." Lorcan mused, like Descartes pondering his famous theorem.

She stopped breathing.

". . . they're like arrows directing a man to where he ought to apply his tongue."

Her body jerked as if he'd done exactly that.

And the stack of Spillikins avalanched.

Daphne stared at it, cleaved into equal parts horror and exaltation.

In absolute silence they regarded the aftermath.

Through the roaring that had started up in her ears, two wicked, remorseless words emerged, in his low, silky, thoroughly satisfied voice: "Oh, dear."

Chapter Sixteen

◦◦◦◦

SHE LEVERED her head up to stare at Lorcan.

Whose eyelids were lowered like a wolf contemplating a meal.

She said nothing.

With leisurely, casual grace, he swept the sticks into his hand, stacked them, and installed them in their tin.

With equally unhurried efficiency, he lifted and slid the little game table aside so that the two of them could easily lunge at each other.

He did all of this as though he had all the time in the world.

While she waited, suspended in silent torment and unbearable excitement.

But then when he turned to her, she understood he was merely heightening anticipation.

Perhaps, improbably, he was nervous, too.

He turned to her.

The swift drum of her heart was nearly painful.

Finally his hand reached out, and he collected a strand of hair spiraling from her temple with his fingertip.

He gently smoothed it behind her ear.

He leaned forward very, very slowly, until his

lips were against her ear. "Tell me you're sorry you lost," he whispered.

Wicked, wicked man.

She nearly laughed at his audacity.

But when the heat of his arms stole about her waist her eyes drifted closed. At last his mouth softly landed against hers; her sigh of relief was unashamed.

And with a sensual precision he undid her, as surely as the point of his knife had spiraled the peel from her orange.

His lips were at first so gentle, so shockingly, lingeringly tender, a low keen of raw yearning hummed from somewhere within her. It shocked her. His hand softly slid up from her waist to cradle her head. She curled her fingers into his shirt and clung for dear life as little by little the kiss became deeper, more demanding, more searchingly, teasingly carnal. The sweet, dark taste of him made her wild, then wilder still. She met him with equal hunger. She pulsed with a restless, frantic need. Her hands slid up, latched around his neck.

"Lorcan." Her voice was desperate and shredded.

His arms tightened around her. She took his ragged groan of desire in her mouth; she could feel it vibrate in his chest. She could no longer feel the confines of her body; she was composed only of the places he touched her, and the places she longed to be touched.

She crashed to earth when he ended the kiss abruptly, with a low muttered oath.

And for a moment he rested his forehead against hers. His breath came in ragged gusts.

Still, he held her. As if he'd just been washed up on shore after being bashed about in the waves.

To stir such a man as this.

The way his back heaved with his breath made her feel powerful. And exhilarated. And frightened, indeed. He could lay her flat on the settee right now, and have his way with her. If he were that sort of man, there would be nothing she could do to stop him.

But what he chose to do instead was to hold her as if she were something he'd rescued at great peril to himself.

Finally he lifted his arms away from her.

She uncurled her fingers from his shirt.

She opened her eyes.

To find his eyes were hazed.

It was a moment before either could speak.

"Thank you," he said quietly. "Now you have a choice to make. Will your next kiss be in the shadow of your cleavage, where your lovely breasts meet?"

His eyes fell to the swell of her breasts and lingered. She felt that gaze as surely as if he'd dragged a finger across them.

He returned his eyes to her face.

"Or high on the tenderest inside of your thigh, as I earlier described."

Shock was like a lightning strike in her mind. She went briefly faint from it.

But the moment he'd said it she knew this was what she wanted.

She wanted to flirt with danger, with vulnerability. She wanted to test the limits of her own control and his.

She hadn't known this madness lived in her.

But when would she ever again have this kind of opportunity?

"The second," she whispered.

Primal satisfaction surged in his expression. His eyes were very dark indeed.

"Very well. If you would be so kind as to lift your skirts, Daphne."

He said it quietly. His tone suggested he'd just asked her to pass the salt. And somehow this made it more illicitly thrilling.

Blood rushed to her head and pooled between her legs.

She hesitated, to tease him. To tease herself.

Their gazes locked. The two of them were balanced, breathlessly, on the knife edge of anticipation.

But they both knew she would do as he asked.

Her hands shaking, she gathered her dress in her fists, and furled it slowly upward.

Until the air of the room rushed over her exposed skin.

Until her skirt lay ruched across her lap.

He watched the entire process unabashedly. His face taut, his eyes dark.

"Now spread your legs for me, Lady Worth."

Every step of the way he ensured she understood her complicity. Every step of the way he made sure she was choosing this.

No longer did a voice in her head suggest to her she could stop at any time.

She could not listen to lies.

This was who she was.

This was what she wanted.

And so she did, like the veriest wanton. Slowly, she opened her legs until she could feel the air of the room caressing her thighs.

When he knelt between her knees, she closed her eyes.

Her breath rushed between her parted lips.

She nearly jumped at the first featherlight touch of his fingertips on her ankle.

He traced with the pad of his finger, a slow, complicated, feathering little shape over it. And from everywhere his fingertip touched, silvery, shivering sensations fanned in tributaries, tiny trails of flame, that reached every point in her body. She shifted to accommodate the simmer in her blood as all roads, as he seemed to promise, led to right between her legs, where she ached.

His single fingertip became a squadron of fingertips, and together they glided up the curve of her calf to the hollow behind her knee. And there his lips and tongue joined the siege.

She sighed, and pressed her hands against the seat of the settee.

And then, to her desperate rejoicing and uneasiness, his lips were on the silky inside of her thigh.

He took his time.

Delicate brushes of his lips, following by delicate brushes of his fingertips, evolved into hot, lingering, openmouthed caresses, and she was on fire with want.

"God," he whispered.

His lips, his tongue, his fingertips against skin

she'd never dreamed harbored such secrets. Or yielded such extraordinary sensation.

Her breath was like bellows now. She stirred, fingers gripping the edge of the settee.

"Christ. I can feel the heat of you," he murmured. He sounded drugged.

He sounded tormented.

When he exhaled a long, soft, hot breath over her damp curls between her legs, her head fell back on a muffled sob of surprised pleasure at the pulse of sensation.

More. It wasn't enough. She needed more. She could sense the bliss that lay in store for her.

But he stopped.

And just like that, he was no longer touching her.

Hideously bereft, she covered her face in her hands. Her shoulders heaved with her breathing.

She was stunned. Overwhelmed. Abashed suddenly, and angrily wanting, though she knew not what specifically she wanted.

She'd had no notion that such gradations of pleasure hid in her own body. That such secrets of sensation could be unleashed.

Some of her fury was over the realization that it was possible she might never have known.

Some of her fury was over the realization that she now knew, but could never dare discover more.

For that way lay absolute ruin.

She was furious that she'd brought it on herself.

"I am sorry to leave you like this." Lorcan's voice was graveled, somber with real regret. His words halting. "Our wager was only for a kiss. As much as I want to . . ." He took a breath. "I shall not transgress. The rest of what you now want involves . . . a good deal more. Perhaps you would like to consider the wisdom of whether you want more . . . when again you can think."

She felt a surge of irrational hatred for him and his sense of honor.

For what he knew how to give her, and what he knew she was feeling, and was not offering now.

For how right he was to stop.

For what should never be.

That she should be in thrall to this madness to the point where she was willing to be taken.

That he should have such control that he could refuse it.

When he stood, she was nearly eye level with the erection straining against the fall of his trousers.

She stared up at him. One hand still pressed against her hot face. Her skirts still hiked to her waist.

He regarded her a moment, his face enigmatic. His eyes were dark with emotion that looked a lot like anger, and a little like wonder. Tension pulled his features taut.

He gently lifted her hand from her face, and placed a chaste kiss in her palm. And then he loosely grasped her wrist and guided her hand to that throbbing place between her legs. There he released it.

"Touch yourself, luv," he urged on a whisper, like the devil himself, with maddening sympathy. "That's what I'm off to do, before I go stark. Raving. Mad."

Seconds later his bedroom door emphatically shut.

ANY OTHER WOMAN.

Any other woman would be on her back now, digging her nails into his shoulders and moaning his name with pleasure while he pounded her into his mattress. In the same circumstances, he could have, would have, taken any other woman.

Any other woman.

It was a plea to a deity he wasn't convinced had ever taken much of an interest in him: *Let me want any other woman. Not this one. Not with a fever I've never before felt. Not with a hunger that makes me feel both savage and almost uncertain as a boy, and panicked, as if I've been abandoned on a ship I do not know how to sail.*

He didn't want any other woman.

And in this moment, after he'd taken care of his aching cock with the help of his old friend, his right hand, he could not remember ever before wanting any other woman, and he could not imagine ever again wanting any other woman. Which was probably pure melodrama. It was just that he'd gone and trapped himself in this sensual net through the measured, calculated, teasing out of pleasure. Through a wicked little triangle comprised of her innocence and his jadedness and Spillikins, of all bloody things. In the excitement of revealing to her the depth of her own sensual nature. And through constant proximity in the sensual den their suite had become.

Because he could not and would not ravish a

virgin. Especially one who had almost nothing else but her virtue to bring to the marriage she was obviously destined for.

Especially one who trusted him.

What a gift it was, her trust.

His chest ached.

He laid an arm over his eyes, but even if he closed them, he saw her face as he'd left her, flushed and yearning, confused and angry.

He had taken selfish pleasure in bringing her gifts: an orange, an astrolabe, the secrets of her body.

The greatest gift he could give her now was to never touch her again.

Chapter Seventeen

❧

Two days of torrential rains later ...

"WHO DO you suppose we'd eat first if we were trapped in here and ran out of food?"

Delacorte said this suddenly in the sitting room.

He'd been reading the part of Mr. Miles Redmond's book which recounted the time he'd almost been eaten by a cannibal.

Angelique and Delilah exchanged a swift glance. More than once they'd discovered there was a razor-fine line between spirited discourse and havoc. It was the thrilling risk they took every night they gathered. Sometimes everyone took turns rhapsodizing about the best apple tart they'd ever eaten. Sometimes, apparently, cannibalism was on the docket.

Occasionally the discourse grew so spirited, so merry or heated, it led to a penny or two clinking into the Epithet Jar, and to this they found they could not object overmuch, since it paid for the morning papers. It was hard to say which direction tonight would go.

"Here now, let me help you dear," Mrs. Pariseau murmured to Dot, who had inadvertently sewn part of her sleeve to her embroidery. Not for the first time.

All the ladies held hoops tonight, and were clustered industriously in the corner.

"We should eat Delacorte," Mr. McDonald declared suddenly, under his breath.

"I am mostly gristle, my friend," Mr. Delacorte said placidly. "Good luck with that." He was sitting across from St. John, who was taking a very long time to decide which move to make next in chess.

"Mar isbean greasy," Mr. McDonald muttered pointedly in what sounded like Gaelic.

Delacorte narrowed his eyes. He didn't know what he meant, and even if it sounded beautiful, it also sounded like an insult.

"We're not going to run out of food," Delilah assured everyone hurriedly, noting that the German boys' heads had whipped toward them with hunted eyes. "We are very, very prepared to feed everybody for quite a long time."

"Even if it's mice on toast," Lucien added, wickedly.

"I hear heirs to earls are tender as a result of standing about and doing nothing, like veal," Lorcan said idly. He'd taken a chair and a brandy and was merely enjoying the ambiance of the room. The soft light. The pretty women. The bonhomie with a bite (that was Captain Hardy).

St. John looked at him balefully. Then he looked back at his fingertips in sullen resentment. It seemed he was developing calluses from practicing the cello, which half appalled, half fascinated him.

"None of you will want to eat me," he said bitterly. "I'll be chewy and leathery by the time this week is out."

Otto rolled his eyes.

"Perhaps it's a philosophical question," Mrs. Pariseau said. "Would we eat people in order of value to the group, or in order of stature?"

"You better stop her, now," Captain Hardy murmured to his wife. "Before there's bloodshed."

Delilah stifled a laugh. "I think I might want to hear some of the answers," she whispered.

"Well, you don't want to eat any of the ladies, because we'll keep everyone's flagging spirits up with inspiring embroidered pillows," Daphne said. She held up her project, which would eventually read "Bless this Home" but currently said only "BLE."

She blushed delightedly when everyone laughed.

Such had the lines of reality blurred that Lorcan felt a genuine glow of pride at how everyone seemed to enjoy her. And a delight in her obvious delight.

As if she was truly his.

"It's going to be pretty," he said, encouragingly.

She smiled across at him, and his heart contracted in an odd way, half pleasure, half pain.

For two days, they sat across from each other for coffee and a scone in the morning.

For two days she had spooned sugar into his cup and poured, and he had cut her scone into pieces.

They were kind to each other, and even amusing.

And though every bit of his body remained exquisitely, nearly torturously attuned to every bit of hers—the way her hands moved, the light on her hair, the curve of her lips, the sway of her hips when she walked—they had not touched each other again.

They were intelligent people who understood self-preservation, and this was how they were going about preserving themselves. So be it.

But he had spent an afternoon teaching her how to use her astrolabe, and he could truthfully say those few hours were among the best in his life so far, for reasons he could not quite articulate. It was peaceful and easy and amusing and nourishing. The way her eyes lit with comprehension. The way she laughed. The speed with which she learned. The pleasure he took in imparting knowledge had been a surprise, but it had a good deal to do with how much she wanted to know and the fact that he could give it to her.

Mostly it was a good afternoon because he was there and she was there and they were together and this realization had subtly, somberly haunted him since then.

"We'll need the strong men to tear the furniture apart for firewood for, er, cooking," Captain Hardy mused delicately from his chair.

"But big, strong men will *eat* the most," Mrs. Pariseau wisely noted. "We can keep a lot of ladies alive for weeks on the amount of food our musician friends here eat in a day."

The boys merely beamed with pride at this.

"A fellow at White's by name of Havelstock told me his wife eats the equivalent of three men now that she's with child," St. John volunteered.

Daphne went so abruptly, rigidly still that Lorcan felt it like a blow.

And then color and light fled from her face so abruptly it was like watching an eclipse. Something had blotted her out, just like that.

Her eyes were blankly stunned. Her graceful hands paused on her embroidery.

He stared, ice gathering in his gut, as she remained fixed in that position for several of his own heartbeats.

Then she glanced up at the ladies and produced a little smile. She cleared her throat. "If you would all please excuse me for a moment. I just need to fetch my . . ." She gestured vaguely with her embroidery and stood.

He thought he detected the faintest strain in her voice.

They nodded and murmured and smiled and she set aside her embroidery and hurried out of the room.

She didn't glance back at him. It was as though she'd forgotten he existed.

He was motionless. Suddenly no other sound in the world was audible but her footsteps crossing the foyer.

He listened until he could no longer hear them.

The room came into focus again. Rustles, murmurs, the slide of chess pieces across a board.

He pondered what to do.

Perhaps she did indeed need more embroidery silks, or a different needle, or her shawl. Maybe she just needed a chamber pot.

But he was familiar now with the way color

moved in and out of her face. And how she looked when visited by emotion she struggled not to show.

His gut remained icy with portent. He strongly suspected it had to do with the name Lord Vaughn had just uttered and the quiet turmoil he felt over this suspicion shocked him.

"I'll just go and see what she needs, shall I?" he said pleasantly to whoever might hear. He waited for no reply. He left them.

"So devoted," Mrs. Pariseau muttered approvingly, and all the ladies murmured in agreement.

DAPHNE WAS SITTING on the settee staring fixedly at the fire when the doorknob turned, and Lorcan quietly entered.

She scarcely looked up.

For a long moment he didn't speak at all.

"Daphne . . ." He sounded almost gentle. "Do you feel ill?"

She shook her head slowly, as if it hurt. A leisurely to and fro. It wasn't quite the truth, and it wasn't quite a lie.

She didn't look up at him, but she could sense that he was frowning slightly at her. It was never going to be comfortable to be frowned at by Lorcan St. Leger.

The silence stretched.

"Who is Havelstock?" he finally said.

She turned her head slowly, in absolute amazement. "He's an earl," she said, with a hint of dry amusement.

He took this in.

"Who is Havelstock to you?"

She gave a short laugh. "Ah, Lorcan. You never do take the long way round with a question, do you?"

"I do not know enough words to clutter up my sentences with them. If I did, perhaps I would. But I do know your face went as white as an Irishman's arse when Lord I-Love-Myself said the word 'Havelstock.'"

She tried not to laugh, but he'd gone and punctured the dark tragedy of her mood, and some of it seeped out.

She sighed instead. "You couldn't have said 'white as a ghost'?"

"Trust me, an Irishman's arse is the whiter of the two."

"Lord Vaughn isn't so bad," she said shortly. "I've met worse."

"I haven't," he lied.

She cast a dry look up at him.

He seemed restless and distracted. He was standing perfectly still, poised and alert.

And she realized, with a little jolt of pure pleasure, that he was genuinely concerned. He had come for her because he couldn't help himself.

She wanted to sit for a moment in the sweetness of this realization.

"Am I right in that something about Havelstock upset you? Or did the eel stew take you the wrong way?"

It felt as though she needed to pull the words up from the bottom of a dark mine, where they were mired in memory. But she managed.

"Lord Havelstock and I were once engaged to be married."

She had dreaded the need to say those words aloud for years. But it seemed safe to do it now. As though when Lorcan was in the room, nearly anything became safe.

Lorcan was motionless and silent. He seemed to be taking this in.

Perhaps comparing it to the things he thought he knew about her. She wondered if all this time he'd thought she was the veriest spinster.

"And you may have noticed that I am not married to him," she added. Dryly.

"How did the . . . not being married to him come about? That was my sorry attempt at being something other than blunt."

"He fell in love with someone else."

Again he went quiet.

She realized there was something thrilling about watching his face when he was merely thinking. She pictured his mind as a blade, parsing things.

"Was she a governess?" was what he came out with.

"How . . ." Her word was nearly arid from shock.

"When we arrived, when Mrs. Durand said the word 'governess.' And you looked as though someone had flicked something hot into your eyes."

She sat for a moment in silence. "I think it's a very good thing we've never played five-card loo."

Their eyes met and in his there fleetingly glinted a thousand little jokes about games and wagers and the price thereof, spicy little innuendos, considered and rejected as not appropriate for the moment.

How astonishing that she'd only realized this because she'd thought of a few of her own.

"She is a very beautiful girl. The governess," she added.

"What a shocking plot twist."

She was surprised into smiling again.

He was still standing before her, motionless but somehow radiating a sort of restlessness. She realized he was once again charged with a need to see her right. It could not be done in this instance. The damage had been inflicted many years ago. The ramifications might very well be permanent.

"If you do not want me to ask questions . . ." he said.

"No. I don't mind. I'll tell you. But I don't want to bore you."

"I can truthfully say you have yet to bore me. You are full of surprises, Lady Worth."

She quirked her mouth. How extraordinary that this was a thing he valued.

She patted the settee near her.

He settled slowly, sat at a proper distance, as if they'd a chaperone, and had never groaned helpless pleasure into each other's mouths.

"Henry—Lord Havelstock—courted me in the usual way. We had so much in common. And I felt we had such an accord." She shot a wry sidelong glance at the man with whom she'd had anything but when they'd first met. "It seemed we could speak to each other of anything. It was the first time I felt someone truly knew me. I fell in love. I was twenty when he proposed, and it was like . . ."

She didn't want to remember that happiness, because now it seemed evidence of her foolishness and naivete. "Walking on air."

She didn't look at Lorcan.

He said nothing. Perhaps the cliché had horrified him mute.

"My family was ecstatic," she added.

"He's rich. Havelstock," Lorcan said finally. In a rather neutral tone.

It wasn't a question. It was a conclusion he'd drawn.

She nodded. "And so . . . well, Henry . . . had a much younger brother. And a short time after we were engaged, about three months, they hired a new governess for him. I remember him mentioning her in passing one day."

Lorcan took this in with a fixed gaze and single, cynical uplifted brow.

"There came the day, a month or so after he'd mentioned this . . . he took me for a walk. The walk we'd often taken in the woods near our home, for there's a little path that meanders down to a sort of pond—oh, this doesn't matter. And that's where he told me he was in love with her. He was perfectly gracious, he was absolutely himself in every way—he'd always been kind and direct—when he told me about her, which actually made it more horrible. I kept thinking it must be a terrible dream. He said he was tormented and ashamed. He wept. He was wretched. I have never been so confused, you see, because my impulse when someone I love is in torment is to do anything at all to make it better for them. And the only thing I could do to make it better for him was to be . . . to be somebody else."

She was trembling now as if she'd just, at long last, regurgitated poison.

Lorcan silently reached for the coverlet folded on the settee and wrapped it gently about her shoulders, cocooning her as she'd wrapped him after he'd rescued the child.

The coverlet smelled like him. She could not say why this was so soothing, when the man before her was a walking disturbance.

"He told me he hadn't slept a night through in months. But he said because he knew me so well, and esteemed me so greatly, that he decided he *must* tell me. Because he knew I would not want to marry a man who could not . . ." She paused. She gulped in a breath. ". . . love me as I deserved to be loved."

She glanced over to see that Lorcan had gone white about the mouth.

"The worst part was—Henry was also absolutely glowing. Despite the weeping. He could not keep his face from glowing when he said her name. Because he was so very in love. And I could full well imagine how miserable he was to hurt me, because we were such dear friends, and we always told each other our happy news and he could not tell me about her and . . . Lorcan . . . are you quite all right?"

His face was fully pale now, and his skin was stretched taut over his features, and his eyes were flat and hard.

He looked . . . murderous.

It was the expression, Daphne thought, her attacker must have seen when he'd dangled from Lorcan's fist.

"Go on," was all he said. In a tone so pleasant it ironically made her uneasy.

"Some people in town were kind, but the pity . . ." She shivered. "I could not abide the pity. I had a few very close friends, but they were engaged, and it was as though they didn't want my disaster to taint their happiness."

"A pox upon the pitiers of the world."

She smiled faintly at his inimitable brand of solidarity. How bolstering his unequivocal approach to the world.

"And the shame of it. It was such delicious gossip, you see, when he went off and married her. Of course, everyone outwardly agreed it was a scandal, but so many saw him as such a romantic figure. Defying his father's wishes for true love, and so forth. I went from being admired and emulated to 'poor Daphne' overnight. No one knew what to say to me, even people I thought were my friends."

His mouth was a thin line now.

"Lorcan . . . In my wildest dreams I could not have imagined anything so horrifying as that moment he told me. I could not reconcile this person I loved with this person who was inflicting such terrible hurt. It made me question everything I thought I knew about life."

He said nothing for a long moment.

But this was clearly because he was exercising considerable restraint.

Finally he abandoned it. "Daphne, your beloved was a selfish bastard."

She reeled as if he'd struck her. "How dare—"

He was calmly unmoved by her rage.

"You can tell me to go to the devil if you choose. But I do not know how to say this any other way. A real man would not have asked you to choose. He wanted you to take responsibility for his misery, or for your own. Mostly I suspect what he really wanted was absolution for doing something dishonorable from someone he expected would give it to him. Because you loved him. He's an absolute despicable knave. The *governess*. What a weak bloody fool. How bloody *dare* he."

Daphne went rigid. Her mouth dropped in shock.

She knew at once this was so in essence brutally correct that it scorched away not only any temptation to protest, but another sort of an obscuring mist.

She *always* took responsibility. There had always been some man willing for her to shoulder a burden rightfully his.

But now she could see the whole affair precisely as Lorcan saw it. And he saw it with absolutely no impartiality.

How novel to take strength from someone else's outrage on her behalf. How nearly dizzying, as though a window had opened and new air rushed in.

She felt shy, suddenly. Reflexively she turned her head to breathe the scent of Lorcan clinging to the coverlet.

She stopped herself.

"Did your father and brothers offer to castrate him?"

Lorcan's tone suggested he already knew the answer.

And for the first time in her life, Daphne knew what the answer ought to have been.

It was a moment before she could answer.

"They were embarrassed. I was embarrassed to have humiliated them so. My father was . . . he seemed . . . angry. And distraught."

Angry and distraught with *her,* she understood now. The rejection and abandonment of her, the daughter of an earl, for a governess had reflected badly on him.

Her father had, in fact, fussed and railed as though he'd been thwarted. He'd been in a panic. Of course he'd been in a panic.

He'd been counting on Henry to pay his debts.

She was still subdued. Reeling from her epiphany.

"Oh, I am certain he was," Lorcan said ironically.

Loyalty was the very bedrock of her being. Lorcan's irony landed painfully. She smacked down a reflex to defend her father. But that new, invigorating anger was now quietly bubbling beneath the sludgy strata of memory.

Lorcan was wearing his gambler's face.

Carefully still, giving nothing away. He was watching and waiting for her to make conclusions.

She sat for a moment, turning over in her mind and heart fresh, sharp, stunning realizations.

LORCAN FINALLY SAID carefully, "Do you still love him? Havelstock."

The world felt strange in his mouth. "Love." Farcical, even.

He felt he hadn't a right to it. All his life it had been more of a theory. Like plump pillows, knitted blue coverlets, endless comfort and plentiful food . . . it had seemed a luxury. Or a frivolous plaything for those who had no worries of survival. Or a drug to take when life was grim. That the price he'd paid for peace of mind, for success, for climbing his way out of St. Giles to the top of a secret little empire was dodging it neatly. Satisfying mutual appetites, never making any promises. Avoiding entanglements. Moving quickly on. Thus were his relationships with women.

But now, watching Daphne, he wondered if it was the one failure of courage in his life.

He thought about what she'd said the night he'd first kissed her: "Is it muscle . . . or is it scar?"

He began to wonder which one she'd hoped it was.

Muscle implied you could dive back into the fray, stronger than ever, to try again.

Scar suggested nothing, particularly something like love, could get through anymore.

He found he was tensed waiting for the answer.

Daphne was watching him. "No. I don't know. Surely not? I haven't seen him in years. And *I* am a different person now than I was then. It was just a shock to hear his name in the sitting room and I suppose it's like . . . I suppose it's similar to the way your bones ache when the weather changes.

They remind you of how they came to feel that way."

He nodded.

"But I don't know . . . that is, what are you supposed to do with love when someone kills it at the root? Maybe it just needs to recede, like that flood at the end of the road."

He didn't know. He wanted to offer her solace and answers, and it quietly maddened him that he could say nothing of value.

"Lorcan, I have never told a soul any of this," she whispered. She gave a little laugh.

"I am honored," he said quietly, after a moment.

But abstractedly.

"I think it's upset me . . . more because it seems the point at which everything in my life seemed to have gone terribly wrong. I grieved him so. I tried but I could not disguise it. I wanted nothing to do with men for a few years. And of course this is hardly appealing to new suitors, who didn't precisely clamor, anyway. Something about the whiff of rejection hanging about me, no doubt. There were a few who tried, and then lost heart, it seemed. And then . . . my father revealed to me he'd lost our fortune. Over the past five or six years, he'd gambled it away. We're living in the caretaker's cottage, for now. My brothers don't yet know it has come to this. It was my idea. I was able to find someone to temporarily rent our home. I asked about very delicately, very discreetly. My father told them he prefers to live in a smaller home, now that his children are grown."

"Clever. I am certain *every*one believes him."

She momentarily seemed to have gone mute. Regardless, she did not reply.

"Your father was counting on Havelstock to pay his debts, I imagine."

He imagined her scrambling, discreetly, to find someone to rent their family home, and he knew a fresh surge of fury. Because her father, being an earl, of course could not go begging.

"Yes. And marrying the Earl of Athelboro will at last put an end to . . ." she humorlessly quirked the corner of her mouth ". . . my calamitous fall. And my family's calamitous fall."

He went still. Holy Mother of God.

"The marriage proposal . . . he's an earl?"

He said this as if he experienced no emotion whatsoever about it.

And yet. He had somehow not expected this.

Though of course she was the kind of woman who could, and would, marry an earl. She'd been raised to do precisely that sort of thing.

He ought to be pleased and relieved for her.

"I would be his third countess." She produced a ghost of a very bleakly amused smile.

"Surely, he hasn't a harem? They frown upon that in England. Or is it more of a Henry the Eighth sort of thing?"

"He's just been unfortunate. Or, rather, his previous wives certainly were. He does have five children who need a mother."

Lorcan went still. "Five," he said carefully.

She didn't reply.

"How old is he?" He thought he could guess it pretty well.

After a long moment she said, "Fifty-six." Her voice was frayed.

"Only a few years older than my father," she added dryly when he said nothing.

And then when it seemed he would never speak, she said, "I've only met him once, for a few hours. He was pleasant."

"He decided he could see himself with you for a lifetime after only a few hours?"

There was a peculiar echo in his head when he said it. As though someone else was asking him the very same question.

Only it wasn't a question. It sounded like the voice of truth.

Suddenly there was a strange ringing sound in his ears.

"How long does it take a man to decide he wants to buy a horse?" Her voice was a thread. Her mouth twisted ruefully.

Christ.

"So his long letter wasn't by way of declaring extreme devotion?"

She blinked, as if this hurt her. And he wondered if this had been his intent. Because on the periphery of his awareness, somewhere within him, he could sense a storm gathering, by far more dangerous, more annihilating than the one that had trapped them inside together.

"He was sharing his assets in detail, by way of persuasion. He has fifteen thousand pounds a year, and estates in London, Richmond, and Sussex."

The amount was nearly bludgeoning. It left him speechless and airless.

He would have about twenty-five thousand pounds to his *name* when the auction of the ship they'd recently captured was complete. After a lifetime of work. It was indeed a small fortune. But it was a raindrop in the ocean of the earl's fortune.

"As well he should provide all of that, Daphne," he said gently, finally. "You are . . . worth persuading."

The words felt wholly inadequate.

Her little smile then was lovely and grateful, and it was like nails raked across his heart.

"And this is the life you want?" It was a struggle to keep his words even and conversational.

It was a long moment before she replied.

She drew in a breath and released it at length.

"I want to feel safe again. I want consistency. I want children. I want to belong somewhere and to someone. I want to hold my head high. I want to know my family will be cared for. And I want, very much, something of my old life back."

Nothing about love.

Because love was the anchor that could pull you under and drown you. It was an agonized scream when a child fell into the sea. Love was Daphne shaking violently on a settee purging the memory of heartbreak. Love was his mother, enduring his father's rage when he was a tiny boy.

It was a toxin, a ruse.

Wasn't it?

If she married the Earl of Athelboro, she might never need to worry about experiencing that sort of pain again.

Servants, and a grand house to manage, and fine clothing, and people curtsying to her. Never buffeted by uncertainty again.

What a relief that would be, he imagined. He ought to be relieved for her.

He recalled how pleased he'd been to learn she'd had a proposal. She'd be sorted into the proper category, he'd thought. Where she belonged.

He was oddly careful about the next breath he took. As though the whole of his body hurt.

"All very reasonable wants," he said gently. "How would you explain it if you encounter Delilah or Captain Hardy in the company of your new husband, the earl?"

She swallowed. "Odds are very good I'll simply never see either of them again. We'll move in different circles, you see. And from what I understand, the earl seldom leaves the countryside anymore. If I should encounter anyone from The Grand Palace on the Thames, I'll simply feign polite confusion and suggest they must be thinking of someone else who looks like me."

She'd clearly given this some long, frighteningly clearheaded thought.

"Ruthless," he said admiringly. And rather relentlessly. "It seems some of your lessons in make-believe have paid off."

Her features tensed fleetingly.

But she didn't reply.

"Mrs. Hardy was once a countess," he said musingly, as though he was just recalling it. He paused a beat. "She said she's happy now."

It was as casually cruel as he'd ever been. And his unworthy willingness to be cruel told him how he felt about all of this.

She went still.

And then her eyes began to shine with tears and he felt like a brute.

"You intend to accept the earl's proposal?" His voice was uninflected.

Their eyes locked for what seemed an eternity.

Then the corner of her mouth tipped wryly. "What wouldn't you do for someone you loved?" Her voice was shredded.

She meant, of course, her family.

After a moment, he nodded once.

"Well. So seldom do problems have such a single neat solution," he said finally. "Congratulations." His voice had gone hoarse.

She cleared her throat. And gave her head a little toss.

"He'll be visiting my father at the end of the month, weather permitting. I'm to give him my answer then."

The end of the month was about a week away.

Lorcan could not reply.

He was impaled by a fury that seemed to have as many prongs as the devil's pitchfork. It was akin to how he'd felt as a boy witnessing the carelessness with which others treated things— food, and shelter, and clothing—he viewed as precious, and his fury was somehow directed at Daphne, too. It was laced through with a panic he could not quite identify, and this mystery was part of the panic: so seldom was he uncertain about anything anymore.

And so some of this fury was for himself.

Because it seemed unfathomable that she should be viewed as anything—a pawn, for instance, for her father, or disposable, in the case of Havelstock, or a stepmother and bed warmer, in the case of the earl—other than beautiful and precious and rare.

Which told him definitively that he saw her as beautiful and precious and rare.

He breathed carefully through this realization, as if it were a grave threat to his well-being.

If she was able to see herself this way, would she still tremble over Havelstock's betrayal? Would she trade one life of utility in her family for another of utility with an earl? This girl, with skin like satin, and lips like fire? With a mind like a diamond and a laugh that made him feel the sun rose in his chest?

He did not know to convey any of this to her. He did know that she'd saved herself once before, by lowering herself out the window on bedsheets.

She'd said "enough" then.

Perhaps if another option were presented to her.

"Daphne . . . How much does your father owe?"

For a moment he thought she might refuse to reply.

"Five hundred pounds."

Good God.

He took this in silently. The gold-and-ruby loop he wore in his ear was worth at least that. No wonder she was interested in it.

He considered what he wanted to do, and whether she would recoil in outrage. Or embrace the opportunity for what it was.

So he allowed an interval of silence to elapse, as they sat together quietly.

How he would miss just . . . sitting with her, quietly, in front of a fire. Just sitting with her had become one of the chief pleasures of his life.

He allowed a little more time to elapse before he risked the question.

"I don't suppose I could interest you in a game of Spillikins."

Her head turned slowly and she regarded him at length.

The air between them became at once dense with portent.

And it was a long moment before she replied.

"You could," she agreed lightly. Though her voice was faint.

"What will we wager?" he asked, as if it was the most casual question in the world.

Again, they locked eyes.

"If I win . . ." She inhaled. There was a pause, during which he held his breath. "I want your earring."

He exulted, quietly.

"And if I win . . ." He paused at length. "I will take anything you want to give to me, Daphne."

A moment later, she nodded.

She pulled the little table between them, and shook the sticks out of the tin.

"Would you like to do the honors?" she asked him.

"Why don't you, so I can go first?"

She nodded. Then she collected the sticks in her fist, then released them with a little clatter.

And Lorcan ducked his head to examine the pile. This time there was no narration.

No sound at all but the ceaseless tick of the rain against the windows and intermittent pops of the fire.

But he examined the pile in his usual way, from various angles.

And so did she. She identified several likely prospects she could safely pluck. No doubt he saw those same options, too.

The world seemed to slow as he reached out.

And Daphne realized he intended to choose a stick guaranteed to topple the pile.

Her breath stopped as he swiftly tugged.

The pile collapsed. The sticks clattered and rolled about the table.

He swore softly. "Clumsy me."

As Daphne stared at the little wreckage, the room spun violently.

What wouldn't you do for someone you loved? she'd said to him.

She slowly lifted her head.

She could hear her own staccato breath in her ears as they stared at each other.

"You cheated," she whispered.

"Nay, I *lost*."

"Exactly."

The world swam before her eyes as she watched him slowly thumb from his ear the beautiful earring. The thing that could restore choices to her. A real ruby and gold worth hundreds of pounds.

"Take it, Daphne." His whisper was intense. Willing her to obey him.

He held the earring out to her.

For a moment the only sound was their harsh breathing.

"I cannot let you do it like this, Lorcan." Her voice was thick.

Tears welled in her eyes. She brushed them violently away with the back of her hand.

His eyes flared. His features went tight with a surge of emotion, swiftly tamped.

And for long moments, they merely stared at each other.

When he finally put it back in his ear.

She saw that his fingers were trembling.

She stared.

And a nearly unendurable, breath-stopping elation slowly flooded her.

It was escorted by a near killing fury and despair.

She wanted to howl from it.

It robbed her breath.

The vicious, cruel, mocking *injustice* of it. The injustice that this miraculous thing that had sprung between them was so spike-edged that even looking at it closely was to court terrible pain. *Why?* Why this? Why now?

Abruptly, almost angrily, silently, she gathered the Spillikin sticks in her fist.

She looked down at them blindly.

He said not a word.

Then she carefully, neatly laid the sticks down. She stared down at them.

Her vision was hazed. She could hear her own breath sawing in an uneven rhythm, somewhere between grief and anger.

She reached behind her and with fumbling fingers, tugged loose the laces on her dress.

She looked up at him.

His face was unreadable. He was holding himself rigidly still.

And then leaned slowly forward and gently took his face between her hands. And just for a moment she held it and stared, marveling at its rough beauty.

Then tenderly, slowly, she drew her thumbs along the hard corners of his jaw, savoring the scrape of his whiskers. She delicately traced with her fingertip the shining raised road of his scar. The curve of his lower lip.

His beautiful eyes were filled with pain and wonder and a hope that lacerated her heart. And a desire that could incinerate them both.

And then she laid her mouth against his in a hot, hungry, open kiss.

The iron bands of his arms went around her, and she was engulfed, pulled hard up against his body. She raked her fingers up through his hair and tugged his face closer, closer still, opening her mouth to him, their tongues dueling as she chased her own desire while fanning his. She nipped his bottom lip and he swore softly, and returned the favor. The kiss became nearly devouring, a clash of teeth and a crush of lips, a greedy savoring of textures.

He gasped and took her earlobe between his teeth, lightly, and her breath hitched at the tiny shocking pleasure. She hadn't known such savagery was within her. She shook with a need that seemed fathomless, that welled and spilled and built again and he was there for her. He met her again and again with a hunger the equal of her own. He knew what she wanted.

She gasped when he swiftly lifted her onto his lap and moved her body so that she was astride the jut of his hard cock in his trousers.

He shifted his hips up against her and her head fell back on a gasp of pleasure as a bolt of lightning went through her.

"Aye, lass. It's this. It's this you want."

He moved against her again, grinding slowly, teasingly as he swiftly finished the job she'd begun with the laces of her dress and tugged her bodice swiftly down.

And suddenly her breasts were in his hands.

His eyes locked with hers as he stroked, dragging his thumbs over her nipples.

Bliss forked through her like lightning, and she cried out.

He grinned like a pirate.

And then he urged her back in his arms and closed his mouth over her nipple and sucked, and teased with his tongue. And when she half choked, half sobbed out her pleasure she could feel his animal groan vibrate through her body, in concert with her own.

"Christ, you are beautiful." The words were nearly a groan against her ear, and he followed them with his lips, then his tongue, while his hands coaxed pleasure from her breasts. "So beautiful. Move with me, Daphne." His hands were hot on her bare arse as he pulled her against his cock, still behind the fall of his trousers. "Trust me. Your body knows."

It did know. Something was flooding her veins, pressing against the very seams of her being, like a river churned in a storm.

They rocked together, swiftly now. Eyes locked so she could see when his went black and hazed. His hot breath gusted against her throat. The cords of his neck went taut. His head fell back and his chest was heaving against hers.

"Oh God." His words were tattered. "Oh God, love, I'm going to . . ."

Dazedly, stunned, desperate, she stared into his black eyes, his face as wild and hazed and amazed as hers, his forehead gleaming sweat. His head thrashed back.

"Lorcan . . . Lorcan I . . . oh, please *help* me . . ."

He slipped his fingers down between them and against where she was wet and aching and stroked hard.

The world exploded into fragments of light.

She heard her own scream from somewhere among the heavens, where she'd been launched.

Distantly, she heard him roar his release against her throat.

And as his body quaked in the throes of it, she clung to him like he was flotsam in a shipwreck.

HER HEAD RESTED on his shoulder. Her arms remained loosely looped around his neck.

His hand moved gently over her hair, then glided softly over the blades of her shoulder, down the little pearls of her spine.

"Are you still among the living?" he asked her.

She gave a single soft laugh. "I saw stars," she murmured.

"As did I."

More silence, as she pressed her cheek against his. Lightly, she kissed his neck. She let her lips linger there, so she could feel his heartbeat. Still martial.

"I never dreamed," she whispered.

He pressed a lingering kiss against her bare shoulder. Like a wanton, her breasts were still out and crushed against his chest.

They merely held each other for quite some time.

"Am I squashing you?" she asked.

"Nay," he murmured. "I think I could hold you forev—"

He stopped himself just in time from saying that fateful word.

And it was this that seemed to sober both of them immediately.

She could feel the tension gathering in his body and her own.

A moment or so later, he eased her from his lap. They sat side by side for a moment, dazed and sated and thoughtful, while she tugged up her bodice.

He turned to her and they studied each other in yet another new light.

He smiled faintly.

He reached out and drew his thumb softly, slowly over her cheek. "Consider yourself ravished, Lady Worth."

He stood, and adjusted himself. "I'll bid you good night, shall I?" he said politely.

He saw hurt flash in her eyes when he looked down at her.

But it was followed swiftly by an understanding that made him feel raw: she knew he wanted to be alone with whatever it was he was feeling. He did not want her to witness it. He'd experienced all manner of things in his life, enough so that he'd developed a response or defense in nearly every possible situation.

He simply hadn't one for this. Like a child, he wanted, needed, briefly to hide.

He was ashamed of this, and yet there it was.

Her gaze was searching. Then soft. Then accepting. She swallowed and turned away very slightly.

"Good night, Lorcan. Sleep well."

LORCAN LAY AWAKE tracking the shadows the fire cast on his ceiling and listening to the wind hurl rain at his window. To avoid the stunned and somewhat torturous run of his thoughts, he tried to concentrate on sensations instead: the pillow beneath his head. The very good mattress. Even old aches in his bones would do.

He flexed his hand, and he remembered the soft slip of her hair between his fingers.

He'd just been willing to hand over several

hundred pounds' worth of earring to a woman he'd known for mere days and she wouldn't let him do it.

Moreover . . . he was fairly certain he'd do it again, if she'd let him.

He hadn't anything else to offer her.

He lay, hollow with disbelief. And hungry, still, for her body. For her presence.

Beneath the rain and wind, another sound emerged.

And it nearly squeezed the breath from him.

In the room next to his, she was quietly weeping.

It scored his heart like acid.

Chapter Eighteen

∽᧰᧰᧫᧫∾

"*I*'M SWEATING through my clothes," St. John said. "I've never been so nervous in my life."

He was pacing behind the curtain on the stage of the ballroom in The Grand Palace on the Thames. Delacorte had poked his head through the curtain to see if they were ready to start the recital. They were not.

"You should be," Delacorte told him sympathetically. "I've heard you play."

"I've gotten better!" St. John said, panicked.

"Perhaps when you're evicted the blokes who run the livery stables will let you sleep there until Barking Road clears," Delacorte said kindly. "Unless you can swim. Though St. Leger knows a fellow with a little boat. And you'll need hip waders for the rest of the journey into town."

St. John made a growling sound.

Delacorte removed his face from the curtain and went to join the little audience, which was all atwitter with anticipation. Angelique and Delilah sat in the first row, like a pair of Caesars ready to deliver a thumbs-up or thumbs-down verdict.

Otto and Hans and Friedreich paced like worried parents.

"Not too much bow, St. John!" Otto reminded him, gesturing. "More bow on the low notes! Remember, more bow on the low note!"

"Right. Right right right right," St. John muttered.

It had been an alarming revelation to him that one didn't just saw away at a cello. There was a lot of subtlety and actual technique involved.

"Keep your elbow up, McDonald. Keep your hand straight, McDonald! Watch Frau Pariseau!" Friedreich admonished.

Mrs. Pariseau beamed with the universal pleasure of being the star pupil.

The German boys had proven to be strict and very good teachers. They'd been personally offended any time careless squawking noises emerged from their instruments.

Gratifyingly, none of their pupils were hapless.

And all of them, when they finally strung notes together by dragging bows across strings, had lit up with the magic of creation. Even St. John.

"I've never had to do anything for my *shelter* before," St. John fretted.

"Is daily life of musician!" Otto told St. John sternly. "Be brave!"

FOR THE MORNINGS following what was to be their final game of Spillikins, two mornings, Daphne had spooned the sugar into Lorcan's cup, and then poured his coffee.

For two mornings, he had cut her scone into little pieces with a sharp knife.

They were as careful of each other as they would have been with grenades or rare crystal, solicitous and kind.

He had made a grand, reckless gesture, and she had refused it.

She had thrown herself into his arms, and he had shown her the stars.

For two days after that, she'd seen very little of him.

"I will be gone for most of the day on matters of business. Meeting with my banker. My solicitor. And then I'll need to see about provisioning my ship."

He'd told her so she'd know he wasn't deliberately avoiding her. So that she wouldn't feel abandoned or misused, after riding him and begging him for pleasure while half-naked in his arms. She understood this.

And yet she knew the distance was wise. That even if they didn't speak, the silence was loud. That in not speaking, they were tacitly admitting to something that neither dared name, and to Daphne seemed nearly as indistinguishable from joy as it was from terror. And would end only in grief.

In the sitting room at night, she joined in card games or knitting with the ladies, while Lorcan exchanged bawdy witticisms with the Germans or chatted with Delacorte and Lord Bolt and Captain Hardy, with what to Daphne seemed improved civility. Last night everyone had gathered around to hear the German trio brilliantly play Bach, and Daphne welcomed the camouflage of aching beauty, because her eyes were not the only ones shining with tears. Lorcan's face had been taut.

And then he was off to the smoking room to presumably curse and smoke and whatever the men there did, and she went up to their suite without him.

She would not sleep until she heard him return. But she was in bed behind a closed door when he did.

It would not rain forever. As soon as the roads cleared, she would be going home to her father, and to give an earl an answer to his proposal.

Lorcan would be leaving soon.

And this mad interlude in the strange little fairyland of The Grand Palace on the Thames would end.

THE NIGHT OF the recital and party, she emerged from dressing to find Lorcan standing in the center of the suite. He appeared to be taking it in thoughtfully and rather intently—the hearth, the settee, the little table at which they enjoyed their breakfast scones, the view from the window, as though he were planning to draw a map of it.

"I did not expect to be participating in revelry when I came to London," she said. "This isn't the dress I would normally wear for dancing." She smoothed her green silk skirt. The sleeves were short; and the neckline and waist were trimmed in bronze ribbon.

He turned toward her voice.

A stillness came over him. For all the world as if he were withstanding the impact of her.

And he looked at her as though he were seeing her for the first time.

Or perhaps the last.

You are beautiful, he had said fiercely to her.

And inside her the realization dawned soft and brilliant as a spring day: he believed she was.

She thought, no matter what, she could conjure spring inside her always when she thought of him.

"It's a very pretty color," he said quietly.

"Thank you. I liked it because it's very nearly the same shade of new leaves on the hawthorn outside of our home in Sussex."

His mouth tipped up at the corner as if she'd said something singularly charming.

She didn't know why this should make her blush.

He wore his black suit and waistcoat in a dashing pewter stripe, done up with silver buttons. He was, in essence, a walking advertisement for the lucrative possibilities of privateering. And he still looked like precisely what he was: staggeringly confident, dangerous, piratical, self-made, bursting with life. No one was going to mistake him for an earl or a viscount.

But his majesty was innate. She knew he was destined to cause a ripple in any room he deigned to enter for the rest of his life.

Her stomach twisted with a sudden realization: she might never know what the rest of his life would be like.

For an instant this so blindly panicked her she couldn't speak.

For a quiet moment, they merely admired each other.

"Lorcan, would you like me to help you with . . ." She gestured to his still dangling cravat.

He glanced down. "What's a fake wife for if not to dress me as well as undress me?"

Her face was warm.

"Tie me a fancy knot, Daphne," he said quietly.

He stood obediently still while she deftly wound the cravat around him and tied it artfully.

When his eyes met hers, they kindled hotly. He quickly disguised it.

Her hands were suddenly clumsy.

"There," she said finally. "Now you look like a slightly dangerous birthday present."

He patted his cravat.

He held out his arm. She hesitated, and she looped her arm through it, and thought how odd it was to be familiar with, comforted by, the feel of his huge bicep against her hand. And to feel an ache in her chest at touching him again.

"Thank you. Now let's go throw fruit at Lord Vaughn."

THEY ARRIVED IN the ballroom to find the other guests milling about a table promisingly burdened with a ratafia-filled punch bowl and a variety of little cakes. It had been pushed against the wall.

"Alas, no fruit for throwing," Lorcan said to Daphne.

Present was everyone who lived and worked at The Grand Palace on the Thames and one gentleman they'd never seen before who appeared to already be drunk, and who was introduced to them by Dot as "the man who usually leans against our building." They'd all been given a TGPOTT handkerchief to clutch.

Lorcan steered Daphne into one of the little white chairs arrayed at the front of the room, behind Dot and Rose, the maid.

Finally, Lucien bounded onstage, and called for quiet by extending his arms and pressing the air downward with his hands.

"Ladies and gentlemen, I'm pleased to present to you what we like to call the Chagrin Trio—Lord St. John Vaughn, Mr. Angus McDonald, and Mrs. Pariseau—performing their rendition of *'Ah, vous dirai-je, Maman.'* Conducted by Otto Heinrich."

The audience enthusiastically applauded, and Delacorte put two fingers in his mouth to whistle, and the curtains were whipped open.

"Have you heard the lyrics that were set to this tune?" Angelique murmured to Delilah before they began. "Perhaps we can sing along. 'Twinkle, twinkle little star . . .'"

Lorcan and Daphne glanced at each other. "Star" was always going to be their word.

St. John and Mr. McDonald were as white as their cravats with nerves. Mrs. Pariseau looked confident and cheerful.

Otto's hand waved, and Mrs. Pariseau launched into the tune at a sprightly pace.

Everyone gasped when actual recognizable music emerged from the cello St. John was playing.

Then Mr. McDonald's violin harmonized.

And together they all played a fully recognizable piece of music.

Three entire verses, with charming variations here and there. And while it wasn't flawless—there were a few clumsy muffled places, and squawks—it was competent, and the musicians managed to inject the music with the passion and urgency of people afraid of being thrown out into a terrible rainstorm.

Finally Otto emphatically gestured the end of the piece with a vigorous chop of his right hand.

Thunderous applause greeted them.

They leaped to their feet to curtsy and take bows in every direction.

Already a little tipsy, the audience stomped and whistled.

St. John pushed the cello and the bow into Otto's hands—he had joined them onstage for the bows. "I need a drink!"

And he leaped from the stage and all but bolted for the table of refreshments.

Lucien returned to the stage and cheerfully bellowed, "Let the dancing commence!"

The German trio remained on the stage and launched at once into "The Sussex Waltz" with such competence and verve they were at once forgiven all the flirting, eating, and loud and untoward merriment.

"I've something to confess, Daphne," Lorcan said. "I don't know how to dance the waltz."

She smiled up at him. "I suppose it's impractical to waltz on the deck of the ship."

"Not to mention the dearth of willing partners."

She didn't say, it's likely because you haven't been asked to many balls, which was, in fact, true, and they both knew it. She stayed by him, while the dancers sailed by.

He watched her foot tap out that one two three, one two three rhythm. Her face was alight and wistful.

Lorcan glanced about the room, and noted who had partners and who did not. But he knew instinctively who he needed to find.

Bloody hell. He looked forward to it the way he might look forward to swallowing a nail.

"I'll fetch us some more ratafia, shall I?" He'd rather bolt a little whiskey, frankly.

"Yes, please," she said.

He moved over to the table supporting the punch bowl, where St. John was thirstily draining his second cup of ratafia.

"Lord Vaughn," Lorcan said. "Very moving performance. I fair soaked a handkerchief."

St. John gave a start. He eyed him warily. "Thank you, Mr. St. Leger. I've calluses now."

"Congratulations. If you're not careful, you'll have muscles next."

St. John pressed his lips together.

"I've come to beg a favor of you."

This rendered St. John briefly speechless. "I'm disinclined to jump off the building," he warned.

"I'd like you to ask my wife to dance this waltz."

St. John took this in with understandably great suspicion.

"Are you looking for an excuse to call me out because you haven't killed enough people lately?"

Lorcan took a breath. "She would love to dance the waltz and I find myself unable to accommodate her. And I find it excruciating to deny her the things that make her happy."

St. John absorbed this with admirable equanimity, with just a little hint of a brow furrow. He studied him thoughtfully. "And in exchange?"

"How about you do it out of the kindness of your heart and you'll never have to worry about encountering me in a dark alley."

"Done," St. John said.

AND SO LORCAN stood against the wall, half in shadow, and watched Daphne sail about the room in young Lord Vaughn's arms.

Granted, she'd been astonished when St. John humbly asked if she would be so kind as to dance with him. She was prepared to refuse and remain loyally by Lorcan's side.

She'd been even more astonished when he'd nodded and told her to go ahead.

He admired her loyalty fiercely. Of course, no one understood the value of it better than he did. But it was a quality, like pride, that could either buoy or strangle a person. It was the thing that would ultimately tether Daphne to a life that could very well snuff the light out of her. And maybe that was the price she was willing to pay for certainty after upheaval and struggle.

And just look how bloody happy she was to waltz. It was the prettiest sight. Graceful as a swan, he thought. Well, both of them, really. Because they were, after all, of the same species. It was so abundantly clear from this vantage point.

And suddenly he felt as constrained and separate and alien from her as if he was a painting on the wall in the ballroom. As if it was inconceivable for the two of them to ever enter each other's worlds.

God only knew if one could nimbly fence, and he certainly could, one could manage a few graceful steps with a beautiful woman in his arms.

But the fact that he hadn't wanted her to teach him with anyone looking on told him a thing or two about his own pride. He hadn't wanted anyone to bear witness to the true, vast gulf between who Daphne was and who he was.

She smiled over her shoulder at him. And he recalled what she'd said about the remoteness of stars. *I think maybe that's why we associate them with wishes. Particularly for things we think we cannot have.*

He'd made it a policy not to waste time on regret. It was ballast; it could drag you under like a hungry shark.

He watched, relieved that he could bring her this moment of happiness, even as he was held fast by a sorrow so corrosive he could taste it in his throat. It was entwined with a near impotent fury that someone had finally outsmarted him. That someone was himself. He'd fooled himself into believing there was nothing he'd ever want that he could not eventually get, so clever, so invincible, was he. That there was no one or nothing he now needed in order to conquer life, to live it on his terms. That he might be, in fact, somewhat superior to Captain Hardy in his strength, wiliness, resilience.

He knew a moment of pity for that boy in St. Giles who could never have imagined sitting in a suite in a boardinghouse by the docks while a quietly lovely woman spooned just the right amount of sugar into his cup. Or laid a hand on his brow to see if he was feverish. Or held his face as if she'd at long last found the treasure she'd been seeking.

If he'd been able to imagine it, perhaps he could have saved himself from what was to come. A grief that would reshape his life the way a tsunami reshaped a coastline.

LUCIEN PAUSED NEXT to Delacorte and Hardy to sip at his cup of ratafia. Together they watched the dancers swirl (and occasionally collide), and enjoyed the respite from worrying about the ship.

Angelique had gone to play the piano so one of the German boys could attempt a waltz with Mrs. Pariseau. Delilah had kindly consented to dance with Angus McDonald who, they were astonished to see, was finally smiling.

Dot was teaching Rose and Meggie how to dance the waltz, and they were all laughing together.

Bloody hell, all of this nonsense added up to happiness, Lucien thought. What a good life they had here.

"What's the matter with St. Leger?" he asked Delacorte, gesturing with his chin.

For a moment, they all turned to regard the big man standing quietly against the wall.

"I think he's just in love with his wife," Delacorte correctly diagnosed.

"Ah. Tragedy, that," Lucien said, idly. "A fatal condition, to be sure."

Chapter Nineteen

❧

LORCAN COMPORTED himself enthusiastically during a number of reels. He seemed to mind not a bit when she danced with others. He smiled and laughed. He drank very little.

But throughout the evening Daphne sensed his mood growing gradually more and more remote. As it did, her sense of unease ramped. She thought she understood the reason, but it was as if she were watching him drift out to sea on a boat that had slipped its mooring, and there was nothing she could do about it.

As he grew quieter and quieter, her stomach coiled tighter and tighter in tension.

By the time they left the ballroom, it was knotted completely.

He spoke not at all as they climbed the stairs to their suite.

She found herself chattering anyway, to fill the silence. "What a lovely evening. Perhaps I'll learn to play an instrument, too. I thought Mrs. Pariseau played beautifully. Perhaps she has real talent."

Inside their room, he shook himself out of his coat. Reflexively she took it from him to hang up on the little rack by the door.

"Lorcan, would you like a cup of tea before we sleep? It's not too late to ring for one."

"No. Thank you."

"Some brandy?"

"No, thank you." He had gone to stand before the fire, silently. She stood next to him, but he did not look up at her.

She stared at him, heart in her throat.

"Shall I help you with your cravat?" she asked quietly. She reached for the knot at his throat.

He shocked both of them by seizing her wrists.

And in silence, he held her fast. His expression was dark. And almost cold.

"Daphne," he said.

She was too stunned to speak. Her breathing had gone panicked and swift.

"I. Am. Not. Your. *Husband*."

His volume scarcely raised at all.

But each word somehow hurt her worse than the last, as if he beat her down like a nail in a plank.

Until she was small and flat and lightless.

He uncurled his fingers and released her gently.

She took a step back.

Then another.

AND LORCAN WATCHED her face flash white, then scarlet, then white again.

Two hot pink spots remained high on her cheeks.

Then there was a silence that seemed to whine as if someone had fired a gun next to his ear.

They stared at each other.

She looked blank with shock.

"Good heavens. Of course you aren't. No need to take on so," she said lightly.

He said nothing. He could not. He was flooded with horror. As if he'd crushed a butterfly in his hands.

"Good night, Lorcan." She said it brightly.

If there was a tremble in her voice, it was slight.

She turned. Spine straight, she headed straight for her room.

She quietly closed the door and turned the key in the lock.

HE STARED AT her closed door.

Then covered his face with his hands.

Everything was too loud, suddenly: the fire echoed like whip cracks.

The wind moaning, as if in pain.

The frantic, slamming beat of his own heart, trying to get out of its jail. Furiously pounding its rage at what he'd subjected it to, despite its efforts to defend itself from pain. Furiously pounding as if it wanted to leap out of his chest and go to her.

He was in pain. He was in pain.

DAPHNE LAY ON her bed and held herself very still in the dark.

As if in so doing she could prevent the shocking pain of his words from flooding her entirely. As if she could save one tiny corner of herself from it.

As it was, she felt as though her lungs had been punctured.

She thought she knew why he'd done it. Why he'd said it. How he felt.

And therein lay both salvation and heartbreak.

But she could not know for sure, and she felt like she'd just leaped into the dark from a crate, only to endlessly fall.

"DAPHNE?" HE SAID quietly to the door.

There was no response.

He cleared his throat.

"Daphne, if you can hear me, will you please say something?"

He waited.

He was greeted with the sort of silence that must have preceded creation. A howling nothingness. He could not feel her presence. He realized he'd been able to feel her in the room even when his eyes weren't upon her.

He swallowed.

"Daphne. I do not know what to say . . . or how to say it. So I am just going to talk. By now you know I value my worthless hide more than I ought and I know a thousand ways to save it. But right now I would willingly lay down and die for putting that expression on your face." He stopped. He took a steadying breath and said, more quietly, "For causing you hurt of *any* kind."

There was no reply.

"Daphne?"

Nothing.

"I do not know what is wrong with me. I am . . ." He gave a short, dark, laugh. ". . . *suffering*, lass."

His voice was little more than a hoarse whisper

now. "I cannot say that I understand it. But your pain, lass . . . it seems I've finally found a thing I cannot endure."

He listened; ear pressed against the door. Willed her with all of his considerable spirit to speak.

Nothing stirred or creaked. She could be a statue or a corpse in there.

He sensed her not at all on the other side.

He leaned his forehead against the door.

"I am sorry. I pray your forgiveness."

He said it with the stiff formality of a man delivering his last words before they lowered the noose over his head.

LITTLE BY LITTLE, with every word he spoke, the darkness inside her lifted, until the whole of her felt golden and radiant.

She thought she could actually feel her heart breaking, cracking in her chest.

Or was it instead merely opening? Perhaps a scarred heart could never quite open again fully without pain. Perhaps like a flower, it couldn't help but unfurl, however wretchedly, toward love.

And if it was futile, did it matter?

Was love ever futile?

If they could not keep it, did it matter?

Was it ever a waste?

She didn't know the answers to these questions.

She only knew she could not bear his suffering, either.

So she slid from the bed.

She turned the knob slowly, surreptitiously.

And the well-oiled door glided open silently when she gave it a push.

He was sitting before the fire, head propped on his hands.

His stillness was a revelation. It was at once clear to her how much of his moods and personality animated his body with force and confidence.

This was Lorcan weary and uncertain.

And afraid.

It clawed at her heart even as it sang a dark little hosanna that he should feel such pain all for her.

She understood now, more clearly than ever, that this fearsome man had arranged and lived the entirety of his life to avoid feeling uncertain. To avoid feeling, or showing, weakness. Or fear.

He straightened suddenly. Then swiveled about and saw her.

He was on his feet at once. He straightened slowly, cautiously.

They regarded each other from across the room.

"I . . . don't know why I'm standing here." Her voice was little more than a broken whisper.

With startling speed he strode across the room and closed his hand around her arm.

A little tightly.

He loosened his grip at once.

She hadn't minded his grip. She wanted to be held as though she was desperately wanted. As if she was a thing so precious letting her go would mean the end of his world.

His hand slid down, down, then moved to her waist. His arm curled around her. He drew her into his body, gently.

He tucked his face into her throat. And held her.

"Your heart, Daphne," he said after a moment. "Oh, your heart. How fast it is beating."

The frayed wonder in his voice. As if he could not believe her heart leaped all for him.

He threaded his hand through her hair and kissed her where her heart leaped in her throat.

She slid her hands up, and they lingered over the mighty thud of his heart before they locked around his neck.

His mouth was on her throat, her ear, her lips. Her lips. She fell into the kiss. Surrendered entirely. She was falling, falling. Falling so irrevocably she hardly noticed that her feet had indeed left the ground.

He carried her to her room.

HE REMOVED HER dress with the same startling efficiency with which he'd peeled that orange. She lay shivering and naked. He was out of his clothes just as swiftly. She heard the muffled thump of trousers and waistcoat and shirt hitting the floor.

And for a second loomed, first shadow, then lamplit, then in filtered moonlight let in through the crack of the curtain. He was enormous, terrifyingly beautiful, infinitely stronger than her. Perhaps infinitely more vulnerable. She trembled with anticipation.

The bed sank when he joined her there and they turned to each other in a near frenzy of want.

She entwined her limbs around him, eager to feel his skin over the entire length of hers. He caged her with his arms. They grappled like two people who had tumbled down a cliff, mad with, greedy for, desperate for the feel of every inch of each other; their hands wandering, stroking, searching, while their mouths clung in a deep, hungry, nearly bruising kiss. She wanted to feel every sensation he could offer her. She wanted to touch and taste all of him. She scored her nails across his chest, tangling her fingertips in the curly hair; then pulled away to close her teeth lightly over his nipple. He hissed in a breath of pleasure, his hand rising to cover the back of her head. She rose up to gently bite the great curve of his shoulder; he took her earlobe between his teeth and she gasped. His hands were on her breasts, stroking, teasing her nipples, and she moaned her pleasure.

His hands splayed over her back, traced the nipped curve of her waist, followed it to her arse, spanned nearly the whole of her thigh, his fingers reaching beneath the petal-soft skin there, softly stroking, and she sighed. And then he swiftly rose up on two arms, bridging her. He hovered there, gazing down at her. She reached up to trace his lips, wonderingly. She arched up against his hard cock at the juncture of her legs, reveling in his growled oath, in teasing each other.

And then she escaped.

She slipped from beneath the bridge of his body and rolled away. Strictly for the primitive thrill of being captured again.

Knowing she would never escape him if he didn't let her go.

He pulled her roughly back into his arms, then briefly pinned her, and the strength of him made her weak, weak with desire.

They smiled at each other.

He kissed her. So softly, so gently, a whisper slide of his lips over hers. So tenderly that tears rushed the corners of her eyes.

"Lorcan," she murmured thickly.

Gently she slid her palms over the vast, hard-as-armor terrain of his back, finding the ridges, the scars, the bumps of his spine.

And then he took his lips away from hers.

Trailed them along her throat.

Lingered, briefly, to draw her nipples into his mouth and suck. She cried out.

He smoothed his hands over her belly, and placed a kiss in the center of it.

He spread her thighs with his hands.

And ducked his head between.

And when the hot, satin sinew of his tongue stroked her for the first time a ragged animal groan tore from her.

And there he feasted. A diabolically skillful, stroking rhythm, a collusion between his skillful tongue, his breath, and his clever fingers drove her to the writhing brink of madness.

So much unimaginable pleasure surely could not be survived.

As if from a distance she heard her own voice half sobbing. Begging incoherently. She undulated beneath him, her fingers clawing the counterpane into furrows.

"Lorcan . . . help me . . . it's too good . . . *oh God . . . oh my God . . .*"

And her body snapped upward like the string of a bow drawn back and a scream tore from her throat and she was among the stars.

He left his hand against her to savor the violent pulsing of her release, like a triumphant conqueror. He rose up on his knees, and she gazed up at him as he parted her thighs.

And then he rose up again, and he guided his cock into her.

The shock of him filling her made her head go back on a gasp.

He kissed her, softly.

She swept his hair from his brow, savoring the wondrously strange feeling of being filled by him. Joined with him.

"Daphne . . . lass . . . I do not want to hurt you . . . I shall try to be gentle. I fear I cannot go slow. I have wanted you more than I have wanted my next breath."

She drew her hand along his throat, to his chest, to where his heart thundered.

"I trust you. I want you, too."

She clung to his shoulders, slid her hands down to his hips, to the indents of muscle at his buttocks, and she arched to meet each dive of his hips. To take him deeply. To be as much a part of him as she possibly could, for this moment in time. For a time, they moved like this, almost languidly. And in the amber light of her lamp she could see his clear eyes go dark, and then remote, she watched his release come up on him, and felt within her that same building need, until she was frantic with it. Begging.

"Lorcan . . . Lorcan I . . ." Her voice, hoarse. *"Please . . ."*

And then their bodies were colliding, and their mingled breathing like a storm in which they were trapped.

He roared her name. She clung to him while he shook.

SHE LAY SATED, thoroughly loved, deflowered and ravished, and she seemed to him pale and fragile as a lace glove in his arms. His heart felt too large for his chest. He would kill for her without question.

And he would have to let her go.

But not tonight.

He traced with a finger the delicate bones of her wrist. The pearly underside of her arm. He felt saturated by the beauty of her body, this glorious secret hidden by her clothes, the textures and curves of her, the sweet, satiny curve of her breasts with their rose-colored nipples, the triangle of dark fluff at her legs.

"Listen," he said quietly. "While you are with me, you do not have to be strong. Cry. Laugh. Scream. Be whoever you are. Feel whatever you feel. I am strong enough for both of us."

She turned to him. She touched his face.

"Make me scream again," she whispered.

HE WAS UNDONE. He had never felt so simultaneously weak and savage.

He traced the contours of her kiss-swollen lips with a single finger.

Then he laid his mouth against hers softly.

In him warred two impulses: devour or cherish. The instinct to take what he could before it disappeared, before it could be taken from him, before he could be told such beauty, such bliss, was not for him, burned powerfully. But she had taught him to savor. She had shown him he had the right.

And so, as if by sheer force of will he could alter the flow of time enough to make this interlude of discovery and desire last the rest of their lives, his hands moved over her slowly. Revealing to her that every bit of her skin could be a source of pleasure.

"You can tell me how you like to be touched," he murmured, as silently, slowly, his rough palm skimmed over the unthinkable softness of her skin. Tracing the sweet dip of her waist up over the slope of her hip. Dipping to glide over the curve of her belly. To lightly, tantalizingly, tangle in the damp curls between her legs.

She half sighed, half moaned. Sounding somnolent with pleasure.

"I like . . ." she murmured, tracing his eyebrow with one finger, "watching the way your expression changes when you touch me. And the way it changes when I touch you."

He was too moved to reply. He felt a little raw, knowing that she could see so clearly into him. He was a little in awe of her.

With delicate fingers she followed the bones at the base of his throat. Then circled the bump of his nipples, which she then licked. She smiled with a vixeny delight when his breath hitched and he hissed in a pleasured breath. She followed the furrow between his muscles on his chest, his abdomen. She marked him out like a cartographer, her face a study in wonder. Reveling in her power to quicken his breathing, to make him sigh, make his muscles tense with pleasure beneath her questing hand.

When her hand slid down to his cock, he covered it with his own. Then wordlessly, he showed her how to stroke him.

She circled him in her hand and obeyed.

"Is this right?" she whispered.

"Dear God, yes," he groaned.

In silence, her fist dragged the length of him, harder, and harder still, as she responded to the sounds of his pleasure. She explored the smooth dome of his cock, lightly combed through the curly nest of hair, reveling in all the exotic-to-her textures of him, her eyes never leaving his face. Until he was shifting restlessly, and groaning from the heretofore unimaginable pleasure. Need was like a spear through him.

He rose up over her, and she instinctively slid beneath him so he could enter her again.

He rolled the two of them gently so that they moved, side by side together, their bodies fused and rippling.

The scream of her release ebbed into a little sob, as if such pleasure, such happiness, surely could not be borne.

And as she rested her head on his chest, her

breathing settling, he stroked her hair, and he felt his own eyes burning with tears.

SHE'D CLOSED HER eyes, and he watched her face in the lamplight. Make this night last forever, he willed. But he'd watched her lose her battle to sleep, and he was about to lose his. They slept holding each other, entwined, skin to skin.

They woke to bright light shining through a parted inch of curtains.

The rain had finally stopped.

Chapter Twenty

❦

𝐵ETWEEN THEM, there could only be this—this island of time, the strange stolen interlude at The Grand Palace on the Thames.

And they only had it because they were pretending to be what they were not.

She knew this, and so did he.

She could not regret it.

For the next two days, as the sun rose and shone and the water drew back and the clouds gave way to watery-pale blue skies, they asked each other no questions about the future. No "what if" scenarios were introduced. Nobody used the word that began with "L."

It would have been redundant, anyway.

But they did spend an inordinate time in the suite behind closed doors. Daphne felt nearly permanently drunk with lust, distantly aware of the recklessness of all the abandoned lovemaking. She didn't care. She, like Lorcan, had begun to understand "take what you can get while you can get it."

"Good heavens. Like newlyweds," Delilah whispered to Angelique, observing the sultry aura that suddenly seemed to surround Daphne and Lorcan in the sitting room for the next two nights.

Then came word, via Delacorte, that water had receded from the bridge at the end of Barking Road. Carriages could get through now.

Lorcan grew quieter and quieter as the moment came for them to part. The weight of his silence spoke of the gravity of what they felt for each other and what they were going to lose. The density of it was love itself.

She had told him once before, clearly, what sort of life she wanted. She'd meant it.

She could not imagine a life on a ship. She could not bear the loneliness of waiting, and worrying and wondering whether he would return safely.

He had said he never intended to take a wife. Regardless of what there was now between them, there was no reason not to believe him. He knew who he was.

She did not know how to make a wild rogue into a husband, or an interlude into forever.

Regardless, he made no demands or promises. Neither did she.

They didn't discuss her impending engagement to an earl with five children, which was the reason she urgently needed to be home before month's end. In three days' time.

The reason she would be on the first mail coach available when the roads cleared.

He merely loved her body with his.

The day they were to part dawned clear. They dressed, separately, and packed their belongings, separately. The mail coach that would bring Daphne back to Hampshire, to her father, and to ultimately the man she would marry, would depart at just past eight in the morning.

And Lorcan was expected at the docks before then. He planned to row out to his ship with his crew to begin the process of provisioning it. They would sail by the end of the week.

Lorcan had told everyone in the sitting room that Daphne would be leaving to stay with her father while Lorcan was at sea for the next six months. Daphne was so silent and pale, such a study in grief, that everyone treated the two of them with tender solicitousness.

And as the hour for her to depart drew closer, she wept in his arms.

Quietly, but with abandon. The glorious freedom of surrendering what she felt, knowing he understood and that it mattered profoundly to him, that he suffered when she suffered and rejoiced when she did—she had never before known it, and knew she might never know it again. Sadness poured from her, much the way the sky had split and the rain torrented down the night they'd met.

She could feel the ragged pattern of his breathing, and the hammer-hard beat of his heart against hers, and the heat and press of him as he held her, tightly, as if he could brand himself with the shape of her. As he promised, he was strong enough for both of them. She knew it stormed inside him, too.

They had always known there would be one last kiss, and one last time he saw her face.

He kissed her eyelids, her cheeks, her mouth.

"Look up at the stars if you miss me, Daphne." His voice was graveled. "I'll be with you. Always."

He seized his hat. And for the last time, the door shut hard behind him.

THE WEATHER WAS paradoxically brilliant and beautiful, given that internally Lorcan felt barren as a desert as he walked to the docks. Water had finally stopped falling, but everything was sheened in it. The eaves dripped diamonds, and cobblestones glinted like silver. Huge pearly clouds had moved aside just enough to remind the humans below that the color of the sky was actually blue. The Thames was a shining ribbon. The air remained cold enough so that his breath made white puffs.

The roads would likely be hard going for a few days, and he thought of Daphne stuffed in a mail carriage, jostling her way through the mud and ruts, to get back home again.

She would be a countess by the time his ship reached the waters of Spain again.

At that thought, the sheen was off the day entirely.

The streets near the docks were once more teeming with humans. Somehow he threaded through them, somehow he managed to put one foot in front of another. Reflexively, he returned subtle nods from people who recognized him.

Finally he stopped right where, a mere few days ago, he'd saved a life and nearly lost his. He saw his own bonnie ship anchored, and his heart lifted just a very little.

Suddenly he froze.

He shielded his eyes to peer at a ship that seemed to be all but limping toward port. He swiftly retrieved from his pocket a spyglass and trained it, twisting into focus.

It was clear that the ship had been dismasted— perhaps in some storm well out to sea. Some effort had been made to jury-rig a usable mizzen. He whistled to himself—that would have been extraordinarily hard going, particularly in rough seas, unless they'd made it to another port. A rent in one of the sails was visible. The crew ought to have been able to repair it. Something had clearly prevented them from doing that.

As it drew closer, he thought he noted some damage to the quarterdeck, hastily repaired. Perhaps a burn, or a cannonball strike.

The ship had been through quite a drama. And yet here she still was.

And then suddenly goose bumps rose along his arms when he realized exactly what he was looking at. Even before he saw the name on the prow.

And he turned and ran like hell for The Grand Palace on the Thames.

"HARDY! BOLT! DELACORTE!" He burst into the foyer bellowing. "She's in!"

He heard footsteps running from all directions in the house, thundering down the stairs.

Hardy was the first to appear on the landing, followed by Bolt, who nearly crashed into him.

"She's in! *The Zephyr* is in! She's been dismasted. She might have some more damage to the quarterdeck. But she's sailing in right now."

Both Hardy and Bolt froze in place.

"Are you sure?" Hardy managed a moment later. His voice was hoarse.

"Sure as I've got eyes."

Hardy closed his eyes and a long breath left him. Then his mouth shaped what looked like a silent prayer or an oath. Bolt slung an arm around his shoulders. For a moment they ducked their heads, and appeared to be holding each other up in relief.

Lorcan was fiercely, truly glad for him. For both of them.

"My thanks, St. Leger," Hardy said.

And then they were out the door at a run.

LORCAN REMAINED IN the empty foyer for a moment. The return of the sun meant the crystals on the chandelier were able to scatter little rainbows at his feet. And though his plans to row out to his ship hadn't changed, he found instead his feet were carrying him to the passage to the annex.

He wanted to see if he could feel Daphne there.

With some trepidation, he turned the key in the door.

Without her presence, the silence in the suite seemed to whine.

There was an answering echo in his scraped-raw soul.

He found himself pacing, like a bear emerging from hibernation to discover the forest has been burned to the ground.

He fancied he met the ghost of the scent of orange near the settee. He hovered there a moment, closed his eyes and remembered. And an ache for her started up. He breathed in, against the wanting.

He went to her room and gingerly sat down on her bed.

And then he dragged her pillow to him and held it to his face to breathe her in.

He sat like that, pulsing with love and loss and furiously, furiously thinking.

Now he knew why he'd returned to this suite. It resounded with her absence. It looked cheap, unreal, like set dressing—and he understood that even if he carried her love about like hidden miser's gold, this was how the rest of his life would feel without her.

And therein lay an epiphany. That fancy beautiful word she had taught to him.

Who was he now? Not a coward. That much he knew. He didn't know how much of his courage was innate, or how much he could attribute to experience building his courage up like muscle, the way he'd claimed. He did know nothing in his life had prepared him for what he was considering doing.

Unless it was loving and being loved.

And he burned with the near holy knowledge that she loved him.

The epiphany was this: in loving him, he was only now realizing she'd shown him he had something of value he hadn't yet offered her. Maybe, just maybe, it was what she'd wanted from him along.

What a miracle that would be.

But damned if it was going to be the only thing he brought to her.

He thought of Hardy's and Bolt's ship limping into port. An idea was taking shape on the periphery of his awareness; he aimed the spyglass of his mind at it, and he could feel a thrill stirring in the pit of his stomach when it expanded fully into view. Seconds later, he nearly shouted "Hosanna."

What he was considering was a risk. He was used to risk.

Bloody hell. He was going to do it.

This realization left him genuinely terrified.

And thoroughly exhilarated.

But he felt powerful again.

And he didn't know if he was mad, brave, delusional, or brilliant, or all four.

It was going to be up to Daphne to decide.

IT WAS QUIET in the smoking room that evening, as Mr. McDonald and St. John Vaughn, after thanking their hostesses, had bolted from The Grand Palace on the Thames like hares set free from traps, and Hans, Otto, and Friedreich had been engaged to play at a previously arranged small soiree at the home of a wealthy merchant.

They expected never to see poor Mr. McDonald again, but they all sincerely hoped he continued his violin lessons.

Which left Hardy, Bolt, Delacorte, and Lorcan to wearily enjoy cheroots and much-needed brandies alone in the smoking room.

Bolt and Hardy looked exhausted but more at peace. At least they knew what they were up against: repairs to the masts and quarterdecks. Financial losses from partially damaged cargo. New crew members to hire, and injured crew to compensate—their crew had valiantly gotten their ship into port, but two members had been injured in the rigging when the mast snapped. They would be unable to work for quite some time.

"So the Triton Group needs a ship," Lorcan said thoughtfully.

"Yes," Bolt said.

Lorcan's heart was suddenly a bass drum in his chest. He waited a moment, strategically. He understood the value of a bit of theater, especially when it came to a high-stakes wager.

And then he exhaled smoke. "I have a ship."

It sounded as offhand as "would you kindly pass the peas?"

Almost as if the rest of his life didn't hinge on what happened next.

Bolt, Hardy, and Delacorte stared at Lorcan.

After a long, taut, fascinating silence, Lorcan added, entirely neutrally, "a large and fast ship."

He saw a hard, almost mordant amusement and respect flicker across Hardy's face. And a suppressed excitement. He knew that Lorcan more or less had them in the palm of his hand.

Finally Hardy said, very casually, "What are you proposing, St. Leger?"

Lorcan's palms were actually a bit damp as he reached into his coat for the sheets of foolscap covered with notes and figures he'd prepared that afternoon.

And he showed them.

And told them.

And when he was done speaking there was a different silence.

The quality of hope had entered the room. And it was fast evolving into excitement.

"I suppose my question is . . . *why* do you want to do this?" Hardy finally said. "When privateering is so profitable?"

When we have been more or less enemies, was the unspoken question.

Pride was Lorcan's very spine.

"I want Daphne to be happy. I want her to have everything out of life she desires, because in truth, that's really all I want. And . . ."

Damn. It was never going to be easy to say this next thing aloud to Hardy. But he knew it was the one thing that would convince him of his sincerity. He took a breath. "I want a life a lot like this one."

He gestured with his smoldering cheroot at the smoking room. His mouth dented at the corner, just a very little. Ruefully.

The faces around him were riveted. Bolt's reflected compassion. Delacorte's, pleasure—he loved it when other people admired The Grand Palace on the Thames.

Hardy remained interested and otherwise unreadable.

"All of this, mind you, hinges on whether it's what Daphne wants. I will need to make sure she approves of it first. Because I want Daphne to always be able to hold her head high. I want to be proud of my work, and I want her to be proud of me. And mostly I . . . I just don't want to ever leave her again."

Lorcan delivered all of this in a steady voice. But by the time he'd reached those last words it had turned to gravel.

He schooled his features to stillness. Inwardly, every particle of his being was screaming to get to Daphne before she accepted the earl's proposal.

Another wordless interval ensued. Lorcan maintained his game face in the face of three wondering, speculative expressions.

"Those sound like the best motivations in the world to do anything," Hardy said quietly, finally.

He thrust out his hand.

Bolt and Delacorte followed suit.

And negotiations got underway.

DAPHNE WAS ALMOST blackly amused at how quickly life returned to aggressively ordinary once outside the magical confines of the cozy Grand Palace on the Thames. After two days (which really ought to have been one day; a stuck wheel had kept them all overnight at a coaching inn, where passengers were fed a few careworn shreds of beef and assigned indifferently cleaned rooms) of somewhat shambolic traveling over rutted muddy roads, she finally arrived at the caretaker's cottage where they lived in the shadow of her real home.

Exhausted, sweaty, still somewhat sore between her legs from wantonly rolling about with Lorcan, still numb and grieving and inwardly glowing from knowing she was loved, she tumbled out of the cart that had taken her from where the mail coach stopped, and walked the rest of the still somewhat muddy road to her door, carrying her portmanteau.

She paused. Suddenly reluctant to go in, as if the house was quicksand and the past, and duty, would engulf her once she stepped over the threshold.

The door was flung open and there in the doorway stood her brothers, Charles and Montague.

She gasped and flung herself at the nearest brother, and was scooped up and swung about.

"Daph, you look wonderful and . . . you need a bath!" Charles said.

She swatted him. "It was a rough trip home! Put me down."

It was Monty's turn to hug and give her a quick, critical inspection.

"Is that your sister finally returned from London?" her father called from inside.

She hesitated.

"Here, Papa," she called. Quietly.

For the first time in her life, she was conscious of a profound reluctance to see him. Around her heart there settled a coolness composed of sadness and resignation.

She'd been given new eyes with which to see her father. She did not think things could ever be the same.

Charles seized her portmanteau for her and they filed through the door. He lowered his voice. "We're so relieved to see you, actually. Father has offered his own already unnerving explanation about funds, but I want to hear from you why we're in the *caretaker's cottage.*"

"You're not going to like it," she said frankly. But sympathetically. She was relieved to know that someone else was taking an interest. "When did the two of you get here? *How* did you get here?" she asked him.

"Just two days ago. The channel crossing was one I'll never forget," Monty said.

"He was green the entire time," Charles said. "It was a bad one. I must say, however, it was tremendously odd how your friend was able to track us down."

"My friend?" She was puzzled.

"We were given a message from him saying our sister urgently needs us to come home at once," Montague said. "Who the devil is this Lorcan St. Leger and what the devil does he mean by—"

"I am Lorcan St. Leger."

Daphne spun.

She froze.

She made a sound of stifled, wild joy. Of almost pain. Her hand flew to her mouth.

Lorcan filled the doorway.

There fell an absolute silence.

Daphne didn't think she would ever tire of witnessing people experience Lorcan for the first time.

Her brothers and her father had gone absolutely still and mute. A bit the way little furry animals in the forest might when the wolf strolls into view. But their expressions were very nearly comical. They could not quite reconcile the presence of such a man in their house.

They slid sidelong glances at her.

And then back at him.

Lorcan bowed. Low and beautifully.

They watched this warily, too.

Monty's hand went up to absently finger his earlobe. Probably imagining how *he* would look with an earring.

"The Honorables Montague and Charles Worth, I presume?" Lorcan said pleasantly.

"Ah, yes," Charles said. They bowed, because they had good manners.

He turned toward Daphne's father. "And Lord Worth, I presume," Lorcan said neutrally. He bowed to him, too. Lorcan was generally polite. Until he wasn't.

Her father said nothing. Nor did he bow, and this rudeness embarrassed Daphne. His face was, in fact, nearly scarlet with anger.

Which was really about not liking at all that his will was countermanded. Things had gone his way for most of his life, after all.

Charles cleared his throat. "Mr. St. Leger . . . I'm a trifle confused about what connection you might have to our family . . . and to my sister."

"Your sister and I were introduced when your father saw fit to allow her to take a paying job. She was fleeing for her virtue from one of the people with whom she was employed."

To their credit, her brothers both visibly recoiled as this appalling sentence registered.

Their heads pivoted between her and her father.

"What on earth . . . ? Father? Daphne? Is this true?" Charles was bewildered.

"She wanted to help your third cousin, Mrs. Leggett, who offered to pay her," her father said tersely. "I could see no reason to deny her the wish to help. She would have been paid. Daphne, were you paid?"

Daphne couldn't speak. Her heart broke a little that this was the first question her father chose to ask.

"How . . . how . . . did you find us?" Montague asked Lorcan.

"I have friends everywhere, in all walks of life," Lorcan said. "Many in London, Calais, Dover. I gave my message and your names to the right people and merely asked that it be passed on. It seems it was."

This was not a sentence calculated to make anyone comfortable. It rather made him sound omnipotent, and he was unnerving enough as it was.

"I did this on the same day I found an orange." He turned to Daphne.

"What an efficient day that was," she teased softly.

He smiled at her.

Her brothers' eyes had gone huge, witnessing the two of them smiling at each other.

"Daphne . . ." Her father's voice was trembling with outrage. "Who *is* this man? What the devil is going on?"

This man is the heart of my heart, she wanted to tell him. An outrageously demanding, skilled lover who took my virginity and made me scream with pleasure, then cradled me in his arms as though I was treasure. My rescuer. A peeker into my soul. This man is possessive and vulnerable and brutal and brilliant and funny and he's mine. He's mine.

She longed to say it.

Her voice was lost.

"Daphne," Lorcan said softly.

And suddenly they were the only two in the room.

She smiled softly at him.

She wished she wasn't so weary, and sweaty, and a trifle disheveled, but the night they'd met her hair had stood up fuzzy as a pussycat and he'd fallen in love with her anyway. He was looking at her as if she were an angel sent down from heaven, with that mixture of bemusement, wonder, affection, and frank desire.

He cleared his throat. "I should like to speak privately with you, if you are amenable," he said quietly.

For a moment she couldn't speak.

"Of course," she finally managed on a whisper.

"Now, see here, Daphne . . ." Her father sounded nervous. And incensed.

Lorcan turned to her father and said very politely, "If you would be so kind as to excuse us for a moment, Lord Worth."

It was not a question.

Her father, whether out of astonishment or outrage—or fear—wisely said nothing at all.

SHE LED LORCAN into a tiny sitting room and shut the door. And locked it.

She knew everyone outside that door would press an ear against it. She didn't care.

The settee wasn't nearly as comfortable as the one in their suite at The Grand Palace on the Thames, but it was smaller, which meant they really had no choice but to sit very, very close. Her thigh right up against his hard one.

He took both of her hands in his.

His expression when he touched her nearly did her in. The relief in it. She nearly crumbled.

His thumbs moved in a slow, wondering caress over the back of her hands. As if he cherished every damned thing about her. As if he found everything about her a soft and lovely miracle.

"Daphne . . ." His voice was soft. A little gruff. "You love me, aye?"

She nearly laughed. She loved that he did not present this with any doubt.

She exulted that he knew her heart, and her most precious secret.

Her eyes filled with tears. "I love you. Aye," she said thickly.

She watched these words transform him before her eyes. He was at once radiant and peaceful and certain.

He took a slow breath, accommodating the in-rush of joy.

"I love you," he confided to her.

He said it as though these were the secret words that rolled back the stone of a tomb. Like a vow. As though they were irrevocable law.

Her heart was wild with joy. She felt at one with the sun, she was so ablaze with it. How she'd wanted to be loved this way her entire life.

He cleared his throat.

"Daphne, I am here to tell you I am not going back to sea. I have joined Bolt, Hardy, and Delacorte as a member of the Triton Group, and when our agreement is made binding, I will officially be a land-bound merchant. Here is the draft of our partnership agreement."

Not to be outdone by an earl, he'd brought documents.

She was astounded.

He released her hands, reached into his coat, and laid the documents on the table.

"I know you like an exquisite budget, Daphne. So if you'd like to peruse it, here is our proposed budget. And here are our projected earnings. And here is my expected share of them." He pointed them out.

With a sense of unreality, hilarity, and genuine, delicious fascination, she did indeed take a little time to look at all of them. The numbers were practical yet heady.

"If we continue on this trajectory, we anticipate having a fleet of three to five ships within the next five years. I will be unbearably respectable. I might even run for Parliament."

She gave a breathless laugh.

"I have twenty thousand five hundred and fifty-two pounds and a gold and ruby earring worth seven hundred and fifty pounds to my name. I have countless friends, some with titles and orangeries, some who slink through alleys at night. I doubtless have many enemies."

He claimed one of her hands again.

"And I love you. I love you. I will lay down my body to keep you safe. I will pay your father's debts—but one time only. I will buy you a home in London, lavish you with oranges and stockings, and with laughter and challenge. And I will spend the whole of my days making sure you understand the beauty of your own body and heart. No children will be more loved than ours. At night I will claim you, and make you mine again and again."

He paused. "The pleasure I have known with you, lass . . ."

His voice cracked.

And just like that, Daphne's body was on fire from head to toe.

"These are the terms of my offer, Daphne, and that is the nature of your risk. My fortune. My body. My heart." He paused, and took in a long, steadying breath. "Me. I am offering me." He waited, and what he saw in her face apparently gave him courage to continue. "I have come to ask you to marry me, and they are yours, if you would do me the extraordinary honor of being my wife."

And once again, there it was. The choice to leap from a crate into the dark into his safe arms.

She was already soaring. Her eyes filled and tears fell in little rivers. Words were impossible.

"And I know I am a mad, mad bastard to ask it of you, when you could wed an earl and be a countess and be wealthy and titled. Mark my words, we *will* be rich. And my vow is this: you will not be a countess, but I will treat you like a queen the whole of your life. I will love you as though we invented love. And I will understand if the life I offer is not the one you wish to lead, and I will leave you with gratitude, and deep regret, and with my heart. For I will not give it to another. You will not see me again."

She brushed her hand across her eyes. "Lorcan . . . never seeing you again . . . is the very worst thing I can imagine. Yes. Yes, I want *you*. All I want is you. I want to be your wife. And I cannot imagine a greater honor than to marry you."

He closed his eyes briefly and his head dropped to his chest. His shoulders rose and fell in a great sigh.

"Oh, luv. We are going to be so happy."

To belong forever to the person who had introduced her to herself. Who *loved* her for herself. Who was oranges, black coffee, whiskey, and sex personified. To be given this fierce, precious man to tend for the rest of her days. She'd endure all of it again—the broken heart and window escape, all of it—if it led to him.

He gathered her gently in his arms, which was where she belonged, after all. They had felt like her true home from the moment she'd leaped into them.

He kissed her like a man who knew he'd won the wager of a lifetime.

Epilogue

◦⟋∘⟍◦

Dear Lord Athelboro,

*I should like to thank you for the profound
honor you conferred upon me with your offer
of matrimony, and for the thoroughness and
thoughtfulness with which you presented it.*

*I have taken as my guide the honesty and
forthrightness reflected in your letter to
write this one, and I hope you will not find my
directness untoward: I am unable to accept
your offer, for by the time you read these
words, I will be a married woman.*

*I wish for you the same extraordinary
good fortune with which I have been blessed,
and I hope you find a life's companion
who brings to you the same joy which now
characterizes my every day. I have come to
believe that we all deserve it, at any age.*

 Yours sincerely,
 Daphne St. Leger

DAPHNE READ this aloud to Lorcan before she
sent it via a messenger Lorcan had hired.

He remained motionless for a second or two

after she'd finished, so proud of her elegant way with words, and absolutely captivated by that last sentence. For it was merely true, and this was a miracle to them both.

"You should tell him he was outbid by a rogue," Lorcan teased.

She laughed.

Lorcan quickly obtained a marriage license and they were wed in her local church two days after she'd returned home, without fuss, fanfare, or her father in attendance.

In part because Daphne had chosen to spend the night at the local inn with Lorcan before she married him rather than keep apart for one night, or remain under the roof with her father.

She could not deny the sting of his absence. He had been invited, of course. Nevertheless, she felt for the first time in her life so light she thought she might drift away like a champagne bubble, and clearheaded, and free. And safe. Finally, at last, safe. She understood she had never fully felt this way in her life.

For Lorcan took immediate charge.

"My wife is not and will never again be a solution to any of your financial troubles," he told Daphne's gathered family evenly. "And I am not a bank. I will settle upon you, Lord Worth, an allowance to be managed by my Man of Affairs, and any and all purchases or investments you wish to make will require permission first. I will pay your debt, but only the one time. I will not have Daphne concerned about your welfare." He paused. "Because she loves you."

The words were nearly accusatory. Implicit in them, and both men knew it, were the words, "and you hardly deserve it."

Daphne might forgive her father. Lorcan might forever struggle to, however.

Daphne and her father locked eyes. Hers were sympathetic, and tentatively warm. But resolute. She would not countermand her husband.

The earl swallowed, then turned away. For perhaps the first time, a flush of shame washed his cheeks.

"I'm not a child." Her father was seething. But he knew he had no standing.

Lorcan found it strange how closely the Earl of Worth resembled his beloved wife. His features were perhaps more chiseled. His eyes a bit darker. But the soul which peered out of them was more complicated, and less warm. Understandably, he'd not been treated to any of his vaunted charm yet.

"No, you're not a child," Lorcan said patiently. "You're a grown man who ought to have taken care of his family. But you have demonstrated that you cannot be trusted with money, and harm has come to your family, and someone I cherish, as a result. Honor and a title and an estate are about all that's left of your legacy. If you do not wish to destroy your family name forever, you will cooperate."

Ultimately, Lord Worth agreed to the arrangement. Daphne witnessed his shallow nod, agreeing, with sadness and relief.

They all knew rapprochement would be a longer time coming.

"I expect the two of you," Lorcan said to Montague and Charles, "to remain aware of your father's affairs, as well as manage your own."

Her brothers were shaken when they were apprised of the true carnage done to their inheritance by their father. To their credit, they both seemed to understand that railing about it was pointless.

"We're so sorry, Daphne," they both said. Quietly. They did indeed each have a little money of their own, which they had invested sensibly. It was nothing compared to the inheritance they had expected.

"Sheep," Charles said suddenly. "Wool! We have the land, Monty has the brawn, I have the brains—"

"Ho there!" Montague interrupted indignantly.

"We'll make a go of it. The next generation will be proud."

"If you wish to discuss investment opportunities, or if you need employment, I will be happy to assist," Lorcan told them simply. "And now, my wife . . ." He turned to her. Daphne flushed when he paused at that word. He savored it every time. Imbued it with a universe of meaning. ". . . and I are returning to London. We'll be living there permanently."

"FINALLY HOME, I see. Good afternoon, St. John," the Countess of Vaughn had said to her son as she sailed down the hall of their St. James Square town house, his father trailing her. She paused to plant a kiss on his cheek.

St. John's eyes went wide. He'd frankly been a bit

wounded at the lack of fanfare. He'd been gone—missing!—for *days*. In a terrible storm!

His mother gave a little laugh at his expression. "We knew you'd be in good hands at The Grand Palace on the Thames," she reassured him.

He stared at her. "How on earth did you know I was at The Grand Palace on the Thames?"

"Well, for one, you were out with Mr. Delacorte. We know he wouldn't abandon you," his father told him. "But a most unusual man paid us a call and told us you were sound. He seemed to have gone through some considerable personal effort to get into our part of London through flooded roads on another matter of business—to visit a friend with an orangery—and he said that it had been dangerous indeed. He called upon us on impulse and assured us you would come home when the streets were passable."

St. John could not believe his ears.

"Was this man's name St. Leger?"

"Yes, that's it. He said he couldn't countenance your parents suffering over not knowing where you were."

St. John, who had experienced more challenging emotions in the past week or so than he ever had in his entire life, had never been more flabbergasted.

Suddenly his mother peered beyond him into his room. Her eyes narrowed speculatively. "St. John . . . what is that?"

St. John adroitly sidestepped, blocked her view. Blushing.

His father's eyebrows dove suspiciously and his

voice raised incredulously. "Have you a woman in there?"

St. John hesitated.

Then sighed. "It's a violoncello."

"You . . . bought a violoncello?" the Earl of Vaughn said the word gingerly, as if he'd never said it aloud before.

St. John nodded, and with some resignation, stepped aside to reveal it, leaning against his bed.

His parents stared at it. "You stopped on your way home to buy a violoncello."

St. John almost laughed, so confused did his father sound. "Yes."

"Can you . . . *play* the cello?" his mother ventured.

"Yes. A little."

His parents were modern and for the most part quite accepting people—after all, they managed to like Mr. Delacorte, and Mr. Delacorte was the very definition of an acquired taste—and while he'd made certain his daughters, Lillias and Claire, could properly play the pianoforte, his father thought—not without some justification— that musicians, poets, painters, singers, and the like were at all times about two steps removed from debauchery. (Which St. John knew wasn't too far wrong. They all did indeed seem to know how to enjoy themselves.)

Lord Vaughn heaved a sigh. "Well, I suppose we'll look forward to your recital," he said ironically, shaking his head as he made his way down the hall, wondering if his children would ever cease to surprise him.

"St. Leger had us by the short hairs," Tristan said half admiringly, half irritably to Delilah in bed the night the *Zephyr* had limped into port. He'd told her about the tentative agreement they'd all struck in the smoking room. "He had something we needed, and damned if he didn't know how to work that to his advantage. He was ready with the figures. And I know how smart he is. How effective he is. How good of a leader he is. I was already halfway to yes before he was done speaking. But Delilah . . ." He sighed, and stretched and yawned on her name, and gathered her into his arms, and she burrowed closer into his body. "The main reason I said yes . . . well, the man has nerves of iron. I never knew him to blink at all even when he was tracked for smuggling. But when he first mentioned he had a ship, I noticed his hands were trembling just a very little when he was holding his cheroot. It meant everything to him. Because Daphne means everything to him."

For a respectful moment they basked in the sweetness of someone else's vulnerability and love.

"I'm happy for them," Delilah said softly.

"Be happy for all of us. Inside a decade, we'll be merchant kings. Barring caprices of fate here or there," he murmured.

"One, two, three, One, two, three . . ." Daphne murmured to Lorcan. "Watch Mr. Delacorte and his partner now, they're heading our way . . ."

He had taken to waltzing the way he'd taken to

the sea, and Daphne felt as though she'd boarded a great galleon to sail about the ballroom of The Grand Palace on the Thames.

Hans, Otto, and Friedreich promised to come again as soon as they were able, and were told they'd be warmly welcomed, which was mostly true. Their farewell gift to their hostesses and hosts and fellow guests was an emotional concert, which gave Daphne and Lorcan another excuse to gaze into each other's eyes while in each other's arms, which was one of their favorite things to do. They would be moving on, too: Lorcan had found a very pleasant house to rent while they looked for a permanent home in London, for Daphne longed to set up housekeeping with him now that they were a couple.

"And we'll invite everyone from The Grand Palace on the Thames to a party for your birthday, with dancing, and ratafia, and little cakes . . ." Daphne mused.

". . . and oranges," he added.

Since Lorcan didn't know the actual day he was born, he had chosen the day he'd met Daphne as his birthday. Their winters, for the rest of their lives, would be filled with celebrations.

AND SO THERE ensued a bit of a lull at The Grand Palace on the Thames—a wistful one, as most lulls often were when they occurred, because they were often preceded by the departure of guests of whom all the residents had become fond. But Helga could exhale, now that the German musicians would be departing, and she could loosen, just a little, the constraints around the menu and the food budget. There was now time to mend Mr. Delacorte's waistcoat, to aggressively pursue the drafts to repair them and to perform other loving and energetic acts of building maintenance.

But lulls become unnerving if they go on too long, for The Grand Palace on the Thames depended on new guests.

As it so happened, they were not fated to enjoy a dull moment. For the lull ended and drama began on a Wednesday, during a full moon, when it was finally Mr. Pike's turn to open the door.

Two and a half years later . . .

LORD HENRY HAVELSTOCK plucked up his hat and patted his handkerchief across his damp forehead, something he'd done five minutes ago and would likely need to do again in another five minutes. The fact that the sun seemed to be conspiring to boil everyone in London like crabs in a pot had not deterred his wife from insisting on a shopping trip—shopping was her very favorite thing to do—to The Strand. He found it easier to indulge her, to set her loose with his money and her lady's maid among the shops while he waited elsewhere; he might have to talk to her otherwise, and he had tired of listening to her years earlier. He could not quite say why. He loved his children well enough; both were currently home with their governess. He had realized too late that what made him feel alive was newness and beauty, and he was too young, he felt, for life to become so relentlessly *uneventful*. Still in the prime of his life. Perhaps a mistress would be just the thing. One could always get another mistress if one grew bored. Rather unlike a wife.

As if his thoughts were made manifest, a woman entered the ice shop in which he had taken refuge and he promptly lost his breath.

She was glowingly, arrestingly lovely. Her frock was the color of marigolds. Her bonnet was tied beneath one ear with a satin ribbon of the same color. Her mouth was soft and full and her complexion called to mind the finest pearls.

He stared, suffused with restlessness and longing.

Perhaps the heat was the reason recognition took so long to set in.

When it did, it nearly knocked him off his feet.

"Daphne?" He almost choked the word.

She turned swiftly about at the sound of his voice.

She froze, too, her lovely brown eyes huge with astonishment. But her expression registered not much more than recognition. Certainly it betrayed nothing of the shock he felt. Nor did it convey dismay or pleasure. It was pleasant enough but abstracted, as if her thoughts were entirely elsewhere.

It had been a decade at least since he'd seen her, but Lady Daphne Worth had never before looked at him as if he hadn't mattered at least a little. He was badly jarred.

He could not seem to stop staring. His last memory of her was her face, pale with shock and contorted with an effort not to weep. Some days, when he felt taken for granted by his wife, he conjured that image to remind himself that he had once mattered so intensely to someone. He had been appalled to hurt her. It had seemed at the time it could not be helped.

He had heard, not too long ago, that she had yet to marry. He wondered if she would be amenable to another arrangement of some kind.

Suddenly the sun was nearly blotted out, as though by an eclipse.

Henry's head shot up to discover one of the largest and most fearsome men he had ever seen filling the doorway of the shop.

An earring—an earring!—glinted in his ear. A scar—a scar!—streaked down his jaw. He was riveting, in a sort of primitive way, he supposed.

Henry took an involuntary step backward.

In the man's arms wriggled a little boy, a handsome imp with curly dark hair whose eyes were crinkled with amusement, as were his father's—for the man was surely his father, the resemblance was unmistakable—as if the two had been roaring with laughter just before they entered.

When she saw them, Daphne's smile could have lit all of London and Henry's breath caught at its beauty.

"Mama!" the little one cried in delight, and Daphne reached out to gather him in her arms.

Henry's mouth dropped open.

Lorcan looked from Henry to Daphne and back again.

"Lord Havelstock . . . allow me to present my husband, Mr. Lorcan St. Leger, and my son, Archer St. Leger."

The huge man's arm curved around Daphne and his child and the three gazed back at him. Clearly a snug, inviolable little family unit.

In shock, Henry at first could say nothing.

It was at once clear to him Mr. St. Leger knew precisely who Henry was. And who he had been to Daphne.

"Havelstock," he said politely. His expression changed very little apart from a sardonic eyebrow twitch, but it was cool, and contained a touch of cynicism.

And the faintest hint of pity.

Pity alarmed Henry.

He realized he was looking into the face of a man who was singularly happy because he had everything in the world he wanted: Daphne, and the child.

Henry bowed slightly. "A pleasure to meet you," he said. Seldom had anything felt less true. "Archer is a fine name."

The little boy beamed so brilliantly at him that Henry's mouth reflexively twitched into a smile.

"We named him for the Sagittarius constellation," Daphne told him. The boy had caught hold of her bonnet ribbon. "He was born in December."

"You did like stars," Henry said faintly, after

a moment. She'd liked a lot of things, hadn't she? He'd stopped listening, after a time.

"Oh, yes. Lorcan and I are very nearly star *experts*," Daphne said dreamily, somewhat saucily, tipping her head back to look up at her husband, who was gazing down at her. His smile was possessive, peaceful, and content. Whatever it was between them, they amplified the temperature of the room by about ten sultry degrees.

Henry flushed.

"I hope you're well, Henry," she said, sincerely and politely, as if she was suddenly remembering him. But she said it without much interest, as her arms, and clearly her heart, were full. "Lorcan has recently won a seat in Parliament. Perhaps you'll see him there? We must move on. We promised Archer an ice."

"Ithe!" Archer bellowed.

They left Henry standing alone.

Celebrate the summer with more books selected by Bridgerton's

JULIA QUINN!

UNLADYLIKE LESSONS IN LOVE

> "Sizzling romance with a splash of intrigue."
> —Julia Quinn

The first in a dazzling romantic mystery series, a half-English, half-Indian society hostess must grapple with her past, prove a man's innocence, and face off against a handsome yet infuriating man who seems determined to hate her—or does he?

WE COULD BE SO GOOD

> "A spectacularly talented writer!"
> —Julia Quinn

Colleen Hoover meets *The Seven Husbands of Evelyn Hugo* in this mid-century rom-dram about a scrappy reporter and a newspaper mogul's son, perfect for *Newsies* shippers.

HOW TO TAME A WILD ROGUE

> "I am in awe of her talent."
> —Julia Quinn

In this next installment of *USA Today* bestselling author Julie Anne Long's charming Palace of Rogues series, an infamous privateer's limits are put to the test when he's trapped during a raging tempest with a prickly female at the Grand Palace on the Thames.

DUKE SEEKS BRIDE

> "Simply delightful!"
> —Julia Quinn

Christy Carlyle takes readers to the breathtaking coast of Ireland where a pretty, young countess's secretary agrees to impersonate her mistress to help a duke appease his fortune-hunting family…until he falls for her instead.

EXPLORE MORE OF
JULIE ANNE LONG'S
NOVELS

PENNYROYAL GREEN SERIES

The Perils of Pleasure

Like No Other Lover

Since the Surrender

I Kissed an Earl

What I Did for a Duke

How the Marquess Was Won

A Notorious Countess Confesses

It Happened One Midnight

Between the Devil and Ian Eversea

It Started with a Scandal

The Legend of Lyon Redmond

THE PALACE OF ROGUES SERIES

Lady Derring Takes a Lover

Angel in a Devil's Arms

I'm Only Wicked with You

After Dark with the Duke

You Were Made to Be Mine

How to Tame a Wild Rogue